PARADISE
Ben Tufnell

Influx Press
London

Published by Influx Press
www.influxpress.com
@InfluxPress

Published by Influx Press, London, UK, 2026
© Ben Tufnell, 2026

The right of Ben Tufnell to be identified as the author of this work has been asserted in accordance with section 77 of the Copyright, Designs and Patents Act 1988.

This book is in copyright. Subject to statutory exception and to provisions of relevant collective licensing agreements, no reproduction of any part may take place without the written permission of Influx Press.

This edition 2026
Printed and bound in the UK by Clays
Paperback ISBN: 9781914391583
Ebook ISBN: 9781914391590

Cover design: Luke Bird
Text design: Vince Haig
Editor: Dan Coxon
Proofreader: Pablo Tufnell

This book is sold subject to the condition that it shall not, by way of trade or otherwise, be lent, re-sold, hired out, or otherwise circulated without the publisher's prior consent in any form of binding or cover other than that in which it is published and without a similar condition including this condition being imposed on the subsequent purchaser.

PART 1

Paradise waits.
Paradise has time.
Paradise waits, just as it always has and always will.

(1)

As he waited for them to come, wondering if they would kill him or not, Nash could not rid himself of the growing conviction that it was all a terrible mistake..

If they did intend to kill him, what could he do? He had no weapon. If he somehow managed to elude them, they would find him. He told himself it was best to wait and hope that common sense would prevail. Even so, he could not rid himself of the feeling that what had happened was a disaster, a catastrophe.

He had done as instructed. He had left the hotel and walked to the tube station, taking a meandering route that included a diversion along the canal, where he had dropped the gun into the dark water. As directed, he had not hurried, but had forced himself to walk slowly, even stopping at one point to watch some ducks. The winter sun had seemed unusually bright and, reflecting from the steel and glass of the new developments that lined the canal and off the still surface of the water, it had dazzled him, making him feel lightheaded. He had been glad of his dark glasses. As he walked, his nervous energy gradually dissipated and he began to feel weary. It was unseasonably warm. Catching a glimpse of himself in a reflection, he had loosened his tie and undone the top button of his shirt. As he did so, he noticed spots of blood on his suit. He passed through a scrappy park where people were walking dogs and sitting on benches. The light was weird, but perhaps it was just his heightened state of mind. On any other day he would have enjoyed the strange beauty of the city, the surreal collage of water, glass, steel, tarmac, concrete, trees and vegetation, people and animals, none of which belonged to anything else, but on this day he could not rid himself of the creeping apprehension that it was all a terrible mistake.

He took an obscure route home, changing trains several times. When he reached the road where his flat was, he lingered on the corner, waiting to see if there was anything out of place. Satisfied, he let himself in the front door, checked if there was mail (there was not, there never was), and climbed the stairs to the second floor. For a full minute he stood on the landing, waiting and listening, before unlocking the door and going in. He carefully locked it behind him. He took the envelope from his jacket pocket and examined it properly for the first time. He wondered at the word printed on the heavy cream paper:

ACCELERATION

He set it down on the kitchen table. For a moment, he considered opening it, to see what was inside that was so important. But something told him that would be a very bad move.

He took a chair from the kitchen and wedged it under the front door handle. He quickly undressed and showered, and put on jeans, a plain t-shirt, a grey sweatshirt. His suit had blood on it. He put it in a plastic bag. It would need dry cleaning. His white shirt was also stained. He balled it up and pushed it into the bin. He took a second chair and set it down by the windows that overlooked the street. He poured himself a glass of water and settled down to watch.

He knew they would come. The instructions were very clear. *After, make your way home and then wait. Someone will come and you will receive further instructions.* But now, as he watched the street, he could not rid himself of the notion that they were coming to kill him.

He had no weapon. He thought of the small knife he used for chopping vegetables, and the knife he used to slice bread. Neither would be of any use. If they were coming to kill him, they would have guns. He did not have a gun. His gun was in the canal, where they had told him to put it. Should he have disobeyed his orders, and kept it? *What does it matter*, he thought wearily. *It is all a terrible mistake, and if they are coming to kill me then so be it.*

It was mid-afternoon when they finally came. Nash was beginning to feel drowsy, and his attention was wandering when he noticed a black car draw up on the other side of the road, where no parking was allowed. He watched it and waited. A flare of sunlight angled off the windscreen so he could not see who was in the car, but he knew it was them.

Eventually, they got out. Two men. Gray, of course, and another in black. One tall and thin, the other short and broad. Both wore suits, white shirts, grey ties. He watched them cross the road, the tall one leading the way. When they passed out of his field of vision, he went to his front door and listened carefully. From below, he heard footsteps coming up the concrete stairwell. Of course, they had keys.

They stopped outside his door and waited. There was silence. He strained to hear and could not help but picture them drawing guns and knives from their jacket pockets, gesturing and nodding to each other, preparing to do something dreadful. Eventually, the doorbell rang and the sudden noise made him jump.

'Who is it?' he called.

'Friends,' came the reply. 'You know who it is. You're expecting us. Let us in, Nash. We need to talk. It's urgent business.'

Nash took the chair out from under the door handle and set it to one side. He slipped the bolt, turned the latch, and opened the door. They went past him and into the kitchen and he locked the door again before following them through.

In the kitchen, The Grey Man was waiting, grinning broadly.

'Mr Nash, it is always a pleasure to see you,' he said. He held out his hand.

Nash hesitated and then took it.

'I love what you've done with the place.' Gray smiled sarcastically and gestured at the room, which was bare, austere. No ornaments, no books, the walls empty of pictures.

His face was grey, corpse grey, and deeply creased. His hair, the grey of ash, flecked with white and silver, was brushed back from his high forehead. His eyes were stony. They had heavy lids which gave him a reptilian appearance. Nash saw that even the whites of his eyes were grey, the lower lids pink and raw. His lips were thin and bloodless, his teeth were small and discoloured. He looked down on everything and everyone. Yet now a smirk played across his face, as if it was all highly amusing or perhaps even ridiculous, a cosmic joke. He looked as if he might burst out laughing at any moment.

'Is this it?' he said, pointing to the envelope lying on the table. When he spoke, he over-enunciated some words and sometimes misplaced the emphasis in the sentence. English was almost certainly not his first language.

Nash nodded and The Grey Man picked it up and examined it closely (*he's checking to see if I've opened it*, thought Nash), then slid it into his jacket pocket.

'Do you mind?' he asked, producing a packet of cigarettes.

Nash took a saucer from the cupboard and set it on the table. 'You can use this.'

'Most kind.'

Gray lit his cigarette, inhaled deeply and blew an extravagant plume of smoke across the room. Behind him his companion, the smaller one, was by the window, watching the street, fidgeting, bobbing from one foot to the other. He projected nervous energy and impatience. His face was ruddy, his ears red, his black suit too tight. His neck bulged over the collar of his shirt. He reminded Nash of some kind of compact fighting dog, the ones that were extraordinarily solid and weighed more than it looked like they should.

'Mr Nash, this is' – he paused – 'Mr Black.' The short one nodded in Nash's general direction, avoiding eye contact, and went back to watching the street. 'Yes, Gray and Black,' he continued, 'Black and Gray. That works well, doesn't it? As I mentioned, we have urgent business to discuss with you.'

'Well, I was expecting you, after all,' said Nash. 'I had very clear instructions.'

'Indeed, you did. Exceptionally clear instructions. And did you follow them to the letter?'

'Yes, of course.'

'To the absolute letter?' Gray grinned at him, showing his horrible teeth.

Nash nodded, but he knew that it had all been a terrible mistake and that something had gone very wrong.

'Well, be that as it may. It's not our concern. The directive is very clear. The protocol requires that you be taken to a special place. It's quite a long way from here, so we've got a long drive ahead of us. In that place you will await a verdict. No, not a *verdict*, that makes it sound as if you're standing trial. Let's just say that we're to take you to the place where you will wait to receive your next instructions. Do you understand?'

'Where is it,' Nash asked, 'and how long must I wait there?'

Gray finished his cigarette and ground it into the saucer.

'I can't tell you the answer to the first question and I don't know the answer to the second.' The expression on his face suggested that he was finding this exchange hilarious. 'Mr Nash, please pack a bag. You won't need much. Make sure you have some warm things. I believe it will be cold. Don't forget your toothbrush. Please do it quickly. We'll give you ten minutes.'

Nash went into his bedroom and pulled a bag from the

cupboard. Into it he threw clothing, a pair of boots, some toiletries. That done, he sat on his bed and tried to think. What else should he take? What would he need? What would be useful? Everything could depend on it. But at that moment, thinking was the one thing he could not do. His mind was a stalled engine. On the bedside table was a photograph. A family. He picked it up and examined it before putting it in with the clothes. Closing the bag, he went out to where they were waiting.

Gray was smoking another cigarette, and Black was still by the window.

'Excellent,' said Gray, looking at his watch. 'Well, let us go forth. Do you have everything you might need, Mr Nash?'

Nash nodded. He put on a coat and followed the two men out onto the landing. They watched him as he locked the door and then Gray held his hand and said, 'The keys.' Nash reluctantly handed them over. They went down the stairs, with Gray in front of him and Black behind, left the building and crossed the road to the car.

Black opened the boot and Nash put his bag in.

'Mr Nash, I almost forgot,' said Gray. 'Your phones, please.' He held out his hand. Nash took a phone from his jacket pocket and handed it over. 'And the other one?' Nash took a second phone from the back pocket of his jeans and gave it to Gray. With exaggerated precision, Gray placed the first on the edge of the pavement and then stamped, so that it cracked and bent, and then ground it under his heel, spreading glittering shards of screen. He repeated the action with the second. Then, noticing a storm drain, he took up the ruined phones and dropped them through the slots into the darkness below.

He grinned demonically at Nash. 'Apologies, but as I said, we have our procedures, as you know.' He opened the back door of the car and indicated that Nash should get in. He did so and Black climbed in beside him, secured Nash's seat belt, and then bound his wrists and ankles with plastic cable ties. Finally, he produced a black scarf, which he tied securely about Nash's head, covering his eyes.

'I do apologise,' said Gray, and Nash could hear the laughter in his voice. 'I hope it's not too uncomfortable.'

They drove for hours. At first there was the jarring stop-start motion of heavy traffic as they made their way through the city. Nash quickly gave up on trying to work out where they might be from the motion of the car and resigned himself to his disorientation. The two men in the front did not speak. Eventually, the ride became smoother, the sudden slowing and accelerating less frequent, and Nash knew they were on the motorway, and fell into a doze, despite himself. He tried to stay awake but his nerves had been shredded by what had happened. He was exhausted. He felt himself slumping, and the sound and the vibrations of the car brought back a strange memory – of lying on the back seat of his parents' car, covered by a blanket and with bags piled about him, the world outside the car seen from an unfamiliar angle, turned upside down, counting the orange lights of the motorway, as they made their way back (from where?), towards the home he now barely remembered – and with that image before him, he fell asleep.

He woke as the car slowed and pulled to the left, and found that he was lying on his side, the seat belt digging into his chest and arm and the ties pinching his ankles painfully. He twisted himself upright, and as the car slowed to a stop, Gray spoke.

'Comfort break, Mr Nash. How are you getting on?'

Nash said nothing. He heard the two of them get out and close their doors, then the door next to him was open and there were hands pulling at his feet and wrists and the ties were cut. The scarf was pulled from his face and even in the gloom his eyes were dazzled. He climbed stiffly from the car into cold air and saw that they were in a layby at the side of a dual carriageway somewhere in the middle of nowhere. It was dusk and they were parked in a pool of yellow light cast by a single streetlamp. The sky was dark but just above the horizon a rip of pink light marked the passage between day and night. Some cars went by, and a huge lorry that made the ground shake.

He rubbed his eyes, shook his arms and stamped his feet to get feeling back into them. Gray had walked to the edge of the light and was smoking, his back to them. Black leant against the car and watched him.

'How much longer?' Nash asked.

Black shook his head.

Gray turned and smirked. 'Oh, it's a while yet, Mr Nash.' He flicked away his cigarette, crossed the tarmac to where a gate opened onto a field, and urinated into the hedge.

'Where are we?' asked Nash.

'We're not yet where we need to be,' replied Gray. He lit another cigarette.

Black arched his back, his arms outstretched, and then he too crossed the tarmac and pissed into the hedge, clouds of steam rising around him.

'I'd recommend you do that too,' said Gray. 'We won't

be stopping again.' And so, Nash did, feeling self-conscious, like a kid on a school field trip made to do something humiliating in front of classmates.

He climbed back into the car, and once again Black was beside him to secure his hands and feet and bind the scarf about his head. For a moment, as Black bent to place the ties around his ankles, he considered the possibility of jumping him, of driving his fists down into the back of his head, bringing his knees up hard into his face, breaking his nose, barging him against the door, climbing from the car and running – either through the gate and into the field or, better, out onto the road where he might stop a passing vehicle. But as soon as the thought came, he dismissed it. His limbs were stiff and sore and Gray, despite his years, would be on him before he could get any distance between them. Hopeless. As the car pulled back out onto the road and picked up speed, he could already feel himself fading, falling again into a vague slumber. He told himself to pay attention, to listen for signs that might give a clue to their whereabouts, but even as he did so he was letting go.

They seemed to drive for an age. For long periods the car maintained its speed, and he assumed they were on a motorway or A roads. He was sometimes jerked awake as the car stopped at junctions or leaned around roundabouts. At one point he was aware of Gray giving Black directions in a low voice.

Then something changed, and Nash surmised that they were on small roads, twisting and turning, rising and falling. At this point, despite the discomfort, he fell asleep again and lolled across the seat, held in place only by his seat belt. And then, sometime later, awoke suddenly as the taut belt cutting into his neck became intolerable.

Then they were on what must have been a track, ascending steeply. The car lurched and bumped on the uneven surface. This change brought him to his senses and he realised they must be getting near to their destination. But the track and the rising ascent seemed to go on forever, and, not knowing how fast the car was going, it was impossible to guess how far it was back to the road they had just left.

Eventually, the car swung around in a tight circle, forcing him against the door, and they came to a sudden halt.

'We're here, Mr Nash,' announced Gray. 'Welcome to Paradise.'

The engine stopped and Nash heard the two men climb out of the car. There was the crunch of feet on gravel, then the door beside him was open and cold air broke into the fuggy warmth of the car. His hands and feet were freed and he hurriedly tugged the scarf away from his face, suddenly feeling profoundly claustrophobic.

The interior of the car was lit by a small yellowish light that had come on when the doors were opened. And even that pale glow was too bright. Black was there, regarding him curiously. Gray was nowhere to be seen, lost in the intense darkness beyond the reach of that faint illumination.

Black indicated that he should get out, and Nash wondered if the man ever spoke.

He swung his legs down and, using the door to steady himself, climbed to his feet. His body was stiff and weary and felt decades older than it should. He rubbed his face and eyes and looked about but there was nothing. He could tell they were in a wood – the cold air had an earthy tang – but there was only teeming shadow. Far above, a gradual lessening of the darkness suggested a sky.

Black opened the boot and pulled Nash's bag out. Nash took it and briefly thought about throwing it in Black's face and making a run for it but immediately dismissed the possibility. He could not even see the track they had driven up on.

Black gestured for him to follow.

As they walked away from the soft glow of the car's interior, a light came on ahead of them. Gray was standing in the doorway of an old house. By the door a hand-painted sign said:

PARADISE

They crunched across the gravel and Gray led them into a small hallway lit by a bare bulb. There was a bench for sitting and a row of hooks for coats. The floor was worn grey flagstones. The walls, which were painted a pale green, were criss-crossed by dark wooden beams. There were three doors – one straight ahead, one to the left, and one to the right – and they went through this one into a kitchen, turning on lights as they went. Black positioned himself by the door.

'Well, Mr Nash,' said Gray, 'this is Paradise.' He made a sweeping gesture, as if welcoming Nash to a palace. 'Your home for the foreseeable.'

'For how long?' asked Nash.

'Well, that depends. That depends on a lot of things. There are many variables to consider.'

The kitchen was basic. There was another door, presumably leading out to the back of the house, and windows through which nothing could be seen. A wooden counter with sink, an old cooker with hobs and oven, fridge, cupboard, dresser, shelves piled with a seemingly random collection of plates, bowls and cups. In the centre an old wooden table with four ill-matching chairs. Gray pulled one of these out, sat down and lit a cigarette before getting up, taking a saucer from the shelf, and sitting down again.

'Please sit,' he said, gesturing Nash to one of the other chairs.

'Thanks, I'll stand,' said Nash. He had been sitting for too long.

'Suit yourself. Right, let me explain how it works.' He paused and delicately tapped ash onto the saucer. 'As I said, you are to wait here while your case is reviewed, and a decision is made.'

'My *case*?'

'Indeed, your case. What happened, how you acted, the consequences, and so on.' He smoked and then went on. 'There should be a few basics here already – milk, bread and so on – and tomorrow Owen will come up from the village with more supplies. Owen will come up here once a week. There's electricity but no heating. No phones or anything like that, obviously. No phone signal, either. There's a wood-burning stove in the sitting room and a grate in the upstairs bedroom. I suggest you get a fire going. There are logs by the shed out there. You'll need to chop them. Do you know how to chop wood, Mr Nash?'

Nash shook his head.

'Well, I dare say you'll get the hang of it pretty quickly. Now, Mr Nash, there is only one rule. Term and condition, singular. You must not go beyond the bounds of this wood. Do you understand?'

Nash nodded.

'It's quite a big wood, a forest really. You can wander around inside it as much as you like. Or not. But you must stay in the wood.'

'What will happen if I leave the wood?'

'Serious consequences, Mr Nash. Very serious.'

Nash looked out of the window but there was nothing there to see. Only darkness. And his own face, like a ghost, hovering in the glass.

'Mr Nash, you should know that if you do not comply, we will know. And we will act.'

He stubbed out his cigarette and stood up.

'You'd best get that fire going. It's going to be a cold night.'

There was a silence. Nash waited. He could feel Gray's lizard eyes upon him, assessing him.

Black took him by surprise. He was behind him, and before Nash could react his arms were pinioned at his back and Black had a thick arm around his neck, squeezing tight. Nash tried to twist but Black was strong and kicked his foot away so that he was off balance. He tightened his grip. It was hard to breathe.

Gray watched this curiously. The smile had gone. He crossed to the counter and opened a drawer, carefully selected a fork, and came over to stand very close to Nash, so close that he could feel the heat of his breath, stale cigarettes and something else, sulphur perhaps.

Very slowly, Gray brought the fork up and pressed it against Nash's forehead.

'I could kill you with this, just like that,' he said. 'I could do it quickly or I could do it slowly.'

Nash could not respond. He had no air in his lungs.

'Let me say this once again, Mr Nash. This is a very serious situation. Do not leave the woods.' He pressed harder and something gave, four tiny punctures.

'Do you understand?' said Gray.

Nash made a noise and Black released him. He could feel his legs about to fail beneath him and leant against the table, taking gulps of air.

'Any questions?'

Nash looked up and saw that Gray was grinning, enjoying his discomfort.

'How long must I wait?' he asked, his voice hoarse.

'Who can say? It might be days. It might be weeks. Who can say? You would want the review to be *thorough*, would you not? You would want us to be *diligent*, wouldn't you? Yes? Then it takes time.'

Silence again but for Nash's laboured breathing. The Grey Man regarded him quizzically.

'Might I suggest something? While you are here, use your time. Look around you. Pay attention. Maybe you will learn something.'

'About what?'

'Who can say? Perhaps about yourself, or about the world you find yourself in.' He watched Nash carefully. 'It's up to you Mr Nash.'

He moved toward the door. 'Is that all? Right, we should be going.'

Nash stood in the hall and watched as they went back to the car, illuminated only by the light from the bare bulb hanging above him. At the car, Gray turned back and called to him.

'Good luck, Mr Nash. I wish you a pleasant stay. Remember the rule.'

He climbed in and the car started with a cough. As it backed around, the headlights arced across a dense screen of trees and bushes enfolding the house. Nash saw the track they had driven up, leading into the woods. The car pulled away and disappeared down it. He watched as the headlights receded and then disappeared, and waited until the sound of the engine had gone completely. There was light from the house behind him but outside there was nothing, only the dark unseen weight of the forest. A world he did not know and which he feared. He went inside and closed the door against it.

He went quickly through the house turning on all the lights. From the hallway, the door on the left opened onto a small cold room with a toilet, sink and a stained bathtub. A towel hung on a hook on the wall. The air smelt damp, mouldy. There was a cracked mirror and Nash saw there were four red points in the middle of his forehead, a trickle of blood. He wiped it away with the back of his hand.

The third door opened into a large sitting room crossed by huge black roof beams. At the near end were a table and some chairs, a treacle-dark dresser and a chest on which stood a glass vase of long-dead flowers. At the far end was a sitting area, centred on a large fireplace of mottled brick containing a black wood-burning stove. Two battered old sofas, one leaking its stuffing, and a spindly wooden armchair. In one corner, an ancient hi-fi system, knobs and dials, cassette player, radio and record player, hulking, stupidly big and blocky, on a small table. Below it, two large speakers, black fabric, a tangle of wires.

The room was split by an ancient and rickety staircase ascending across from left to right. The floor was stone flags covered with threadbare rugs. The ceiling was low, so that Nash had to stoop to cross the room safely. He saw with relief that some logs were stacked in the fireplace and there was a basket with old newspapers, scraps of wood for kindling and a couple of boxes of matches. He picked up a newspaper from the pile and saw that the date was from two years before. The headlines announced the beginning of the war in the Red Sea. Record temperatures. Melting ice, collapsing glaciers. Devastating floods in Europe. Decline and fall.

Should he close the curtains? He was undecided. He could see nothing out there, but if a face were to appear at the window, if someone were watching him, he would want to know, wouldn't he? He wasn't sure. He pulled them closed.

The stairs led up to a little landing. To the left was a room with two bare single beds. Wooden floorboards, a small fireplace. On the mantlepiece sat two white ceramic dogs regarding him plaintively. A cupboard – empty but for a pile of blankets – in one corner. A chest of drawers contained only sheets and bedding. Along the landing to the right was a tiny box room with a single bed and turquoise wallpaper covered in brown, orange and yellow floral motifs. An ornate mirror hung above the bed, wreathed with crumbling corn dollies and crosses made of grass, spun with dusty cobwebs. A threadbare one-eyed teddy bear and a horrible doll with blank porcelain features leant against each other on the bed. At the end of the landing – above the kitchen, he guessed – was a larger room with a double bed, which was made. There was a bookcase with a jumble of books, a chest of drawers – empty – and a fireplace with a grate.

Finally, returning to the kitchen he tried the back door. Having turned on all the lights in the house, some illumination was cast out onto a small patch of lawn, and beyond that masses of foliage, and beyond that the night. He heard the trees swaying and knocking and some unknown and unknowable creature called out, a sound that seemed to express a primeval agony. He shivered and realised for the first time just how cold he was. He closed the door.

No keys.

No heating, Gray had said.

With some difficulty, he got a fire going in the stove. It was the first time he had ever set a fire.

He sat before it for some time, watching the flames and occasionally feeding it logs. As the cold receded, he realised how hungry he was. He had not eaten a thing in all this long, strange, frightening day. This day that seemed to have gone on for days, for weeks even.

In the kitchen he found bread, butter and milk in the fridge, a box of teabags and tins of baked beans in the cupboard. He made tea and heated beans in a pan and cut slices of bread. The butter was so hard that he had to carve it.

He carried the food through and sat again before the fire and ate it.

When he finished, he inspected the old hi-fi system. He plugged it in, turned the switch and the display lit up, a sour green. Dials and lights, like something from an old sci-fi movie. He switched on the radio and spun the tuner across the entire range. Nothing. He flipped from AM to FM. Still nothing, just hiss and whisper. The cassette player would not open, but there were no cassettes anyway. He lifted the needle arm of the record player and the turntable began to spin lazily. Some LPs were propped against the speakers, and he inspected them. None of the names were familiar. Most of the sleeves were empty and the few records present were badly scratched. He tried one, and after a single bar of music the needle bucked and skidded across the vinyl with an angry cough, straight to the centre of the record. The player decided it had finished, and the needle arm lifted jerkily and set itself back down on its cradle. Defeated, Nash turned it off and sat down again before the fire.

The flames were hypnotic.

Eventually, he got up once more. He felt that he should be doing something, preparing in some way. In the kitchen he went again through the cutlery, seeking something that would serve as a weapon with which he might defend himself. There was a small chopping knife, its old blade only as long as his index finger; the bread knife; a corkscrew.

Surely, he thought, once they went over the facts, once they considered all the evidence, they would conclude that he had done no wrong. He may have acted in error, but he had not done anything *wrong*. It had been someone else's fuckup. He was sure of that. And he had taken the only course available to him. They would see that, would they not?

He carried newspaper, kindling and the last few logs up to the bedroom and made a fire there too.

Later, lying on the bed, unable to sleep, Nash watched the pale light from the dying fire dance upon the ceiling.

·:·

He has never known a place like this. He knows cities: tarmac, streetlights, neon, the reflections of headlights off glass and metal, the tang of petrol, frying chicken and cigarette smoke. The percussion of building sites and roadworks. He thinks of the boxy house he grew up in, part of a development created after the last war, rows of regimented houses, all reassuringly the same, lined up along identical streets, all reassuringly the same. Other childhood homes, all ordered, clean, modern, neat. He thinks of the house he briefly shared with his father after the accident. Even his own small apartment, which he last saw all the way back at the beginning of this endless day, is neat and regular. He finds comfort in order. But here everything is awry. It is *off*. There is a not a single straight line in the entire house, which seems to lean and slump drunkenly. Dust and cobwebs are everywhere. As are strange charms, misshapen signs and symbols, peculiar crosses of yellowed grass and horseshoes of tarnished brass nailed into the age-old wood of the beams. Now, as the cold reclaims the house, it begins to groan and creak, as if it is a living thing.

This house is terrifying, he thinks. But not as terrifying as what lies outside.

Outside the house, enfolding it, is a world that is utterly alien to him. It is impossibly old, disorderly and unruly. The night shadows out there are dense and impenetrable. Who could know what might be lurking, watching and waiting?

Where is the aquarium glow of the night city, the reassuringly soft amber of the streetlights? Where is the persistent murmur of traffic, the lulling signification that the world at large continues?

At first, lying there, he had thought there was silence or, at least, quiet. But then he heard it. The calling of unknown creatures. The rushing sound, something like the sea, of the wind in the trees that ring the house like sentinels. The cracking and tapping of branches knocking against each other, the shuffling of unseen beings moving about in the undergrowth.

It is a cacophony. *All the terrifying things of the woods: spiders, snakes, armies of ants, bristling beetles and millipedes, clouds of flies, leathery bats and oily crows, weasels, wolves, ghosts, scorpions.* His imagination runs riot. *Murdered by witches, fiends, demons. Lost, abandoned. Alone.*

The house shifts, uncomfortable.
It is old and set in its ways.
Yet, there is a new presence within.
It breathes deeply.

(2)

Nash woke to the pinch of cold on his nose and ears, disorientated. He had dreamt that he was being pursued through a dense forest. But who or what it was that pursued him, he could not say. Every time he stopped and turned, expecting to see the pursuer, he could see nothing, despite knowing it was coming on, coming always closer. He could hear it crashing through the trees, getting closer, and so he would run again, always running, stumbling blindly through clinging thickets, often falling to his knees as the ground suddenly gave way beneath him. Running, running, with a growing sense of panic. And it, whatever it was, came on, relentless. When he woke, something of the dream remained and he was bewildered, wondering, just for a moment, if it had really happened, was still happening. And then he remembered where he was. He saw the pale light in the cold room, his breath clouding the air.

The fire in the grate had long since gone out. He had slept in his clothes, wrapping the blankets tightly about himself, but had somehow slept well, despite the dream, for he felt rested and alive.

He went to the window and looked out, hopefully. Below him was the gravelled area where the car had parked. There was a blackened patch where a fire had once been. A massive winter-bare tree stood beyond it, and below the spreading branches Nash saw the shed that Gray had mentioned. Beside it a huge pile of logs and twisted branches. Beyond that were the woods.

Wrapping the blanket about his shoulders, he descended to the kitchen, where everything was icy to the touch and feathers of frost spread across the windows. He made tea and drank it, cupping his hands about the mug for warmth, and then rubbed the window clear and looked out at the woodpile. That was the priority. By the back door was an empty log basket.

Before crossing to the shed, Nash made a circuit around the house. *What a wreck,* he thought, surveying it. It was ancient, that was clear. Squat, compact and ugly. Old beams, flaking dun-coloured plasterwork, cobwebbed eaves and broken brickwork. Ivy clung to it all over. The slate roof sagged and was speckled with lichen and moss. To the back, the side facing *up* the valley, were the remains of what must once have been a formal garden. A ragged patch of lawn and then a series of stepped elevations, the remains of flower beds lined with unruly and shapeless box hedging, everything gone wild, gone over. What he saw was rot, ruin, decay, and it appalled and repelled him. Some large white objects, which at first he took for enormous fungi, lay in the long grass. He saw they were marble statues, stained with green and brown, that had fallen from their plinths. Steps led up under iron arches wreathed in unnameable climbing tendrils. He went up and saw that the upper level was bounded by a row of dense and tangled bushes flanking an opening onto what would once have been another lawn, now overgrown and dotted with the crooked husks of huge thistles. Two white statues, draped in ivy, faced off across the remains of the lawn, or would have if they had not been headless. Their heads – with their blank staring eyes and strangely serene expressions – lay concealed in the grass at their feet. Beyond this lawn was a wooden fence threading between skeletal trees. Beyond that lay a small meadow. After that were the woods, seemingly endless.

He continued around the house. At the side there was a gate in the fence and a path that led off between the trees. At the front of the house, the side that faced *down* the valley, was an open space – one could not really call it a lawn – of yellowed grass, knee high. The fence looped around the house, back to where the track came up from the valley. Even though most of the trees were leafless, the woods were still dense and impenetrable. They crowded in close so that there were no views.

Completing his circuit, he went over to the shed. It was green with mould and its roof was covered in moss. Inside he found a work bench covered in old clay plant pots, completely bewebbed. There were tools hanging up and in boxes, and he was able to locate an axe and a rusty saw. The blade of the axe was dull but there was a whetstone and he set to sharpening it.

Outside, a lump of wood the size of a bass drum served as a chopping block. He took some good-sized logs that were not too damp from the woodpile and went to work trying to split them into manageable sections. Each log took several blows. Once he had a decent number, he took the saw and cut some of the smaller branches to use as kindling. He filled the basket and carried his spoils into the house. He piled the logs around the wood-burner and returned to the shed.

The manual work felt good. He quickly warmed up and enjoyed the chill of the air in his throat as he breathed hard. There was a knack to chopping wood, he saw. It would take time to master it, to not waste energy, to become efficient. For the single strike – accurate, smooth and true, using the weight and balance of the axe – to become the standard rather than the exception.

As he worked, something would sometimes make him stop and look about. He had the sensation that he was being watched. Once, he looked up and saw that a large black bird, a crow of some kind, its wings slick with an oily blue sheen, was regarding him keenly from a branch of the tree, its head cocked to one side. It was unperturbed when he met its gaze and instead of flying off it just nodded, as if to say, go on then, you keep going.

Three times he filled the basket and carried it in, piling the logs beside the wood-burner. As he filled the basket for the third time it began to rain. First a dampness, then drizzle, and finally a drenching.

He carried the axe back across to the house and leant it carefully by the back door. With the rain rattling on the tin roof, he went through the tools in the shed again, looking for something that might serve as a weapon. He had the axe, of course, but it was large and unwieldy. He weighed a hammer in his hand and carried it back to the house.

It was fucking cold. He lit a fire in the sitting room and another in the bedroom upstairs.

In a cupboard next to the bathroom, he found an old immersion heater and switched it on. He might risk a bath later. As the house became warm, or at least as the cold began to slowly recede, Nash felt that he had made some progress.

He wondered when 'Owen' would appear.

She arrived at midday. Going into the kitchen to put the kettle on, he looked out of the window and saw a figure on horseback emerging from the track, through the sheets of rain, hunched beneath a crooked umbrella. He went to the back door and watched as the horse halted and the rider dismounted. It was a woman. She had a rucksack and there was a basket tied to the saddle. She undid the knots with difficulty, still holding the umbrella above her head, then she dug in her pocket for something which she gave to the horse, who looked unbearably sad. She came into the hallway, shaking off the umbrella as she tried to close it against its will.

'Nash,' she said. It was a statement, not a question. She spoke with a lilting accent. She looked him up and down, assessing him. 'Not quite what I expected,' she said.

'What did you expect?'

'A grown-up. A killer.' She shrugged. 'Pleased to meet you,' she said sarcastically. 'I'm Mary.' She held out a wet hand and he took it.

She was not quite what he had expected either. Indeed, it was hard to reconcile her with the people he worked for. With the people she worked for too. She looked like something from another century.

She could have been anything between forty and sixty. Her round face was pink with the cold and much lined, especially around the eyes, and her hair, which was long and greying, was tied in a ponytail. She was wearing an overcoat of indiscriminate colour which she took off and hung up in the hall. Beneath, she wore brown corduroy trousers tucked into muddy wellington boots, a heavy woollen jumper, dark brown with paler flecks. She was of the earth, it seemed, but he saw that her eyes were an extraordinary blue, like pieces of sky.

'I've just put the kettle on,' said Nash. 'Cup of tea?'

She nodded.

He went into the kitchen and took two mugs from the shelf. She followed him in and put the basket on the table.

'So, who did you kill?'

He looked at her with surprise, and was about to explain that the whole thing was a terrible mistake when she said, 'Don't mind me, I'm just teasing. How are you settling?'

Nash nodded. He did not want to reveal that he found this place, this whole process, whatever it was, strange and terrifying. He wondered if she knew what had happened, why he was there.

'Well, I've got some things for you.' She began to empty the basket. 'Can you cook?'

He nodded.

'Good. This is all basic stuff. If there's anything particular you're after, within reason' – she winked at him – 'let me know and I'll bring it next time.'

'Do you know how long I'll be here?' he asked.

'That's none of my business. I just follow the instructions. Keep you alive, clear up after you once you've gone.'

'Milk, sugar?'

'Just milk.'

He offered her the steaming mug and she sat.

'Can you tell me where we are?' he asked.

'Paradise. This is Paradise. But you know that already.' She paused. 'I can't say any more than that. You know how it is. He told you the rules, didn't he?'

Nash nodded.

'Warm enough?' she asked.

Nash nodded again. 'I've been chopping wood.'

'Good man. We're in for a cold spell so you'll need to keep that fire going. Probably snow tomorrow or the day after. Weather's coming.'

As he stowed the tins in the cupboard, he asked, 'How far do the woods go for?'

'Far enough. You be careful. It's easy to get lost.'

They sat in silence.

After a while, he asked, 'So, what am I supposed to do?'

'What do you mean?'

'While I'm here, what am I supposed to do?'

'Why, anything you like, love. Read a book. Do a puzzle.' She went through into the sitting room and he followed. She opened up the dresser and pulled out a pile of old jigsaw puzzles, the pictures on the boxes faded. 'These'll keep you going for a while. Be warned, though, I expect there's pieces missing.'

She piled the boxes on the table. They went back into the kitchen and she finished her tea in a single go. 'Right, I should be going,' she said. 'This rain isn't stopping.'

She got her coat on. 'Anything I should be bringing next time?'

Nash shook his head. He could think of nothing. His thoughts were racing, unfocused. Too many questions.

'Whisky,' he said, eventually, and then, 'and music too, if possible. Some records, for the hi-fi. The radio doesn't work but the record player seems okay. I just need something to play on it.'

'Any preference?'

He shrugged.

She nodded. Outside, the horse was waiting stoically in the rain, its eyes closed. It hadn't moved. She mounted and wrestled the umbrella open. She took up the reins in her free hand and nodded to him and then urged the horse on. Nash watched until she was lost from sight amongst the trees and then went back inside.

Later, as the light faded, he went upstairs and examined the bookshelves. In his flat there were no books, and as he thought about it this fact caused him a pang of regret. He had not read a book since the accident. He did not own a single book. Yet he used to love reading. When he was a child, he would go to the library every weekend with his mum and choose as many books as he was allowed, mostly sci-fi novels with lurid covers, or thrillers, stories of secret agents, usually ending with a big shootout. He liked the sci-fi ones best. It was pure escapism. But the accident put an end to all that, somehow. It was like something in his head had switched off. Now he was in a kind of despair. *There is no TV and that is a disaster*, he thought. And so, the books or the puzzles. The prospect of another night looking into the fire and waiting for someone to look in at the window, or worse, filled him with dread and he knew he must find some distraction.

There were mostly volumes on natural history. Field guides to birds and fungi, the *Shell Book of the English*

Countryside, Wildflowers of The British Isles, little *Observer* books of shells, trees, stones and suchlike. He hoped there might be a map or guidebook that would tell him where he was but there was nothing like that. One shelf was of novels, mainly old paperbacks. He took a book entitled *The Trial* – the description on the back made it sound like a thriller – and sat before the fire with it. Two pages in, he fell asleep.

He must know the extent of the wood. And he must know his way through it and out of it. If they came and he had to get away, he must know how to do it. And so, the next morning, seeing that the rain had stopped, he put on boots and coat, opened the gate in the fence and followed the path that led away from the house into the trees. It was much overgrown and wound confusingly across the head of the valley. The ground dropped away steeply on one side and in places, where the woods were more open, he had views looking down the valley, long and wide and filled with trees. In the distance he saw hills, but no roads, no buildings. Above, the hill climbed steeply, and he resolved to try to go up there and find the crest another day. From a high viewpoint he would be able to understand his surroundings better.

As he walked, he began to see that the valley in which the house squatted was one of a series that fell from a long line of hills. The path tracked across the hillside, rising and falling as it crossed gullies and ridges.

He walked for an hour, pushing through bushes and tall grasses, scraped by branches that had sagged across the way, trying to maintain a level passage across the hillside. At times, the path disappeared, only to inexplicably re-emerge twenty feet or so on. *People do this for fun*, he thought, incredulously. Everything was slimy, wet and heavy, dingy, black and brown, not even green, and he was soon soaked, his feet squelching in his boots. He felt enveloped and encroached upon. The sheer abundance and entanglement, the overwhelming *presentness* of so much life, so much growing matter (and its opposite, rot and decay), unnerved him. It was disgusting. Every time he came into a clearing, he hoped he had reached the edge of the woods. But there was no sign of it, the forest appeared to be endless, and so eventually he stopped. He sat on the trunk of an old tree that had fallen across the path and considered his situation. Above him the sky was heavy, and he knew it would rain again.

He would make a map, he decided. But then, as he thought it through, he wondered about those who had been before. Had someone else, one of his predecessors, had the same idea? Perhaps there was a map already?

When he got back to the house, he built up the fire and then began to search. Where would one hide a map?

The kitchen table had a drawer. In it were pens and pencils and a notepad missing half its pages. There were some old newspapers, their pages brown and crispy. String. A screwdriver and some screws. He took a sheet of paper and drew an approximation of the ground he had covered.

Nash woke from terrible dreams in the middle of the night and knew that something had changed. It was freezing cold and for the first time there really was silence outside. It was as if the volume had been turned down. He went to the window and saw that it was snowing heavily, just as Mary Owen had predicted.

In the morning, the windows were swirled with frost flowers and the snow was already lying deep. Outside was just black and white. There was no colour. For the first time, Nash felt his fear give way to a strange kind of contentment. It was even nice to be in the house, cosy and warm, with a fire going and a hot cup of tea to hand, while outside the snow fell.

By midday a wind had come and was driving the snow against the windows. He lay on the sofa and tried to read *The Trial* but fell asleep. When he woke the light had gone and the only sound was the wind. It swirled in the chimney, a mournful music.

For four days it continued to snow intermittently, and the drifts grew deeper, keeping Nash inside the house. He began to worry. Would Mary Owen be able to come back? He was already beginning to run low on some things.

Every day, he cleared snow from the woodpile and chopped logs, building the stack beside the wood-burner so that they could dry. He kept the fire going all day long. It was the only way to keep the cold out. At night he would build it up before lighting the fire in his bedroom, but by morning both fires would have burned down, leaving only cold grey ash.

Stubbornly, he forced himself to read *The Trial*, hating it. It seemed plotless. Or, at least, it never progressed, only looping round and around, pointlessly. *Do people really read this stuff for fun?* he wondered. He abandoned it halfway in, and started an ancient hardback called *The Count of Monte Cristo* instead.

He began a jigsaw puzzle of an oil painting depicting a horse and cart crossing a river. Scanning the tabletop for a piece of blue sky, a fragment of water, was meditative, dreamlike even. He found he could easily lose a couple of hours like that.

On the third day he went again to chop wood and saw that there were tracks in the snow. As far as he could tell, someone had come from the trees, through the gate at the side of the house, had circled the building, and had then headed down the valley on the track.

On the fourth day he completed the jigsaw puzzle. Inevitably, there were two pieces missing. It seemed somehow appropriate. He would have been amazed if all the pieces had been present.

As he waited for Owen to come again, it began to dawn on him that he might be in this place for some time. At first, he had thought it would only be for a couple of days, perhaps a week at the most. But gradually, he realised, he was beginning to think of it in terms of *weeks*. Something that The Grey Man had said, about being thorough, *diligent*, suggested there was no rush. He must be patient. Yet, he must prepare.

In the void spaces of the house, spiderwebs as old as oak trees are still, soft with dust.

Within the old walls, embedded in mortar, the ancient corpse of a cat, as dry as parchment, eye sockets blind and empty, wrapped in leather and bound with twine, shivers imperceptibly.

(3)

Thinking it over, Nash kept on going back to his recruitment, his *calling*, whatever one termed it. It was a moment that had come to seem like a pivot about which his life had been turned. In truth, there were many such moments, such turning points – the accident, of course, being the most important of all – but that moment, that first meeting with The Grey Man, was looming larger and larger in his thoughts.

Recruitment. Was that even the right word? Had he been hired? No, not really. It seemed there was more to it than a simple contractual arrangement. (And what contract, anyway? He had signed some pieces of paper, but they had not had anything written on them.) Engaged, summoned, *called*? He could not say for sure.

He had been in the pub. At this particular time, he was living in a terrible shared house with Mooney, who he had met on the night shift at a supermarket supply warehouse, and a bunch of hard-drinking builders from eastern Europe who spoke almost no English. The rent was cheap and the accommodation correspondingly nasty. His room matched his state of mind. The carpet was threadbare. There was only a mattress in one corner, an unsteady chair with some clothes thrown over it, and a clothes rail with a single coat hanging from it. The walls were bare and mottled with damp. One corner bloomed with a thick black mould like soot. He had no pictures to put up. He had no trinkets or nice things to improve the ambience. But that was fine. The bareness of it, the rawness, suited him. He spent long hours just lying on the dirty bed, brooding. The lead-up to the accident, the consequences. He still occasionally wrote letters to his father, but he never posted them. He felt lonely but didn't know what to do about it. At the same time, he felt that the loneliness, the meanness of his surroundings, were a kind of penance. It was something he had to endure. It was necessary.

This particular evening, he had gone to the pub with Mooney. There was not much conversation (there never was), and when Mooney left to get ready for the shift, Nash stayed, feeling entropic, not caring if he missed the signing on and lost another shitty job. He sat at a corner table, sipping a pint. A man at the bar, talking animatedly with one of the bar staff, kept turning and looking at him. He thought nothing of it.

Finishing his beer, he went to piss. As he washed his hands, examining his weary face in the mirror above the sinks, the door into the toilets suddenly exploded, kicked in with astonishing force. The man from the bar was there. His face was red-hot, a massive bruise, a knot of rage. He pointed a shaking finger at Nash, like a gun.

'You fucker!' he said, through gritted teeth. 'Don't. You. *Fucking*. Mess. With. Me. Son! *Don't*.'

Nash thought it was very strange how he seemed to enunciate every word separately, as if there were a full stop between each component part of the sentence. He was sure he had never seen him before. Yet he clearly meant him harm. He was obviously drunk. Raging drunk.

Nash was surprised by how calm he felt.

'What?' he asked, evenly. And then, after a pause, 'I don't know who you are.'

This seemed to infuriate the man. He took a step forward. 'I've. Told. You. Before.'

'No, you haven't.' Nash raised his hands in a gesture of openness. 'I've never seen you before,' he said, gently. 'You've got the wrong person.'

The blow landed before he even saw it coming. Perhaps he had blinked, but the man's fist came from nowhere and crashed into his face. It was like something had exploded inside his skull. For a moment everything was bleached white and white-hot and the roaring was unbearably loud. He staggered backwards and regained his balance, his ears ringing. Then something very strange happened. The man stepped forward again, his fists clenched, getting in close enough to strike. Nash felt very calm, despite the hit he had taken and the damage. It didn't hurt, but he was vaguely aware that something had broken – a tooth? his nose? – and that there was blood. And yet, without thinking about it in the slightest, without being fully aware of what he was doing, he stepped to one side, wrong-footing the man who, he saw now, was wearing a t-shirt with a smiley face on it, which seemed odd, and whose skin was cratered and raw, and whose ears sprouted wiry tufts of black hair, and Nash hit him. He hit him in the face, his fist connecting just below his eye, and even as he hit him, he was surprised at how hard he was able to hit him. It was a hammer blow. It was not something he had ever done before.

As if someone had flicked a switch and disconnected the power, the man fell straight to the tiled floor and didn't move. Still, Nash felt unusually calm. He touched his face and looked at his fingers, which were covered in blood. It didn't hurt, which seemed very odd to him. It *should* hurt, he thought. Everything was happening extraordinarily slowly, it seemed.

The man lay very still. That was strange too. Blood was coming from a cut below his eye. Nash wondered idly if he should kick him or stamp on his head or something, but, seeing that he was not moving, it didn't seem necessary.

After a while, the man lurched to his feet. He leant unsteadily against the door, his eyes closed, blood slowly staining his t-shirt. Nash wondered if he was going to come at him again, if he should hit him once more, pre-emptively. But no, the man did not even seem to be aware of his presence. With great effort he got the door open – which, Nash noticed, had buckled when he had kicked it – and staggered out into the passageway. The door swung shut behind him.

Nash steadied himself against the sink and saw that the white porcelain was speckled with a fine spray of blood. He couldn't bring himself to look in the mirror. He spat into the sink, a clot of blood, and walked the passageway back into the bar. The room was silent. Everyone was looking at him. His assailant lay prostrate on the floor in the middle of the room. Nash crossed to the bar and spoke to the barman. 'He attacked me,' he said. 'I've got no idea who he is. I've never seen him before.' He was conscious that his voice sounded unusual, as if he was using a stranger's mouth to speak.

The barman handed him a beer towel and he mopped his mouth and chin, which seemed to be very bloody. Still, it did not hurt. 'I'll call the police,' the barman said.

Nash sat on a bar stool and looked around. Everyone was staring at him and the room was quiet.

'He got the wrong person,' he said to no one in particular. 'I don't know who he is.' He could hear someone somewhere on a phone, talking urgently.

'This might help,' someone said, and there was a glass of whisky in his hand. He drank, and it did indeed seem to help in some indefinable way. His ears were ringing but it still did not hurt.

'The police are coming,' the barman was saying.

The man he had hit climbed to his feet and staggered across the room to the front door. His face was a mess of clotting blood and his eye was already closing up. His t-shirt was awash with blood, obscuring the smiley face. He seemed to be buffeted by gale-force winds.

'Bye,' Nash heard himself saying as the man opened the door with difficulty and lurched out into the street.

Someone was beside him. He turned and saw a man, a grey man in a grey suit.

'Forgive me,' the man said to him, and his voice was odd, foreign. 'But I think this might be of interest.' He held up a business card and slowly placed it on the bar next to Nash's whisky glass, which had mysteriously been filled again. Nash stared at it in confusion. 'We have opportunities for people with your…' The grey man talking to him paused, searching for the right word. '… your particular *talents*.'

Nash nodded. He pocketed the card without reading it.

'Call the number,' the man said.

Nash nodded. (And later, much later, he would think to himself, *that was the beginning of it all*.)

Everything then stretched out interminably. At some point someone pushed a clump of tissues into his hand. 'Yours, I think,' they said. Nash unfolded the delicate white paper – like a flower, he thought to himself – and there at the centre, crusted with blood, was a tooth. 'It was on the floor,' someone said. Nash nodded. He ran his tongue around the inside of his mouth and felt the unfamiliar absence. Still, it did not hurt.

The police arrived and carried away his attacker, who had somehow got himself out of the pub but had collapsed on the pavement, where he was surrounded by onlookers. Two officers began to ask him questions. Nash explained what had happened several times. They kept on asking if he was absolutely sure he had been hit first. Of course he was. And yes, he was sure he had never seen the man before that evening. No, he had not said anything to him before he had gone into the toilet. They then explained that Nash would probably be required to attend some kind of court hearing at an unforeseen point in the future. They were keen to press charges against this man who, it seemed, had a record for this kind of thing, attacking people in pubs after too many pints.

'Some people are just angry,' said one of the policemen.

'Some people just like fighting,' said the other. He shook his head, sadly.

Once all that was done, Nash was taken to the local hospital where he waited for two hours for a nurse to put three stiches in his upper lip. 'Take Paracetamol,' she said.

It was only now, some hours after the event, that it was beginning to hurt.

Indeed, his whole face felt swollen and tender. He got a taxi home, feeling unutterably weary. At the house, the eastern Europeans were gathered in the sitting room, smoking and drinking beer from cans while watching some kind of talent show on the television. He knocked on Mooney's door, forgetting that he would not be back from the warehouse until the morning. Nash would be in trouble for his absence. *Fuck that*, he thought. He climbed into his filthy bed and slept until noon the next day.

Two days later he found the business card in the pocket of his jeans. There was only a phone number. No name. He thought about it and then called. The phone rang three times before it was answered. There was a pause, which was longer than was comfortable, and then a voice asked, 'Yes?'

Nash hesitated. 'You gave me your card in the pub, The Crown, a couple of days ago. After I was attacked. You said I should call. That there might be an opportunity.'

'Ah, yes.' The disembodied voice sounded pleased. 'Of course, I do remember. You were attacked. But you retaliated, didn't you? How could I forget? You were very impressive. Can I ask what your name is?'

'Nash, I'm Nash. Who am I speaking to?'

The voice ignored the question. 'Well, Mr Nash, perhaps we can arrange a time to meet. Are you free tomorrow?'

'Yes, I work nights at the moment.'

The voice named a café and a time and suggested they meet for a conversation over coffee.

Nash agreed. 'But who am I talking to?' he asked again.

'Don't worry,' the voice replied good-naturedly. 'I'll explain everything when I see you.'

When Nash arrived at the café he was already there, seated at a corner table. He was *grey*. Vaguely old, with greying hair, combed back from a high forehead. The pale grey complexion of a heavy smoker (and indeed, Nash inhaled the scent of old smoke, stale cigarettes, ashtrays). Cold eyes, drooping eyelids that made him look disdainful. He rose to shake Nash's hand and he saw he was wearing a dark grey suit, white shirt, dark tie, and was very tall and thin. Yet his handshake was firm and there was about him an air of power, a lack of doubt, that was quietly impressive.

'Good morning, Mr Nash,' he said, looking down his nose at him. 'Thank you so much for coming.'

'Not at all. Thank you for meeting me. I'm curious to know what this opportunity you mentioned might be.'

'Well, it depends.'

'On what?'

'On this conversation. You see, while you certainly have the skills we're looking for, this is not a role that is suited to anybody. I'll need to ask you some questions.'

'Of course,' said Nash.

'How old are you?'

'Twenty-four.'

'Really, so young! I'm surprised. I thought you were older.'

'How old?' asked Nash, curious. 'Does it matter?'

'No, of course not. I don't know, I thought perhaps you were in your late twenties, perhaps early thirties.' He grinned, horribly. 'Mr Nash, you're little more than a child! One of God's children. Of course, it doesn't matter. If necessary, we can teach you. We can mould you...'

They ordered coffee and there followed an elliptical conversation. First, Nash was asked about his family and education, his present circumstances and his work on the night shift. Why had he not taken up his place at the university, which was surely such a wonderful opportunity? Nash explained about the accident and how that had changed everything. Did he have any dependents, a girlfriend or boyfriend? No. Siblings? Again, no. Did he have a criminal record? No, he did not. Was he religious? Nash considered this one, sipping his coffee. 'No, not really,' he said. 'But sometimes I think that there might be something else. I can't quite explain.'

'A spiritual dimension?' asked the man.

'Something like that.'

'How interesting.' He had taken a small notebook from his jacket and now made some notes. 'Personally, I think God, *if* He exists, has let us down. Yes, He's let us down rather badly. His creation, such as it is, has gone off the rails, has it not? We are tumbling towards the abyss.' He watched Nash for his reaction. 'Perhaps we always have been. Perhaps that was His intention all along. To test us. What do you think?'

'I wouldn't know.'

'The question is, what is to be done, given that chaos, not order, is the guiding principle now. Perhaps we should encourage this Fall, help facilitate the inevitable endgame. What do you think of that? Might it not be our duty?'

'I really don't know.'

The Grey Man nodded. He was smiling.

'Very well. And what about politics?'

Nash shook his head.

'Don't you read the newspapers, keep up with current affairs, that sort of thing?'

'Not anymore. There doesn't seem to be any point.'

'Well, I take your point. Politics is a nasty little game, is it not? A dog fight. An undignified brawl. A race to the bottom. We might well be lost, Mr Nash, given the state of things as they are now. There is only a thin layer of ice protecting us from a deep ocean of chaos and darkness. And we are walking upon the ice. And cracks are beginning to form.' He paused. 'Well, perhaps we can do something about that.'

Nash nodded and waited.

'What do you think? Should we stamp our feet and break the ice?'

Nash shrugged. He wasn't sure where this was going.

'And the incident in the pub, has anything like that happened to you before?'

Nash shook his head.

'Tell me what happened.'

Nash told him. He explained how the man had burst into the toilets and screamed at him. How he had known immediately that it was an error, a confusion, that the man had mistaken him for someone else. And how the blow, when it had come, had surprised him, and had somehow not hurt, at least not until much later.

'And he hit you first?'

Nash nodded. 'He hit me and there was this strange sense of calm. And I hit him. I didn't know I could hit him so hard. I never punched anyone before, not really. He went straight down.'

'And you walked away.'

'Yes. I thought about, you know, finishing it, but it didn't seem necessary. I just wanted to get away from him. He repelled me.'

'Were you angry?'

'Of course.'

'But you were in control?'

'Yes.'

'I have to say, the way you reacted was really very impressive. And after, in the bar, you seemed so calm. Did you know you would be like that?'

Nash shook his head again. 'No, to be honest it surprised me. It was like an out-of-body experience in a way. I mean, it didn't hurt – my face where he hit me or my hand where I hit him – until much later. It was like I was anaesthetized. But I still had absolute clarity of thought and action. My head was clear.'

'That is interesting. That is a very interesting ability to have. We might call it a talent.'

'Thank you,' said Nash.

'You have a great capacity for... *action*,' said The Grey Man, smiling. Even his teeth were grey. 'But it's well hidden. It's all below the surface. Normally, with people who can do what you did, it's on the surface. You can read it in the face, the potential for violence. Like that chap in the pub, your assailant. I dare say one could have predicted he would do something like that, just by looking into his eyes. It's like a terrible badge they wear, and that is why people are intimidated by them. But you, Mr Nash, you are different. You go under the radar. You don't look like you would be capable of it, but you are. That can be very useful.'

'But I don't like it,' protested Nash.

'No, of course, you don't have to like it. You just have to acknowledge it, understand that it's a power you have and that you can use it. That you can *learn* to use it.'

He wrote something in his notebook.

'If I were to tell you that we – the people I work with, our organisation – can use this talent you have, and reward you for it, how would you feel?'

'I don't know.' Nash considered. 'I'm not sure it's something I want to embrace.'

'It would be a shame not to realise your potential, would it not?'

'Well, I can think about it.'

'Very good. I can't ask for more than that.'

They talked some more about generalities, abstractions. Finally, it seemed there were no more questions. The Grey Man leaned back and regarded Nash. 'Very good,' he said.

'So, what is it?' asked Nash. 'What's the job? Can you tell me about the job? Is it security?'

'Something like that.' He was looking over his notes.

'Government?'

'No, not really. Though we do have connections.'

'Is it above board?'

'Oh yes, of course.'

'And have I passed? Do you want me?'

'I'll need to consult with my colleagues, Mr Nash. Could we meet again? Same time tomorrow? Would that be possible?'

Nash nodded. The Grey Man rose and they shook hands again. After he had gone, Nash sat and mulled over what had happened. He was confused. He still didn't know his interviewer's name. He had been asked a great many questions, and while he had asked some in return, he had received no answers.

They met a further three times. The first two times consisted mainly of The Grey Man (who told Nash, 'You may call me Gray, with an *a*, but it's not my real name') asking questions. At the end, Nash would ask again what the job entailed, and if he had 'passed'. Each time he was frustrated. Gray needed to 'consult' further. Nash had the sense that they – whoever *they* were – were probably running various checks on him. That was how it worked, he supposed. The longer it went on, the more he began to think that this might be his chance to make everything right again. Finally, at the fourth meeting, Gray said, 'Okay, no more questions. Let me explain.'

He paused as he gathered his thoughts.

'This is the sort of situation where one learns on the job, so to speak. Let me say this: we have to be very discreet. And for that reason, it is best you don't know too much until we know you are fully committed. Let's say information is disclosed on a need-to-know basis.'

'Is it Intelligence?' asked Nash. He had started to wonder if he was being recruited by some sort of secret service agency, MI5 or 6. He had heard of this sort of thing. The way they did it. The secrecy of it.

'Not exactly,' replied Gray.

'Not exactly? What does that mean? Is it dangerous?'

'It might be. Probably not. Certainly not at first.'

'But it's not illegal? You know, *criminal*?'

'What do you take me for, Mr Nash? Some sort of gangster?'

'No, of course not. I'm sorry, I didn't mean to suggest…'

'It's nothing.' Gray dismissed it. 'Now, Mr Nash, let's talk terms and conditions.'

And that was how Nash came to work for them. At the time, it seemed, there was nothing to lose.

(4)

Mary Owen came again on horseback on the first day it didn't snow. She knocked on the door and waited for Nash to let her in. He was pleased to see her.

She was dressed exactly as she had been before, but with the addition of mittens, a thick scarf striped with various shades of brown, and a woolly hat which was pulled down low over her ears.

'Hard work for Charlie, with all the snow,' she said, blowing and stamping her feet. 'Poor old thing. I always forget it's quite a climb up the valley.'

Nash took the basket from her and carried it through to the kitchen. She took off the hat, mittens and scarf and put them on the bench in the hallway and followed him in, hoisting her rucksack onto one of the chairs. He put the kettle on to boil and she unpacked his things in silence.

When the tea was ready, they sat holding the mugs cupped with both hands.

'I couldn't come sooner,' she said.
'That's okay, I'm still here.'
'Were you worried?'

'A little,' he said. 'I was beginning to think I might go hungry.'

'With the snow it would have been hard to get up here, even on Charley. And there was a lot to do on the farm, you know, with the animals.'

'You farm?'

'Well, not really, just the basics. A smallholding, I suppose you would call it. Chickens for the eggs and the meat. A cow for the milk. A couple of sheep and a pig. Vegetables and so on. It's not much but it keeps us going and it keeps us busy. Especially when the weather's like this and we have to bring the animals into the barn.'

'We? Is that you and your husband?' asked Nash.

'No husband, not anymore,' she said sadly. 'Just me and Brigid.'

'Brigid?'

'My little one. Not so little these days. She's not allowed up in the woods so don't get any ideas.'

'Why is she not allowed in the woods?'

'Because people have a way of getting lost up here. And also on account of what happened before.'

'What happened before?'

'There was some nastiness.'

'Nastiness?'

She shook her head. 'Never mind that. How are you coping? You lonely?'

Nash shrugged. He wanted to say that the woods were terrifying, just too much – too wild, too dark, too *alive* – and he hated the house and thought it was almost certainly haunted or animated in some way, and also he didn't know what the hell was going on. But he didn't say anything, only shrugged.

'I feel sorry for you,' said Mary Owen. 'Boy like you should be down the pub of an evening. There's a lovely pub down in the village.'

'I'll survive. I'm an only child so I'm used to being alone. In some ways, I prefer it.'

'Well, that's something. But even so, I dare say you feel lonely sometimes.'

Nash shrugged.

She looked at him slyly. 'So what happened? You screwed up, did you?'

Nash shook his head.

'Usually, they come here when they've screwed up.'

'It wasn't me,' said Nash. 'It was someone else.'

'Whatever. None of my business.' She stood up. 'Look, I know you asked for records but that'll have to wait. I haven't got any. I'll go to town in a week or so and there's a couple of charity shops I can look in. They always have vinyl, don't they, old LPs? Okay, is there anything else you need me to bring next time?'

'You brought whisky?' She nodded. 'Then I'm okay for now.'

She got ready to leave.

'Thanks,' said Nash, and he suddenly felt tender towards this woman, who he didn't know, but who, for now, was his only link to the outside world.

'By the way, what's the pub called?'

'The Black Prince.'

He nodded. A good name. He could picture it. Fire in the grate, the shine of brass, the hum of conversation. The smell of beer.

'You're sure there's nothing else?'

'Shaving stuff.' He ran his hands over his chin.

'Of course, got to keep up appearances. Busy social life, isn't it?'

He grinned, sheepishly.

'Anything else?'

Nash considered. 'If I write a letter, could you give it to them?' he asked.

'I suppose I can pass something on.'

'I just want to ask what's going on. How long it might be,' he said.

'Please yourself,' said Mary Owen. 'Not my business. Like I said last time, I just keep you alive and clear up after you're gone.'

'How did you get the job?' he asked. 'I mean, how do you know them? How did you come to work for them?' He was going to say, *you don't seem like the type*, but stopped himself. *Perhaps she doesn't really know about them*, he thought.

'Can't say, Mr Nash. I've already said too much, I expect.'

'Tell me this then,' he said. 'Why is it called Paradise? Is it some sort of a joke?'

'I expect it's always been called it,' she said. 'Adam and Eve lived in Paradise, and I suppose that all over the world there are special places that have been named for it, that people think either *are* Paradise, or which are some kind of echo of it. Some say Paradise is a garden, as simple as that. Some say Paradise is a place where the souls of the righteous await resurrection and the final judgement. You know, there's an old story that somewhere in these woods is a gate and on the other side is the Garden of Eden. The actual one from the Bible. The Hole in the Wood, they call it. I'm not sure about that. There are lots of stories, Mr Nash. Around here people love to tell stories. There's a spring at the head of the valley and the waters have healing properties. There's the standing stone they call Old Nick's Finger. There's the barrow. Lots of stories about that one. Paradise has its fair share of tales and legends.'

'What's a barrow?'

'Long barrow. Burial chamber. Very ancient. Could be King Arthur, who knows. They call it Arthur's Door, but it's probably nothing to do with him. No, to be honest I don't know why it's called Paradise. The wood is Paradise and the house is Paradise. Always has been. Simple as that.'

'And do they own it? Our employers?'

She shook her head. 'I really don't know the answer to that one.'

'Let me ask another question,' he said. 'What if I just go? What if I just walk away? Out of here. Down the valley to the road. What will happen to me? Will anyone try to stop me?'

'I couldn't say, Mr Nash. Not my business to speculate. You know that. But I will say one thing: I don't think you should try it.'

'Has anyone tried it before?'

'Well, you know I can't say.'

'Have there been many?'

'Many what?'

'People kept here. Staying here.'

'There've been a few. It's been a while though. You're the first in a while.'

She put on her hat and was about to wrap the scarf about her neck when she paused. 'Are you keeping warm enough? Here, take this.' She offered it to him.

'No, I couldn't.'

'Yes, you can. Go on, love. I've got plenty more, but I suspect you didn't bring half enough clothes with you, did you?'

He took the scarf and tied it about his neck. It was thick and he immediately felt the warmth.

'Thank you.'

'My pleasure.' She smiled for the first time and Nash felt a rush of gratitude.

'Before I forget, I brought something else for you.' She opened one of the rucksack pockets and drew out a strange object, a cross woven from green grass or reeds, about the size of her hand. It was like the old and yellowed ones that hung from various beams about the house, and over some of the windows, but was new.

'What is it?'

'It's for the year's turning, for Imbolc.'

Nash frowned, uncomprehending.

'One of the old days, from before. Supposedly it's the beginning of spring, though it don't feel like it this year, does it? I'll put it over the front door.' She hung the cross on an old black nail driven into the door frame. 'It'll keep out illness and evil spirits.' She winked at him. 'Given your situation, I should say you need all the help you can get in that regard.'

Nash smiled. He thought she was joking.

'Who's to say if it works or not,' she said sternly. 'There's comfort in traditions, reassurance in ritual. So don't sniff at it. I won't.'

Nash looked closer. The cross consisted of a central square with four offset arms, each the same length. She had hung it diagonally, not vertically like a church cross.

'Thank you,' he said. 'I mean it.'

He came out with her and watched her get on the horse. 'Charley won't bite,' she said, and he went over and stroked its neck. It was the first time he had been so close to such a big animal, and he was awed by its mass and power, and also its seeming gentleness. It sniffed at him and nudged his hand when he stopped stroking.

'Doesn't he get cold?'

'He's okay. He's a tough one is Charlie.' She nodded. 'I'll see you again soon, Mr Nash,' she said. 'Look after yourself, love. Keep well wrapped up.'

Nash watched her go, and when she was out of sight he went and chopped wood. The scarf wrapped about his throat smelled strongly of her.

A hole in the wood, he thought. *What does that even mean?* In the kitchen, he unscrewed the cap from the bottle of whisky and drank deeply, feeling the fiery warmth spread through his body.

The next day, when Nash rose, the cold was absolute, hard, making his jaw clench. His hands shook as he filled the kettle. When he went to piss, he saw there was ice in the toilet bowl.

No one can be out in this, he thought. *They can't be watching when it's like this.*

He put on almost all his clothes and set out to walk the lane, to know how far it was to the village, to the road, to the outside world.

It was bright, despite the greyness of the sky. The snow was deep and had a crust, giving way to softness beneath.

It was piled deeply upon everything, branches and bushes, creating a world of peculiarly rounded forms.

He could see the horse's tracks and followed them.

From the house, the way descended quickly, carving through the woods that pressed in on both sides, curving across the hillside, before crossing a small stream and then straightening out. It then followed the side of the valley in a gradual descent. Occasionally, smaller tracks branched off, but he ignored them. The trees leant in on both sides, weighed down with snow, and wherever it was more open the snow had drifted across the way, making it hard going. Sometimes he saw animal tracks and wondered what kind of beast had left them: fox, badger, deer, *other*.

He walked for an hour, sometimes forcing his way through deep drifts, and then stopped to rest. A gate led into a small field above the track, and from there he had a good view up the hill above the house. The trees continued all the way up to the ridge. Away to his right, the hillside rose up out of the trees and was criss-crossed with stone walls. Beyond the ridge a mountain loomed in the distance, snow-clad. Thick clouds hung there.

After another hour of walking, making slow progress in the snow, he saw a church steeple ahead, rising above the trees, and knew that he was finally coming to the edge of the wood. It was a relief to see open space; he didn't like the constant encroachment of the trees, the feeling of enclosure. He came to a gate and saw that the way continued across an open field, an expanse of pure white snow unsullied but for the horse's tracks, then passed through another gate and became a road. There was a row of houses and a church.

Farm buildings and more houses lay beyond. Nash hesitated. He wanted to go on, but it would mean leaving the woods and he feared the consequences. As he watched, a figure, a child perhaps, emerged from one of the houses. It stamped its feet in the snow and then, looking around, caught sight of him and stopped. It was too far away to tell if it was a boy or a girl, or how old he or she might be. They watched each other for a long moment, and then the figure raised an arm and waved to him. He waved back.

It took him two hours to get back up the hill to the house. By the time he reached it he was exhausted and soaked to the skin. The light was fading and he knew that it was going to snow again. Soon enough, it began.

He sat at the kitchen table and carefully added the track and village to his putative map of the woods. Then he ran a hot bath and luxuriated in it, chasing the cold from his bones, before collapsing into bed and falling straight into a deep and dreamless sleep.

(5)

At the end of their last meeting, The Grey Man produced a mobile phone, one of the old ones, from his briefcase and handed it to Nash.

'This is for *us* to reach *you*, so we can give you your instructions. Don't call us. Ever. We call you. In fact, don't use this phone for anything else. Do you understand? It's very important.'

Nash nodded. 'So, what happens now?' he asked.

'Someone will be in touch to sort out the paperwork. And once that's done, you can make a start.'

'Make a start?'

'Yes, make a start.'

'What will I make a start on?'

'Whatever it is we ask you to make a start on.'

'Okay, so I just wait for the call?'

'Indeed.' Gray paused, looked Nash up and down, and grimaced. Nash was wearing jeans, a black t-shirt, a puffer jacket. 'Mr Nash, do you have a suit by any chance?' he asked. 'This present outfit is' – he searched for the right word – '*inadequate*. Inappropriate.'

Nash shook his head.

'We'll have to do something about that,' said Gray, wearily. 'There are standards to maintain. It is important to give the right impression. If you look businesslike, like you mean business, people will treat you accordingly.'

He stood and they shook hands.

'Very well, Mr Nash, I suppose it has been a pleasure. I don't expect to see you again from now on, unless something comes up. Let's hope nothing does.'

'Thank you,' said Nash. 'I'm grateful for the chance.'

Nash told Mooney he was done with the night shift. When Mooney asked what his new gig was, he shrugged and realised he didn't quite know what to say.

'I've got a job. Government department, I think.'

'You think? Don't you know who you're going to be working for?'

'It's very secretive.'

'Doing what?'

'I can't really say. It's a bit, you know, hush-hush.'

Mooney guffawed. 'Oh right, really? MI5, is it?'

Nash nodded. 'Got to be better than nights in that shithole.'

'Fair enough.' Mooney thought about it and then asked, 'But why would they want you?'

'What do you mean?'

'Well, there's not much to you, is there. No offence, mate, but there's nothing to you really. You're like a blank page.'

'Perhaps that's why they want me,' said Nash.

Two days later the new phone rang and a voice introduced itself as 'Browne, with an e.' They made an arrangement to meet the next day at the same café where he had met Gray.

When Nash arrived, Browne was already there, sitting at the very same table, and Nash did a double take: Browne looked like Gray's brother. In fact, he looked like Gray's *twin*. The same hooded eyes, thin lips, the same dark suit. The same way of looking both aloof and amused.

Browne stood and they shook hands. 'This won't take long. There are just a few formalities.'

He produced a manila envelope from his briefcase and pulled from it a sheaf of papers. Each was blank except for a printed box towards the bottom of the page, below which was Nash's name.

'If you could just...' said Browne, offering Nash a pen and gesturing to the papers.

Nash leafed through them to ascertain if they were indeed all blank.

'Is it a mistake?' he asked, hesitantly.

'I'm sorry?' said Browne.

'There's nothing on them.'

'Oh yes, of course, I see! No, no mistake. Ha ha. Standard procedure. Completely normal. Can't have you seeing what you're signing, can we?' Browne chuckled at the very absurdity of such a thing.

This seemed all wrong to Nash, but he didn't want to jeopardise the opportunity that was before him, so he took the pen and carefully signed his name at the bottom of each sheet.

'Lovely,' said Browne, tucking the papers back into the envelope. 'Now, you'll be picked up tomorrow at nine by White. You'll be working with him, at least in the first phase.'

'Picked up?'

'Yes, he'll pick you up. From your place. Nine a.m. sharp.'

'Okay. And he'll explain things?'

'He will.'

'What about payroll? Don't you need my bank details or something like that?'

Browne laughed again. 'Good lord, no. You are amusing, Nash. No, you'll be paid in cash. Cash for Nash. Ah, but that reminds me.' He rummaged in his briefcase and produced a second, smaller envelope. 'This is for you,' he said, laying it gently on the table. 'Orders. You're to get a suit. You've got to look the part if you're going to play it properly.'

Nash looked into the envelope and saw that it contained banknotes.

'Excellent.' Browne smiled as he stood. 'Then we're done here. No questions? Good.'

He offered his hand before Nash could say anything.

'Good luck, Mr Nash. Remember, Mr White at nine tomorrow morning.'

Nash finished his coffee and walked to the high street. The envelope contained enough money to get a cheap suit, two plain white shirts and a tie. He congratulated himself. He had enough left over to treat himself to a takeaway and a four-pack that evening. For the first time in an age, he felt happy and optimistic.

In the morning, Nash rose early, shaved and dressed carefully. The suit and shirt and tie were unfamiliar, and he felt self-conscious. But also, he thought to himself, it was true, you felt different dressed up like that, you felt *professional*. He drank tea in the filthy kitchen and at ten minutes before nine he went outside to wait.

In the street a young man in a smart suit and tie was leaning against a black car, drinking a takeaway coffee. Seeing Nash, he came over.

'Nash?' he asked. 'You're early! That's a good start. I'm White.'

'Pleased to meet you.'

They shook hands and walked back towards the car. White was tall, slim and athletic looking, with a surety to his movements that made Nash think, just for a second, that he was playing a well-rehearsed part. He was handsome, with clear eyes and high cheekbones, a sliver of moustache and carefully trimmed goatee. His head was shaved and burnished. His suit was nicer (meaning more expensive) than Nash's. He wore a pale blue shirt and a knitted navy tie. 'Righto,' he said, 'let's get going.' He was well spoken. Public school, thought Nash, who, when younger, had always tried not to pick up that particular manner despite attending one himself.

They drove for about twenty minutes and then parked in a side street.

'Wait here,' said White, getting out of the car but motioning for Nash to stay. 'I won't be long.'

Two minutes later he was back, carrying a parcel the size of a shoe box, wrapped in brown paper. 'Here,' he said, thrusting it towards Nash.

They drove across town, spending almost an hour in traffic moving at no more than walking pace. The traffic was definitely getting worse. Soon it would grind to a permanent standstill. *Who would even think about driving in this city?* thought Nash. *Quicker by tube.* As they went, White explained to Nash that for the next few days they would be mainly on courier duty. Picking packages up, dropping packages off. 'Pretty boring stuff,' he said, 'but easy going. That is, unless someone attempts an *interception*.' He said this melodramatically and winked at Nash. 'Next week we might be on surveillance. I prefer that.'

White explained that for now, their daily instructions would be phoned in to White. All Nash had to do was be ready at nine and follow White's lead.

'And then will I be assigned somewhere else?' he asked.

'Who knows? Operatives always work in pairs, so we may end up sticking together. At some point I'll have to write you up, so we'll see, won't we?'

The first day and the second and the third passed uneventfully. White picked him up at nine and they spent the day driving from location to location, from pick-up to drop-off, always in the dreadful traffic, crawling slowly through thick clouds of exhaust fumes. Sometimes Nash was allowed to go and pick up the packages – usually this involved knocking on a door or ringing a bell and taking whatever was handed to him – sometimes he made the drop-offs. There was never any paperwork, no chits or receipts, and neither was there conversation, banter, or even the basic courtesies of please and thank you.

Often, as they waited for White's phone to ring with the next set of instructions, they would drink coffee and work on a crossword or sudoku puzzle from one of the broadsheet newspapers White always had.

Nash tried to ask White about the people they were working for, but he was always vague. He usually referred to their employers as the Company, or the Organisation. Once he called them the Order. No names were mentioned, even when Nash asked who was in charge. He tentatively asked White if he had encountered Gray when he had started. White nodded, but then explained that within the organisation no one ever used their real names. So, it was possible that the Gray he had met was not the one Nash had been interviewed by. Nash had the vague feeling that this was all some sort of joke at his expense.

It was all very vague. And that was the only thing that could be said with any certainty, if he stopped and thought about it (which he did a lot). Neither could Nash come to a clear understanding of what it was they were doing, who or what they were doing it for, or, indeed, what the purpose of any of it was. It was all very vague. And possibly vaguely hazardous. He fretted about this, thanks to White's talk of interceptions, covert operations and enemy surveillance. He wanted to know what the project was, what it was all for. He needed a sense of purpose, for purpose had been missing from his life for a very long time. And indeed, he wanted to know what his and White's roles actually were, and how they fitted into the bigger picture of whatever the project was. *I'm entry level*, he supposed. *White is a level or two further up. But for now, we're dogsbodies, that sort of thing.* He still hoped that it was some sort of branch of one of the secret services – and so assumed there was therefore a necessity to keep new employees in the dark about the exact nature of their activities. It would be policy. Yes, he suspected he was in the midst of some sort of vetting process. And all would be revealed in due course as he progressed. He imagined some sort of hierarchy of information, a pyramid of secrecy.

Nonetheless, despite his attempted optimism, his natural pessimism got the better of him and he found that he could not shake the ominous notion that it was not government at all, and nothing to do with espionage or counterterrorism or whatever, but something somehow essentially dodgy. Criminal? It felt possible. Worse still – he conjectured in his most fevered reveries – it might be some kind of religious thing. He reflected that White sometimes used words like *Congregation* and *Confirmation*. Didn't the Vatican have its own special army and secret service? He was sure he had read that somewhere. He remembered The Grey Man's words about God and chaos.

White maintained an easy-going facade and Nash found that he could tolerate his presence well enough. But if White was elusive about their employers, he was more so about himself. If Nash asked him any questions – where he was from, what he had done before – White deflected. Eventually, feeling confused, he resolved to adopt the same strategy going forward and evade instead of giving anything away.

However, White never asked about his own background. He didn't need to evade. They nattered about films they had seen and liked, complained about the traffic and the dreadful state of the city, speculated about the news they heard on the car radio, or read in the papers – the war in Central America, the collapse of Democracy in the US, rising sea levels, the energy crisis – but nothing that went beyond the superficial. *Perhaps it's all on file,* Nash thought to himself. After all, he'd gone over a lot of that with Gray during the interviews.

At the end of the first week, at six o'clock exactly, White parked the car in Nash's street. He turned off the engine, opened the glove compartment and took out a brown envelope.

'Well done, Nash,' he said. 'Week one. What do you make of it?'

Nash shrugged. 'It's fine,' he said. 'I like it. Even if I don't really know what it is we're doing.'

'It'll all become clear,' said White. 'Don't overthink it. One step at a time, okay? Look, this is for you.' He handed Nash the envelope. 'It's always cash.'

Nash nodded. He didn't want to count it in front of White.

'Have a good weekend,' said White cheerfully. 'I'll see you on Monday. Nine sharp.'

'Of course.'

Nash climbed out of the car, and as he fumbled for his keys at the front door, the black car drove away.

The second week went much like the first: deliveries and pick-ups. But one day White came back to the car with another man, also suited, who sat in the back in silence as they drove. Nash studied him in the mirror but there was a kind of blankness there that revealed nothing. Eventually, White pulled the car into a car park and the man climbed out.

'Thanks,' he said as he closed the door.

They never saw him again.

At the end of the second week, White again presented Nash with an envelope containing cash. Taking it, he said, 'I'm going to move. I can't stay in this shithole any longer.'

'I did wonder how long you'd last,' said White. 'I think we might have something for you. I'll check and let you know on Monday. Can you wait that long?'

Nash nodded, both relieved and grateful.

The following Monday, White greeted him with a smile. 'It's all sorted,' he said. 'You've been allocated a place. Get your stuff.'

Nash went back inside and bagged up his few things. He wrote a note for Mooney on a scrap of paper and slipped it under his door – he would never see him again. They drove to another part of town and parked. White showed him to the small flat on the top floor and handed him the keys.

'You can get sorted tonight. We've got work to do.'

Driving, crawling, in the interminable traffic, Nash saw the city in a way he hadn't before. It was in a shocking state. The trees, such as they were, were hideous, skeletal. Litter piled up everywhere. Even the sky seemed to have given in. But the pigeons were the worst. There were so many of them, crowding around overflowing rubbish bins and fighting over discarded bones, that even with the car moving as slowly as it did, they would often run them over.

'Flying rats,' said White.

Nash shook his head. 'The rats aren't that bad.'

It was rare to see a pigeon that was not disfigured or maimed in some way. None of them had both feet intact. Instead, they hobbled around on stumps. White explained to Nash that this was because they roosted in their own shit. It was an example of how fucked up nature was, he said. Pigeon shit was so corrosive it would even eat into masonry (which was why people placed spiked deterrents and daubed pesticides on the parapets of buildings, to ward the birds off). Where they roosted, they shat. All over their own feet. And then they happily sat in it, until one day they got up to fly away and the rotting feet stayed where they were.

'If it can rot brickwork,' said White, with a grimace, 'imagine what it does to flesh and bone.'

Not only were the pigeons missing their feet, many were also missing patches of feathers (displaying horrible bare grey skin), and many had broken or twisted wings that meant they flew at eccentric angles.

The pigeons made Nash feel sick. Worst of all was the sheer number of them. Sometimes it seemed as if the ground was covered and the sky filled with them, vast flocks of hundreds of thousands of diseased birds, stupid and oblivious, all over everything. Not only did the cars run them over, leaving them smeared across the cracked and potholed concrete, but people in the streets would unwittingly step on them, often leaving them maimed and immobile but still alive, broken-backed, broken-winged, footless, twitching.

This city, thought Nash, watching a particularly abject bird with almost no feathers at all attempt to inhale a crisp packet, as they crawled through the dreadful traffic, bumper to bumper, cloudy with exhaust. *It's awful.*

'Why do we drive?' he demanded. 'It would be so much quicker to go by public transport.'

White looked at him as if he had taken leave of his senses.

'Public transport? Really?'

'This is hopeless.'

'We have our orders. We have to look the part. We can't be going on buses and trains, can we, like a couple of fucking amateurs?'

For a moment they surged forward into a gap in the traffic, and then just as quickly slowed to walking pace again.

Actually, thought Nash, the pigeons were not the worst.

The worst were the seagulls. They were terrifying. Fearless and unhinged. It was well known they would happily take a finger off, swooping and snatching at a hand-held sandwich or ice cream. They were awful scavengers. Stuck in a traffic jam, Nash and White once watched, fascinated, as a seagull, with painful effort, swallowed a dead pigeon whole. On another occasion, they saw a flock of them fighting over the corpse of a dead dog.

What are they even doing here, he wondered, *so far from the sea?*

Halfway through the third week, White collected Nash and explained that they had an important task to carry out. They were to drive a very senior colleague to a series of appointments. They would need to be punctual. But they must also be vigilant. Their charge was apparently a potential target.

'Target for who?' asked Nash, alarmed.

'For our enemies, our rivals,' said White.

'We have enemies? Who are they?'

'Who knows. Frankly, they could be anywhere, anyone.'

'Anyone?' said Nash, incredulously.

'Anywhere,' said White, firmly.

'What, so we're like security?' asked Nash.

White nodded. 'That's it. This week, we're like security.'

They drove to the pick-up point. A tall, thin, grey man in a dark suit (bearing an uncanny resemblance to both Gray and Browne) was waiting. *Is it actually Gray*, thought Nash uneasily, *just somehow different?* He could not be sure. He got out and opened the rear door of the car.

'Good day, Mr White, Mr Nash. I'm pleased to make your acquaintance.' Gray's double shook hands with both of them and settled himself on the back seat. He named the destination – which would take an hour or so to reach, given the state of the traffic – took some papers from his briefcase and began to read. White pulled the car out into the interminable congestion.

After a while, Nash noticed their passenger had stopped reading and was gazing abstractedly out of the window. He turned in the seat.

'Excuse me, sir. Sorry to disturb. Can I just ask something?'

The man in the back seat nodded.

'What is it we do?'

'What an odd question, Mr Nash. Today you are escorting me to my meetings. It's simple stuff, really.'

Nash considered this and then tried again.

'Sorry, sir. I mean, what is it all for, what we do? What is the goal?'

'The goal, Mr Nash? I'm not quite sure what you mean.'

'I mean, what are we all working for, working towards?'

White nudged Nash viciously in the ribs with an elbow and glared at him.

'I'm sorry, sir,' said Nash. 'I'm not putting it very well. You see, I'm new. Relatively new. And I can't see the bigger picture.'

He nodded and regarded Nash with curiosity. Beneath the heavy lids, his dark eyes gave nothing away.

'The bigger picture. I mean, it would be helpful to have a sense of it. What's it all about? What's it for? What are we up to? *What's it for?*'

'The greater good.'

'The greater good?'

'Indeed.' He seemed to gather his thoughts. 'Are you familiar with the notion of the *Anthropocene*?'

Nash shook his head.

'It is a time, a geological epoch, no less, during which mankind is reckoned to have substantially altered the planet, to have influenced and even destroyed some of the Earth's natural systems, to have upset its equilibrium. Well, there are some who believe that the Anthropocene has now reached its zenith, its apex, and there is no going back. It is, in fact, time to usher in the *post-Anthropocene*.'

'What does that mean?'

'A natural paradise. There are some optimists – deluded people – who believe it may be possible for *Homo sapiens* to somehow reach a more enlightened state of being, to finally work towards achieving some kind of balance with nature and to live on in harmony with the planet. But the people we work with believe such a thing is simply impossible. No, *Homo sapiens* is a mistake, a category error. The only way forward is to take it out of the equation. Let the garden recover. Let it flourish.'

He watched Nash carefully for a reaction. 'No one has explained any of this to you?'

Nash shook his head.

'Let me put it another way. We are at the end of Capitalism. This is the end of the current order. Recent events in America have confirmed that quite decisively. What we are witnessing is the end of the systems and structures, even the very *beliefs*, that have sustained Western Democracy, the hegemony of the West, for the last century. Yes, Capitalism and its erstwhile partner in crime,

Democracy, have entered their decadent phase. And their demise, or mutation into something *other*, is without doubt imminent. And that, we believe, is an opportunity.'

'An opportunity?'

'To make a change for the better.'

'Meaning?'

'A new world.'

'What? I don't understand.'

'For the better.'

Nash considered. 'But what comes after?'

'Well, they say that nature abhors a vacuum…'

Nash nodded. This was neither intelligence work nor (it seemed) criminal activity, but something altogether stranger. What did it mean? He was about to ask another question, about how such a goal might be achieved – and White was about to deliver another jab to his ribs – when the man in the back seat cut him off.

'I'm sorry, Mr Nash, I must prepare before we reach our destination.' He bent over his papers again.

The rest of the day, which involved visits to three separate locations where their passenger would disappear into a building for an hour or so, was conducted in silence.

Well, there was something in that, at least, thought Nash. *The greater good.* For he had started to wonder if they were for the greater good in some way, or if they might actually be for the opposite. This talk was unnerving, but he could take reassurance from *the greater good*.

'You idiot,' said White, as they drew up at Nash's new place. 'What the fuck was all that about?'

'What do you mean?'

White put on a snivelling voice. 'Please sir, *what's it all about*? I mean, honestly. What the fuck were you trying to do?'

'But it's a valid question. I just want to know what the hell is going on.'

'You're lucky he's a pretty reasonable guy.'

'What?'

'He had more important things to be thinking about than your stupid questions.'

'Don't you want to know?'

'Who says I don't? Maybe I *do* know.'

'Why don't you tell me, then?'

Nash got out of the car.

'You dickhead,' said White.

Over the course of the following weeks there were similar assignments, accompanying senior colleagues to meetings and on one occasion waiting outside a conference room in a hotel with instructions not to let anyone in under *any circumstances*. Their charge that day, another tall, thin grey man, was in the room for almost two hours and looked haggard and exhausted when he emerged. That was the day, too, when White revealed to Nash that he was carrying a gun, a small, squat, black thing that glinted when he drew back his jacket to show it.

'Jesus,' said Nash, surprised. He had never seen a gun in real life before, only on TV and in movies. Somehow, its small size made it seem all the more malevolent.

White hushed him. Raised voices were coming from inside the room. Moments later their passenger emerged, and they headed for the car.

At the end of the day, Nash said, 'No one knows anything,

do they?' He watched White warily. 'No one knows what the others are doing. You certainly don't, even if you think you do. None of us even know what the big picture is, what the *goal* is. I've been thinking about it, and the only thing I'm sure of is that the organisation is run on the principle of keeping all its component parts at arm's length from each other and as ignorant as possible of everyone else's activities. It's like a blind network.'

'A blind network,' repeated White. 'Yes, you could be onto something there.'

Later, he asked White what he made of it, the talk of a new world, of gardens and category errors. Was it for real or just some kind of front, a cover for what was really going on?

'Oh, it's for real,' he assured Nash. 'Things have to reach their natural, their inevitable conclusion.'

'And that is?'

'The end times. Chaos. The end of days.'

Nash shook his head. None of it made sense.

'You think I don't know, but I know. It's coming,' said White. 'We did it to ourselves. But someone needs to push it onto the next stage, take it over the edge.'

'Look,' said Nash. 'Give me this, just this. Do we work for the good guys?'

White laughed so hard he had to pull the car over.

(6)

The woods are overwhelming. The forest is chaos. It is anarchy. Bedlam. He cannot comprehend the intricacy of it.

Dripping, sodden, seeping, teeming, crawling, abounding, rotting, sprouting, saturated, oozing, collapsing, growing, disintegrating, growing. The woods are disorder, incomprehensible disorder. But they are conscious too, he knows, in a way he could never understand.

At night, in the borders between sleep and waking, he sometimes wonders if the woods are dreaming him into being. If he is just a figment of their centuries-old reverie, their lucid slumbers.

It is all too much. The woods are too much. A path is only a brief imposition of order, a tenuous line made by walking. He often has the sensation, as he picks his way along dim trails, that if he were to turn about, the way he came would have disappeared, obscured by foliage, fallen branches, fallen trees, knots of undergrowth and impassable tangles. The paths – all but the widest tracks, the old roads – feel contingent, temporary. It is disconcerting, this instability. It gives him the feeling that something else, a greater (higher, older) power is ascendant. He is only a speck, insignificant, a visitor, allowed here under duress, on borrowed time.

(7)

The snow had almost completely melted when Mary Owen next came. This time she drove. Her car was an ancient Volvo, dirty with mud and blooming with rust. She carried in a cardboard box filled with supplies, set it on the kitchen table, and then sat to watch as he stowed the things in the cupboards.

'How are you getting on?' she asked.

Nash nodded. 'I'm coping,' he said. 'It's better now it's not so cold. I just wish I had some sense of how long I'm to be here.'

'They don't tell me that either.'

'I know. So, I've written a letter, like I asked. When I was recruited (if that's the right word for it) I dealt with a man called Gray, so I've addressed it to him, though I don't know if he's the right person for it.'

'I've never heard of him, I'm afraid. I'll pass it along and I'm sure it will get to whoever it needs to get to, whether it's Mr Gray or someone else.'

The letter said:

Dear Mr Gray,

I am writing to ask how your enquiry into the incident at the hotel is proceeding. I feel certain you will determine that the events that took place were an unfortunate mistake, and that I am not to blame. I acted in the only way open to me. Someone else must take responsibility for what happened.

Can you let me know when everything will be resolved? I feel enough time has already passed for you to have completed your investigation (although I am curious as to why no one has come to ask for my version of events). Moreover, I am keen to return to work. Either that or move on and seek employment elsewhere.

I look forward to hearing from you.

Etc.

Nash had drafted the letter several times. At first, he had felt a need to plead his case, to protest his innocence, to set out the facts as he saw them, but eventually he concluded that a simple request for clarification would be most effective. He worried that anything more forward might jeopardise his position, perhaps even prejudice them against him.

He handed the folded piece of paper to her.

'I'll get it to them,' she said.

Nash thanked her and filled the kettle. When the water had boiled, he made tea and they sat at the kitchen table to drink it.

'So, what's going on, out there in the real world?' he asked. 'Since I've been here.'

'Just the usual stuff. War. Catastrophe. Disaster. Riots in Paris. An earthquake in Armenia. Another massive iceberg broke off from the Antarctic ice sheet. This one is, apparently, the size of a small country.'

'Nothing particularly exciting, then?'

'Not really, unless misery and tragedy excite you.'

'Can I get a newspaper, next time you come?'

'I don't see why not. Can't be any harm in that, can there?'

'I like to keep up,' Nash lied. 'And the puzzles will be a distraction.'

'You got a preference?'

'No, I don't mind. What about some books too?'

'That's harder. There's no bookshop near here. But I'll see what I can do. Write a list and I'll see. Might have to go to the library in town and get them out for you.'

'Don't trouble yourself too much.' But as he said it, Nash thought that library books would be labelled and so might give him a clue as to his location.

'That's okay. I'll probably go at the weekend with Brigid. She likes the library. Loves her books. Always has a stack on her bedside table. Mainly nature stuff. Right little scholar, she is.'

'You must be proud.'

'Of course. She's a good girl.'

Nash refreshed their mugs of tea.

'You got a sister, or a brother?' she asked him.

He shook his head. 'No, I'm an only child. I used to want a brother, to play with, but it just never happened.'

'Parents?'

'Both gone.'

'I'm sorry. So, you really are alone.'

Nash nodded.

'Is that why you joined?'

'Maybe.' He thought about it. 'It just seemed like an opportunity. But I can see now that I didn't know what I was getting myself into.'

'How so?'

'I don't know. Too many unanswered questions, I suppose.'

'Well, don't ask me. I haven't got the answers.'

She got ready to leave. 'Do you play cards?' she asked.

Nash shrugged.

'I'll bring some next time. We can play. I'll teach you.'

'I'd like that, thanks.'

When she left, she called him 'love' again and for a moment he thought she was going to hug him, but she didn't. Nash felt another pang of tenderness. He was sorry to see her go. It seemed he did like company after all. Or perhaps it was only that he was suffering from an excess of isolation, which exaggerated the contrast between his lonely days and her friendly chat. He tried to read, but wherever he sat in the lopsided house it seemed dark and dank and he felt restless, so he put on his coat and her scarf and went into the woods. The melting snow meant that everything was wet – muddy, slimy, rotting – and the air was filled with dampness and the smell of mould. He stumbled along the winding paths, walking without direction, walking to try to dispel a sense of inertia, of dread, and eventually came to a clearing. Here the snow had gone, and among the dead and collapsed vegetation tiny green shoots were beginning to emerge.

Time passed. Sometimes the days stretched out interminably. Yet, sometimes, Nash was surprised to find that a week had gone by, without him really noticing it. It was as if time moved at different rates within the woods, sometimes fast, sometimes slow.

Most days, of course, nothing happened. Boredom, nothingness. The drag of the hours. Nash was invariably woken early by the infinite variety of sounds that enveloped the house – the rustling and scratching of small animals, the tapping and knocking of branches, the wind in the trees (which always reminded him of the sea), the cooing, screeching and calling of birds. A group of crows or rooks – malevolent-looking creatures, he thought, coal-black, all sharp angles – were in residence in the trees that ringed the once-formal garden, and their harsh croaking and forty-a-day coughing in the mornings and in the evenings when they returned to their roosts was loud and piercing. At first, the sound grated and jangled his nerves, as if they were crying and shouting with the sole purpose of getting a rise out of him, taunting him, even. But they were not calling to him. Later, when the signs of the coming of spring were more obvious, Nash would watch them rebuilding their nests in preparation for the mating season, carrying twigs and grasses up into the canopies of the trees, and he marvelled at their industry and ingenuity. It seemed incredible that the nests were not flung to the ground when the wind blew and the trees bent and swayed. He came, with time, to feel tenderly towards those birds. They were not malevolent at all, he saw, but bright and curious, and highly social. One of them in particular would often come and watch while he chopped wood. Nash called him Crowley and would chat to him as he worked, though of course he gave no reply, only cocking his head on one side and regarding Nash as if he were insane.

So, Nash would wake or be woken and then lie listening to the world, sometimes for as much as an hour, before rising and leaving his own warm nest and descending to the cold kitchen to make tea. While the water boiled, he would see if there were still embers in the wood-burning stove and if there were he would carefully revive the fire. Then, with a mug of tea, he would return to the warmth of the bed and read a little.

The books he read were a welcome distraction from his inner being: his nerves, the waiting and worrying. With so much time and so little to do, at least at first, his thoughts coiled and writhed, formed labyrinthine configurations, bifurcated, looped back upon themselves, and repeated again and again. His ruminations were invariably bleak, paranoid, fearful. He longed for a sense of inner peace and sometimes the books gave him that.

He would wash (splashing ice-cold water on his face and under his armpits) and dress and take a simple breakfast. Then, as long as it wasn't raining, he would chop wood. It was a good way to start the day, to shock his body into wakefulness and warm his muscles. He kept the fire in the sitting room going all day long, and while he only lit the fire in the bedroom in the evenings, he needed a good supply of logs.

He always chopped more than he needed, and having stocked the piles in the sitting room he began to build a second log stack against the wall by the back door, which he covered with a piece of old tarp he found in the shed. The logistics were thus: there were two stacks inside, one on either side of the burner. He would feed the fire with wood from the left-hand stack, and by the time it was finished the wood in the right-hand stack would have had several days by the side of the fire and so would be nice and dry. He would then replenish the depleted stack from the stack by the back door, with logs that were not quite dry. The freshly chopped logs, which were generally damp from the rain, would go onto the stack by the back door. He found this simple system very pleasing.

Mary Owen came and went. Twice a week he made a pot of soup – following simple recipes that she wrote down for him – and that was lunch. In the evenings he prepared simple dishes – pasta with sauce from a jar, sausages and mash. If Owen had been kind enough to bring him whisky or cider he would drink it slowly before the fire, looking into the flames and allowing them to transport him. The alcohol stilled his boiling brain.

In the afternoons, if it was not raining, he would walk in the woods. It was, in many ways, a simple life, and after a while he came to find it strangely satisfactory. Or he would have, if it were not for the shadow that hung over him: the expected arrival of the verdict (now, he always thought of it as the *verdict* or the *judgment*). In the back of his mind was always the thought that he must prepare for this eventuality. He must be ready. Yes, his expectation was that they would come and he would be exonerated. *Congratulations, Mr Nash!* Gray would say. *As we all expected all along, you've been cleared. Apologies for the inconvenience. Welcome back into the fold!*

But he could not shake the feeling that it would not play out like that. They would come with guns. They would come to kill him because of what had happened in the hotel. So, he must be prepared for this second, terrible possibility.

He considered two options. Firstly, fleeing. He did not like this idea. They would know where he was – somehow – and would follow him, find him, kill him. Of this, he was certain. Secondly, resistance. If they came to kill him, he would have to kill them first. It was simple, really. He liked this idea even less.

He kept trying to map his surroundings, but the mapping was harder than he had thought it would be. As the snow began to melt, he dedicated himself to going out and walking those tracks and paths he could find – the well-defined tracks and the obscure and winding paths – sometimes even counting his steps, and then making notes when he came back to the house. Not knowing which way was north or south, he used the valley and the ridgeline to orientate himself. It was confusing. And indeed, after a while, he realised that many of the 'paths' he was following and attempting to map were not paths at all. Rather, they were the ways used by the animals of the wood.

Moreover, as he mapped the wood, he increasingly found that it resisted comprehension in some way. It seemed to defy his understanding. His maps proved strangely useless, hopelessly inaccurate. At first, he concluded he was simply in error, but after a while he became certain that this something else was happening. The spatial dimensions of the wood did not add up. It was as if the landscape shifted while he was in the house. Thus, a pathway he felt sure he recognised, that ran past a familiar tree before dipping to cross a remembered stream, would not do so but would lead him instead to the edge of a sharp drop, crags and scree below. He knew this could not be the case, but the maps he drew convinced him it was so. The landscape was deforming and reforming; shifting, slipping, changing. It was impossible. The conviction grew that it was defying him. It resisted. It would not be mapped. Nonetheless, he kept going. He had no choice.

Close to the house, everything seemed fixed. In fact, he felt he was beginning to know the ways, the trees, that lay within a stone's throw of the house. But beyond that it felt different every day.

As he wandered, he sometimes heard the distant tolling of the church bells coming up from the valley below. It was a melancholy sound and served only to reinforce the sense that he was removed (had been removed) from the real world. The pealing and clanging seemed to reach him from a great distance, travelling across a vast void, which gave it a strange hollowed-out feel. In the woods, in the house, time was beginning to lose any tangible quality, whereas out there, down below, it was *Sunday* again. Life was going on.

Something else. Nash had a sense that he was being monitored, that someone was close by in the woods, watching and waiting. He started to notice signs: occasional footprints in the mud, a crossing place of two trails where someone had arranged sticks into an arrow, pointing down the valley (though as he looked again at this peculiar augur, he began to think that perhaps it was just chance, that the sticks had simply *fallen* in that shape, and that he was trying too hard to read into something that was not, in fact, there).

Then one day, as he walked one of the paths, he was sure he saw a figure, tall and thin, dart between trees; but when he came closer there was only a small deer standing quite still in a small clearing, watching him curiously. The deer turned away and disappeared into the trees. He looked carefully at the ground to see if there were footprints but there was nothing.

Over time, the sense of being watched, followed – tracked, even – only increased. Yet somehow, he knew it was not Gray and Black or anyone else from the network.

One day he opened the front door and there on the step was an apple. He picked it up and examined it. It was small, dull brown and leathery, not at all like the taut and shiny apples, green flecked with red and brown, that he sometimes bought from the supermarket at home in the city.

He wondered at it. Who had left it there? And should he eat it or not?

He bit into it and found it to be delightfully sweet.

Several more apples appeared in the days that followed.

In this way, the days passed, and the weeks too, and Nash was amazed by how quickly time went. Before, with nothing to do, the days had dragged, like moving through a viscous liquid. Now, as he settled, the weeks seemed to race past, measured by Mary Owen's visits.

As time passed, he came to look forward to these visits more and more. It was, after all, the only human contact he now had. And she was maternal towards him, asking concernedly how he was, if he was warm enough, what had been occupying his thoughts. And she always bought a treat – a jar of homemade jam, a fruit loaf, a bottle of something.

Nash saw that the weather was changing. Colour was coming to the woods. The air felt different, not only less cold but less dank. The sense of rot began to recede.

'Yes, the Wheel of the Year is turning,' said Mary Owen. 'Spring is finally coming.'

(8)

A week after he had handed Mary Owen the letter, Nash returned from walking in the woods and was amazed to see a familiar black car parked on the gravel. He concealed himself behind a bush and watched. He couldn't be certain, but he thought it was perhaps the same car that he himself had arrived in. Lights were on in the house, but he could not see anyone through the windows. White smoke trailed into a grey sky from the chimney. *So*, he thought, *is this it?*

Being careful to conceal himself, he moved around the house but could see no movement inside.

He waited and tried to work out what to do. Were they here to finish things, or had they come to let him know that everything was okay, and it was time to return to the city? He had to assume it was the latter. In which case, best to just get on with it.

He walked boldly up to the front door and went in. The axe was there in the hall, and he thought for a moment about taking it up but decided not to. Too risky. The kitchen was empty. In the sitting room, The Grey Man sat before the fire, smoking, inevitably. 'Mr Nash,' he said slowly, standing up. 'Good to see you again. I hope you've been keeping well.'

Nash nodded.

'Have you been keeping well? How *are* things?'

Nash shrugged. 'What do you think?' he said. 'I'm having the time of my life.'

Gray's smile was completely without mirth. *He has the eyes of a dead thing,* thought Nash.

'Is this it?' he asked.

There were footsteps and Black came down the stairs, watching Nash like a dog.

'"Is this it?"' asked Gray. 'What do you mean?' He threw his cigarette into the fire.

'Have you come to tell me what has been decided?'

Gray grinned. 'Alas, no, Mr Nash. I'm afraid not. We received your missive but no, we're not quite ready yet. Discussions are ongoing. There are many points of view to consider. I'm sure you understand. This is just a courtesy call. To check that you're keeping well and that you're *behaving* yourself.'

He had Nash's map in his hand and held it up. Nash cursed himself for leaving it out on the kitchen table.

'What *is* this?'

'I thought it would be interesting to map the woods. Just to pass the time.'

'Really?' Gray seemed to think this a singularly strange notion. 'Nothing to do with getting away? Getting *out*?'

'Of course not.' Nash made an effort to sound light and breezy. 'I'm certain I'm going to be cleared, so why would I want to get away? I'm looking forward to getting back. Picking up where I left off.'

'Well, where you left off is the problem, isn't it Mr Nash? It's why you're here.'

Gray contemplated Nash's incomprehensible map, turned it this way and that, and then crumpled it into a ball and tossed it onto the fire.

'Have you seen anyone other than Owen?'

Nash shook his head. 'No. There's no one. The weather's been bad. No one comes up here. There's nothing up here. Just trees and rocks and that fucking mountain. What would anyone want to come up here for? I've been walking in the forest, but you know, I've never even come to the edge of it. And I've not seen another soul. It's a fucking wilderness.'

'What have you been doing, apart from walking and making maps?'

'Chopping wood. And I've been reading.'

'Very good, Mr Nash. Bettering yourself.' Gray sneered, sarcastically. 'How admirable.'

'How long is it going to be? Before there's a verdict?'

'I couldn't possibly say.'

'Fucking hell,' said Nash, feeling his temper rising. 'How long can it take?'

'It'll take as long as it takes, Mr Nash,' said The Grey Man, evenly. 'You must be patient.'

He examined one of the little brass charms – a figure on horseback – nailed into the old black wood of the roof beam.

'Well, we'll be off. As you know, it's a long journey back.'

'Mr Gray?'

'Yes?'

'Can you ask them to hurry up? I thought I'd be here for a few days, but it's been weeks already. I just don't see why it has to take so long. The whole thing is pretty simple, after all.'

'Be that as it may, things will take as long as they take. It's the way, Mr Nash. It's how we do things. You know that.'

He took a fork from his jacket pocket and aimed it at Nash's forehead. The tines flashed in the dim light. Gray was very still, intent. Nash froze.

'Remember the rule, Mr Nash,' said The Grey Man, quietly. His eyes were like black holes. There was in his voice both threat and promise, the promise of something awful. Nash nodded, slowly.

Gray dropped the fork to the floor. The tinny clatter it made seemed extraordinarily loud. He turned and walked back through into the hallway and opened the front door. Black followed him. Nash stood on the doorstep watching as they got into the car. Fleetingly, he considered taking up the axe that was propped there, dashing across the gravel and bringing it down hard on the back of Gray's head, cleaving his skull. But instead, he did nothing. The car drove off down the track and he was alone again.

*The bones of the house shift and settle.
It groans, as if enduring a bad dream.*

(9)

Nash met the girl for the first time the very next day. It was morning and he was walking in the woods, following a path he had not found before as it dropped down into a narrow dip in the hillside. At the bottom was a clearing and she was there, standing, looking intently at something in her hands. That place was different somehow to the rest of the forest. For one thing, it was filled with light. It had evidently been cleared at some point. The ground was dotted with tree stumps, now covered in moss and fringed with balconies of plate fungi. It was bounded above by an outcrop of dark grey rock ringed with ferns. At the base of the rock, a pool of clear water reflected the sky. A narrow stream formed from its lip and ran through a boggy area filled with reeds, and then curled away downhill and was lost among the trees.

He watched her for a few moments. She was examining a feather, turning it slowly so that the light caught it. As he stepped into the clearing, she turned to face him and smiled.

'Hello, Mr Nash,' she said. Her voice was deep, almost masculine.

Nash did not know children, young people, and could not tell how old she was. Thirteen, fifteen, sixteen? It was impossible to say.

She was tall and thin. She wore narrow jeans, hiking boots, a dark blue waterproof jacket and around her neck a long woolly scarf that was similar to the one he wore himself, the one Owen had given him.

'Did you like the apples?' she asked.

She had long, curly hair, dark brown, parted above her forehead, falling over her ears to her narrow shoulders. Her eyebrows were two crescents, high, which made her look somewhat surprised or amused. Her eyes were dark, very dark, and her skin was not pale, like Nash's, but tanned. She looked, he thought, Mediterranean, like one raised upon parched hillsides scented with rosemary, among olive and lemon groves, not in the dank and forested enclosure of the valley, with its tolling church bells, heavy skies and incessant rain. With her wild hair and bright eyes there was something feral about her.

'It's an owl's,' she said, holding up the feather for him to see. 'Tawny, I think. Isn't it beautiful?'

He stepped forward and took the feather from her, noting her long, slender fingers, the dirt beneath her fingernails – the traces of nail varnish, a different colour on every finger – and held it up to the light as he had seen her do.

'It is,' he said. 'You must be Brigid.'

She laughed, her voice surprisingly deep for one so young and slender.

'Did you like the apples?' she asked again.

'Yes, thank you.'

'Did you know it was me?'

'No, of course not. How could I?' He thought of the figure he had seen, or thought he had seen, in the clearing where the deer had stood and watched him.

'Who did you think was leaving them?'

'I had no idea. Wood fairies?' He grinned.

'They've been in the cellar for the winter so they're not as crisp as they might be. But I think the flavour is better. Do you want one now?'

She took off her rucksack and rummaged inside it. 'Look, I've got two.' She offered one to him and he took it. She was right, the flesh had a softness to it, the skin was slightly wrinkled, but the taste was amazing, the very essence of appleness.

'This is the spring,' she said, gesturing at the pool and the clearing, settling herself on one of the tree stumps. 'It's one of my favourite places in the woods.'

He looked about. The water in the pool was perfectly clear. 'Your mother mentioned it,' he said.

'It's a special place. It is said that the water can heal.'

'I should have some then,' said Nash. He crouched at the edge of the pool and cupped his hands in the water and drank. It was cold and pure.

'Why, are you ill?'

'In a way.'

'That's a shame.'

She poked with a stick at a mass of fungi growing out of the stump on which she sat. 'How long are you going to be at Paradise?'

'I wish I knew.'

'Do you like it?'

Nash pondered this. No, he did not like it. He hated it. He couldn't bear it. But in some ways, despite himself, he was beginning to get used to it. He was acclimatising. He wasn't as freaked out by it all as he had been at first. But he was still scared. He was nervous. The woods were still an unknown. At times – most of the time – they overwhelmed him, the sheer abundance, the chaos. They had no limits, a notion that sometimes kept him awake at night. True, he liked the simplicity of his days, the routine he had, the physical work of chopping logs, but the open-endedness of his situation was also gnawing at his nerves, the idea that *they* could come at any time. And what would happen when they did finally arrive.

'In a way,' he replied.

'I know you've been exploring,' she said. 'I've seen your tracks. Did you find the standing stone yet, or Arthur's Door?' He shook his head. 'I can show you if you like,' she offered. 'I know the woods really well.'

'Your mum told me you're not supposed to come up here.'

'Do you do everything your ma tells you to do?'

'Fair enough.'

He watched her. There was a stillness about her. He had not spent any time with children, not for years, but those he had known had been wild and unpredictable creatures, swinging between nervous excitement and activity and a kind of frazzled melancholy. But not her. She was alert, filled with energy, but somehow self-contained. She might be fifteen or sixteen, he thought, watching her.

'Do you have a phone?' he asked.

'No, I'm not allowed one. Ma says they rot kids' brains. Only adults have skulls thick enough.' She laughed. 'I don't know where she heard that. I'll get one soon. You know there's no signal up here? You'd have to go all the way down to the village to make a call, even if you had one.'

He looked at her carefully, trying to work out if she was being straight with him.

'Also, you should know that Ma never brings her phone with her when she comes up here. It's one of the rules.'

He shrugged. The rules. The rule.

'Look, it's nice to meet you, Brigid. But I should get back to the house now. I'm not supposed to talk to anyone but your mother.'

'I know the rules. I'll walk with you. But listen, don't tell Ma. That you met me.'

'Of course I won't.'

She led the way back up the hillside. At the gate to the garden, she stopped and turned.

'So, would you like to see the stones, and the barrow?'

'I don't want to get you into trouble.'

'Don't worry about Ma, she won't know. Unless you tell.'

'It's not your mum I'm worried about.'

'You mean *them*,' she said, and for a moment she was very serious. 'Look, it's okay. Ma usually gets a call before they come. It'll be fine.'

Nash shrugged. 'You're sure?'

She smiled. Her teeth were fine and white.

'Of course. I can't come tomorrow as I've got things to do. But I'll come the day after.'

Nash nodded.

She headed off down the track to the village, her long strides carrying her quickly from his sight. Going inside, he realised he was still holding the owl feather. He examined it again and then placed it carefully on the kitchen table.

It was mid-morning when she knocked on the front door. Nash opened it and she pushed past him.

'Can I come in?' she said. 'I haven't been in here for ages.'

Before he could say anything, she was in the sitting room, looking about.

'Nothing's changed,' she said, disappointed.

'What did you expect?'

'Not sure. Something.' She picked up a photograph that was on the table and looked at it. It showed a family. 'Is this yours?'

He nodded. 'That's me, with Mum and Dad. I was sixteen.'

'Cute. Your ma's pretty.' She put it down. 'Are you ready?'

He nodded, put his coat on in the hallway, and they went outside together. The bitter cold of recent weeks had passed, and while it was not warm, there was a pleasant freshness in the air. Most of the snow had gone now and Nash could see that new growth was pushing through. There were slashes of bright green. The sky was grey, but the light was bright.

'Come on,' said Brigid. 'Ma's gone to Much Abbey for shopping, but I should be back home by the time she gets back. I haven't got all day.'

'Much Abbey?' queried Nash. It was the first time a location had been named.

'Down the valley,' she replied. 'Come on, let's go.'

She led the way down the track that led to the village, but after just a hundred yards she veered off onto a small pathway that Nash had never noticed before, climbing quickly up across the hillside. Nash saw that she walked easily, stepping lightly, moving smoothly, whereas he slipped and stumbled and slid on the mud and stones. She went easily where he had to constantly stoop beneath branches or adjust his weight and position to avoid falling or getting caught on brambles.

The path led them through a wild tangle of bushes and gnarled trees, and then the forest opened out. Here the trees were massive and old and there was more space between them. It was a part of the wood he had not seen before. Brigid moved confidently, and even though the path was faint, she never hesitated.

After about thirty minutes of steady climbing, they came to a crossing place. Another path – much larger, wider – met the one they were on, contouring across the hillside. The gentle wind had grown as they climbed higher and above them thick grey clouds crowded the sky.

'Which way now?' asked Brigid.

'No idea,' said Nash. 'I'm following you. Lead on.'

'Straight on, dummy,' she said, smiling. 'It's not far now.'

They came to a place where the trees began to fall away, revealing a raw landscape of stunted and windswept trees crouched low to the ground, thorny and abject-looking, grey with lichen. The hillside was covered in dead bracken, broken with stands of gorse, and Nash saw that they were coming to a sort of shoulder, a levelling of a ridge falling down from the high mountain above them, which, he noted, was still dusted with snow.

Nash hesitated. 'I'm not supposed to leave the woods,' he said.

'Well, it's just here,' she gestured ahead. 'And anyway, to be honest, who can really say where the woods end and where they begin?'

There seemed to be an inarguable logic to this, for the trees continued up the hillside above them, becoming sparser, but still providing occasional cover. The last tree might be said to be the edge of the woods, he reasoned. One *could* argue that.

He followed her and two minutes later they were on a broad shoulder, open and grassy. Some sheep were there and moved off quickly as they approached. Boulders lay about haphazardly, as if they had been dropped from the sky, but as Nash looked, he saw that they had been cleared from a central circle of cropped and pale grass, where a single large stone stood upright.

'There he is,' said Brigid, and looked to Nash for his reaction.

He took it all in. He had never been in such a place before. Turning, he saw the expanse of the land beneath them, the forest, like a thick blanket laid across the ridges and valleys falling to the deep valley below – he could just about make out the church steeple, far far below – and beyond that only hills and valleys, a rolling wave receding into the far distance. No towns, no cities, no motorways, no railway lines or bridges. Nothing.

He swallowed his discomfort. 'It's magnificent,' he lied.

Brigid looked pleased.

She sat on a stone and took off her canvas rucksack. She took out a water bottle and drank deeply before passing it to him. She had some jam sandwiches wrapped in silver foil, and she offered him one.

He sat on the stone next to hers.

'Homemade jam,' she said.

'It's good. Thanks.'

They ate in silence and Nash contemplated the vastness before him, the unnerving emptiness. When he finished the sandwich, he got up and slowly circled the standing stone. It was undeniably impressive, mottled grey and mapped with lichen. It stood about three metres high and something about its shape reminded him of a figure, a man, tall and erect, proud, with broad shoulders and straight back.

'What do you think?' asked Brigid. She was watching him curiously.

'Impressive. What's he called?'

'Oh, he's got lots of names. And there are different stories as to why he's here. Most of them involve either the Devil or King Arthur. The usual stuff. There's a lot of Arthurian lore around here.'

'And what do you think?'

'I love the stories, I really do. And they're important. They're part of this place and the people who live here. But I think he's a marker. As simple as that.'

'A marker?'

'Yes, like a signpost. I know, sorry, it's not quite so mysterious. But look, see the way the path comes up, the way we came? If you take a sight line up the path and past the stone, what do you see?'

Nash squinted. 'There's a dip in the skyline.'

'Exactly. That dip is the pass over the ridge to the next valley. If you were coming up here in mist or cloud, a cairn wouldn't necessarily be visible enough. So, they propped him up. That's my theory anyway. I noticed the stone and the pass lined up the first time I came here.'

She went over to the stone and pressed herself against it.

'Maybe it's not as exciting as King Arthur tricking a giant, or the Devil throwing boulders at the Black Prince, but anyway, it doesn't diminish his power.'

'What do you mean?'

'Come here.' Brigid beckoned him and he went and stood beside her. 'Touch it,' she instructed.

He reached out and pressed his palm against the rock, half expecting a mild electric shock or charge of energy, but there was nothing, only the roughness and chill of the stone. He could not help but feel a little disappointed.

'I can't feel anything,' he said, doubtfully.

She smiled at him. 'You're just not tuned in yet.'

They sat back down on their stones and contemplated the view.

'Where are we?' he asked. 'Your mum won't tell me. She says she's not allowed. But you can, can't you?'

She thought about it, then nodded.

'On the other side of that mountain is Wales. It's the borders, see. Up there, that's the Black Mountains. Down there, my village is called Drybridge. It's tiny.' She pointed. 'It's down there somewhere.' Nash followed the direction of her finger but could see nothing, only the rise and fall of the wood, ridges and valleys. 'Apart from the pub and the church there's nothing there, really. And at the bottom of the valley, about six miles on, is Much Abbey. That's the nearest town. That's where I go to school. If you were thinking of getting away, that's where you'd need to get to.'

Nash smiled.

'I'm not thinking of getting away,' he said. 'At least, not yet.'

She nudged him with her elbow. 'Really?'

He shrugged and considered what she had told him.

'If I *were* thinking of getting away, where's the nearest train station?'

'Aber, you'd have to get to Aber,' she said. 'You could get a bus there from Much.'

'Okay, thanks. Good to know.'

'*Will* you try to get away?' she asked after a bit.

'I don't know yet. You see, I think when they come for me, they'll have good news. Everything will be okay.'

She considered this then asked him, 'So why are you here? What did you do?'

'Probably best I don't tell you. Let's just say I was put in a difficult position and had to make a decision.'

'Did you make the right one?'

'I think so. But they're not sure, which is why I'm here.'

Brigid led them back down the hill, picking up a different path at the edge of the woods. In the depths of the forest, as they neared the house, she kept stopping and looking about.

'What is it?' he asked.

'I'm just seeing if there's anything for us.'

'What do you mean?'

'To eat.'

Nash was surprised. It had not dawned upon him that in this alien place, amongst all this strangeness, this chaos, there might be things to eat. It was a peculiar notion.

'Over here,' she said.

Beneath some spreading oak trees, the hillside was covered with clumps of low plants with waxy green leaves.

'Ramsons, aka Wild Garlic,' said Brigid.

She pinched a leaf between her fingers and held it for him to smell. It was pungent, herby.

'Have you got eggs?' she asked.

Nash nodded.

'I can make us an omelette.'

He watched as she picked a handful of the leaves and carefully folded them into the foil that had held the sandwiches.

Further down, the path crossed a stream, and again Brigid paused and began to cast about along the edge of the water, where the ground was soft and long grasses grew.

'Good,' she said, and showed him young shoots with purple-tinged leaves. 'It's water mint. We can make a tea with this.'

Nash was astonished.

At the house she took charge. She told him to beat eggs, which he did. She put a pan on to boil water and shredded the mint leaves into it. Next, she took a knife and roughly chopped the garlic leaves, releasing a delicious scent.

'Have you got bread? Yes? Make toast then.'

He did what he was told. She melted butter in the frying pan and poured in the egg and then mixed in the garlic leaves, keeping the pan moving.

When it was ready, they ate at the kitchen table.

'This is really good,' said Nash.

Brigid looked pleased.

'How did you learn that?'

'Oh, it's nothing. You just get to know what's what after a while.'

'I'd be scared to pick the wrong thing and poison myself.'

'No, with the garlic and the mint it's easy. You can't miss them. There's the smell too. With mushrooms and things like that you do have to be more careful.'

The tea, sweetened with a little sugar, was delicious and refreshing.

'Right,' she said, standing up. 'I'd better be going.'

She put her coat and scarf on. The familiar scarf.

'Thank you, Brigid,' said Nash. 'That was nice.'

It was clear to him then how much he had missed society. He had thought himself almost content in his solitude, or if not content then *stable*, but Brigid's presence was pleasing. Something about her lifted his spirits.

'Shall I come back?'

'Yes, please do.'

'After all, there's still the barrow.'

'King Arthur's?'

'That's the one.'

'Yes, I'd like to see that.'

'Okay. I don't know when. I've got a school trip tomorrow and there's other stuff too. But I'll come back. But you might see Ma before you see me.'

On the doorstep, she said, 'Remember, don't say anything to Ma.'

He nodded. She smiled and he watched as her long legs carried her confidently off down the track to the village.

Nash went inside and built up the fire. He took the *Shell Guide to the British Countryside* from the bookshelf, lay down on the sofa and began to leaf through it. He read about wild garlic and water mint and marvelled.

(10)

'Something a bit different today,' said White, as Nash got into the car. 'We're going to see someone.'

'Who?'

'You don't need to know who it is. Just follow my lead.'

They drove out into the suburbs. White parked the car, and they walked a couple of blocks. He led Nash down a narrow alleyway. At the end of it was a courtyard. White knocked hard on a door.

'Remember, follow my lead. Don't say anything.'

Nash nodded and White knocked again, harder this time.

'He may make a run for it so be ready for that.'

'What should I do if he does?'

'Stop him.'

Someone called from behind the door, 'Who is it?'

'Friends,' said White. 'Open up.'

The door opened a couple of inches.

'I don't know you,' said the man behind the door.

'Hauser, isn't it?' said White. He leant against the door and pushed it open, forcing the man to step backwards.

Hauser looked worried. He was smartly dressed in black trousers, black shoes – shined – and white shirt, the collar open. He was tall and dark and had a neatly trimmed beard. His face was sad and gentle-looking. Nash instinctively felt sorry for him. 'I don't know you,' he said again.

'We just need a quick word, Hauser,' said White. 'Is that okay? Can you give us two minutes of your time?'

Hauser nodded, cautiously. Nash readied himself for something.

'Thank you. So, the thing is, the people we work for, the people *you* work for, aren't happy.'

'What do you mean?'

'Just that. They're not happy. They are beginning to question the extent to which you are committed. To the cause.'

'I don't understand.'

'Yes, you do.'

'But I haven't done anything.'

'Well, perhaps that's the issue.'

White put his hand on his hip, and in doing so drew back the lapel of his suit jacket. Nash was standing behind him and knew that this movement would have revealed the gun pressed against his side.

Hauser saw it and his eyes widened.

'You need to make amends,' said White.

Hauser nodded.

'That's all,' said White. 'Can I report back that the message has been delivered and understood?'

Hauser nodded again. He looked unsteady on his feet and Nash thought he might sink to the floor at any moment. He was certainly not going to make a run for it.

White watched Hauser and waited. After what seemed

like a very long time – though it was probably only a few seconds – he stepped back.

'Very well, I think we're done here. Thank you for your time, Mr Hauser.'

Hauser looked like he was about to cry, but with a visible effort he held it together. He nodded to them and gently closed the door.

As they made their way back to the car, Nash was trying to understand what had just happened. He was unnerved by what he sensed was the potential for savagery. He felt as if he had just stood at the brink of a chasm. And in the chasm, deep in the chasm, at the bottom of the chasm, was a disaster. Woundings and pain. Murder, even.

'What the fuck was that?' he said, angrily.

'That, my friend, is *business*.'

'What kind of business?'

'Let's call it Communications. Or Relationship Management, if you'd prefer.' White grinned, evilly. 'Sometimes it's necessary to remind a party of the commitment they've made.'

'He works with us?'

'No, not *with*. He works *for* the people we work for. There's a difference. He provides a service. What that service is, I have no idea.'

'Need-to-know basis. The blind network?'

'Exactly.'

'But what would have happened if he'd made a run for it, or if he'd pushed back?'

'Well, that's when we would have had to lean on him. You know, exert a little pressure.'

Nash considered what this meant. As they reached the car White's phone rang, and he listened intently to whoever was on the other end. When the call finished, he turned to Nash. 'Right, next job. Simple pick up and drop off back in town.' Nash felt a wonderful sense of relief. He had half-expected White to say, *we've got to mess someone up*. Or something worse.

They got into the car, and as they crawled through heavy traffic back into the centre of the city, Nash pondered what would have happened if Hauser had tried to get away. Or worse, if he had not acquiesced to White's demand. He thought of White's gun. Would he have used it? Yes, he did not doubt that White would use his gun. In fact, he was sure that White *wanted* to use his gun. He was just waiting for an opportunity to use the gun, and if the chance came, he would not hesitate. Yes, White would relish using his gun.

On another occasion, they paid a visit to a man called Amis. 'Something's amiss,' joked White.

As before, he stressed that Nash was to follow his lead. And to be ready should Amis 'try something' or make a run for it.

Amis's place was on a run-down industrial estate. White knocked hard on the metal door with the number 13 daubed on it in red paint, and after a minute Amis appeared. Unlike Hauser, he stepped straight out and faced up to White confidently, angrily. He was a bulky man with tiny dark eyes. He wore jeans and a t-shirt pulled tight over bulging muscles and his pink head was shaved, revealing a criss-crossing of pale scars.

'I know who you are,' he growled, before White had a chance to speak. 'And you can fuck off.'

White coughed. 'If you know who we are, then you'll know why we're here.'

'A misunderstanding.'

'No, the reason is clear.'

There was a horribly long pause. Amis and White stared at each other, and Nash knew that something was going to happen. A calmness settled upon him, and with it, clarity.

White's hand went to his jacket and Amis took a step forward and headbutted him. Nash had only ever seen it done in the movies and had always assumed it wasn't real, wasn't a real *move* (for wouldn't it hurt the attacker as much as, if not more than the victim?). White went down. Amis – there was now a bright red smudge in the centre of his forehead – turned to Nash and rushed him. It was all very clear. Amis put his shoulder down, but Nash anticipated and side-stepped so that the big man didn't crash into him but went under his arm without the impact to check his momentum. He stumbled and came to a halt and steadied himself and turned, and as he did so Nash hit him hard in the face. Amis stepped back, a look of surprise on his face, a smear of blood across his cheek, and Nash hit him again. This time he went down.

Nash steadied himself for the comeback and was aware of White behind him.

'That's enough.'

White came around him and stood over Amis, his foot pressing down on his chest. His gun was out, and he pointed it straight at Amis's face, which was dissolving in a wash of blood. Nash had the horrible feeling that White was going to fire.

'The message is simple,' White said quietly, and pressed his weight down on Amis's chest. 'You have a week to sort it out. Understood?'

Amis writhed on the ground and groaned.

'Do you understand?' demanded White. He moved his foot to Amis's neck and pressed.

Amis made a strangled sound and seemed to nod his head.

White stepped back. He studied the man lying below him intently, waiting to see what he might do next, but it was clear he wasn't getting up.

'Come on,' said White, and they walked away.

In the car, White dabbed at his forehead gently with a handkerchief. An angry red bump was forming there. He turned to Nash. 'That was impressive. Now I know why they brought you in. *Very* impressive.'

Nash nodded but felt nauseous. His fingers were tingling and there was a dull ache in the hand he had hit Amis with. He looked down and saw that his knuckles were red. He didn't feel himself.

He had not particularly liked White when he first met him, but he had not found him too disagreeable. But as the weeks passed and the artifice of their relationship and the oddness of their work became more apparent, he was increasingly wary. He knew nothing of him, not even his real name. He did not trust him. The man was wearing a mask.

He asked him about his beliefs, if he had any. White said he didn't understand the question.

'When you were interviewed, they must have asked you what you believe. Gray asked me about belief a lot. It seemed very important.'

'Nothing,' White replied, shrugging.

'You mean they didn't ask you about it?'

'Oh, I can't remember. It was ages ago. No, *nothing* is the answer to your question.'

'You don't believe in anything? You believe in nothing? What does that make you, a nihilist?'

'Just so. What evidence is there that there's anything beyond this, beyond chemical and physical processes, the mere facts of life and death? Belief doesn't come into it. Belief is a delusion. What is it the man you call Gray always says? *The universe is indifferent.* We're just a step away from complete chaos. Imagine, Nash, the slightest tear in the veil…'

'It doesn't bother you that some of the stuff they have us do is, what's the word, immoral?'

White laughed, briefly. 'What is morality? Another delusion. The universe is marvellously indifferent.'

They fell into silence, and then White asked, 'And you, Nash, what do you believe?' There was a sneer in his voice.

'I don't know anymore,' replied Nash.

He wondered if he should try to contact Gray. But he had no way of doing so. In the blind network the communications flowed in one direction only. And currently, their instructions all came via White. Nash's phone, the one they had given him, had not rung a single time.

In the days that followed the Amis incident it began to feel more and more like a dream, a bad dream. Yes, he was well paid, but there was something unreal about it all. Sometimes, when he lay in bed at night, Nash was convinced that none of it was real, that it was all a fiction, that he had seen it in a film, or dreamt himself into a film that he had once seen. Following this train of thought, an absurd idea came to him: Hauser and Amis were actors, perhaps even White too. The whole thing had been a play, a construction set up for his benefit. The guy playing Hauser had put in a good performance – at the verge of tears, weak-kneed with fear – but had it been completely convincing? Really? Hadn't there been something fake about the dialogue? He wasn't sure. Amis had been more convincing. And he had hit him. But perhaps that was only because he, Nash, had gone off-script?

When he shaved or brushed his teeth, he looked at himself in the mirror and felt a strange disconnection. *Is that actually me?* he asked himself, wonderingly. He felt like he had slipped through a crack in things, into a parallel universe. *Do I have blue eyes?* He would poke at his face, to ascertain it was indeed tangible, or pinch the skin of his neck. But the nagging feeling that none of it was real would not leave.

At weekends he stayed mostly in his new flat. It was small but comfortable and was the first place that felt like *his*. He bought weights and worked out, building definition in his arms and body. In the evenings he watched films on the television late into the night, drinking slowly, heavily, until he dozed off, waking to find a different film playing to the one he had started to watch, or the appalling news, the doomscroll rolling across the bottom of the screen, a litany of disasters. Many times, during the days, he lay down on the sofa and, with his eyes closed, daydreamed, only to fall asleep and then wake, thinking, confusedly, *I am more asleep than I am awake*. Or was it the other way round?

His dreams were vivid.

He went to the shops and purchased another suit – better, more comfortable, less shiny, more like White's, – more shirts and a second tie.

One day, they had been sitting in the car in silence for hours, watching and waiting, when Nash turned to White.

'Your gun,' he said. 'Can I see?'

White considered and then drew the pistol from inside his jacket and handed it to Nash. It was matt black and not as heavy as he had expected. It nested snugly and comfortably into his hand.

'Glock,' said White, proudly. 'Nine millimetre. Punchy. Small enough to carry concealed but still packs a punch. Super reliable. Six rounds. Punchy,' he said again.

Nash moved it from one hand to the other, feeling the weight of it, then he sighted it at a streetlamp on the opposite side of the street, aiming it through the windscreen. He wondered what would happen if he were to squeeze the trigger. He wondered what would happen if he were to swivel in his seat and point it at White's grinning face.

'Keep it down,' said White, pulling his arm down.

The street was empty, but Nash understood. 'Have you used it?' he asked.

'Couple of times. Generally, it's enough to just let them know that you're carrying. The possibility of it. Remember when we went to see Hauser?'

Nash nodded. 'I've never fired a gun,' he said. 'I'm not sure I want to.'

'First time for everything,' replied White. There was something predatory about his grin.

(11)

Some days of rain followed the visit to the stones and Nash found himself becoming melancholy. The gloom, the heavy skies and the dank shadows between the trees that surrounded the house, all filled with unknowable things, mirrored his mental landscape. His spirits were low. He was beginning to think that the terrible mistake that had kicked all this off would be compounded by a further error and they would not understand the implications of the situation he had found himself in. The verdict would be negative. He would be found guilty. But guilty of what? And what would the sentence be? Was that even how it worked?

On the first clear day he retraced the route he had taken with the girl, up to the ridge where the standing stone watched over the world. He sat and contemplated the wild vista below him; valleys, woods, crags, all veiled with mist. His situation seemed hopeless, the world confusing and unknowable. Running was impossible. The landscape was empty and vast, and he would be lost in no time at all.

When he returned to the house, he found Mary Owen waiting for him in the kitchen. She was playing cards, laying the suits out in columns ranged across the table.

'I'm sorry,' she said, as he took off his coat in the hall. 'I would have just left everything, but I wanted to see that you're okay. And I needed a hot drink. I made the mistake of walking this time.' A coughing fit shook her, and she pulled a handkerchief from a pocket and blew her nose noisily.

'That doesn't sound good,' he said. 'Are you alright?'

'Just a cold. It's going round.'

He made himself tea using the water she had boiled and began to put away the things she had brought. He was relieved to see a bottle of whisky amongst the tins and packets.

She coughed again. 'How have you been?' she asked.

'To be honest, I've been a bit low. Probably the weather doesn't help but it's the waiting. I can't stand it.'

'Poor thing. I expect you're missing people.'

He nodded. 'I guess so.'

'You got a girlfriend back in the city?'

He shook his head.

'No? Handsome young fellow like you? I'm surprised.'

He shook his head again and sipped his tea. 'I don't mind being alone, you know.'

'Well, I remembered the cards. Let's play, it'll cheer you up.'

She took a pack from her bag and began to shuffle them. She taught him Rummy and they played for an hour, with her winning every round. Soon they were laughing and joking and Nash was groaning melodramatically every time he lost.

'Time I should go,' she said, eventually. 'Before I do, let me teach you Solitaire. You can play it on your own. It's a nice diversion.'

She explained the rules, coughing frequently.

She blew her nose again. 'Better get going.'

Nash watched her make her way down the track, and then sat at the table and played a couple of rounds.

Later that afternoon, as he chopped logs, he noticed that the great tree that rose above the woodpile was beginning to come into leaf. Leaflets of a brilliant iridescent green, almost luminous, were appearing at the tip of every branch. A thought came to him, and he went inside to get the *Book of the Countryside*. He carried it back to the shed and, sitting on the chopping block, he went through it until he was able to identify the tree as a horse chestnut.

There was something very pleasing about this, he found, being able to name a tree. And so, the next day, he carried the book into the woods and spent some time learning the names of other trees and bushes: ash, oak, hawthorn, dog rose. After this, he began to take one or more of the books with him every time he went out and, finding a new plant or spying a bird or insect, he would try to identify it. He took to making notes in the margins of the books and lists of what he had seen (and then, what he hoped to see), and something about this simple and seemingly pointless activity made him happy.

(12)

The city was grey. The day was grey. Everything was grey. It was still not fully light, and getting up was an effort. Getting up was getting harder and harder. As he waited for the kettle, he pulled aside the curtain and saw that the black car was already there, waiting on the other side of the road where the yellow lines were. Nash groaned and swore. Most days now, he vainly hoped that White would simply not turn up, that he would be forgotten about. But the car was always there at the appointed hour.

He made tea and looked at his watch. He had five minutes. He poured some of the tea into the sink and topped it up with cold water, making it cool enough to drink quickly. In the bathroom, he watched his face in the mirror. What was going on? He couldn't say with any certainty. Everything was vague, confusing, contradictory. *How has this happened?* he asked himself once more. *How did I get into this? And more importantly, how am I to get out of it?*

In the car, White was drinking a takeaway coffee and had a newspaper propped on the steering wheel, open at the crossword. Nash climbed in beside him and White checked his watch, raising his eyebrows in mock exasperation.

'Six across. Four letters, beginning with D. Informally, father takes drug.'

'*Dead*,' said Nash. 'What are we on today?'

'Good.' White carefully filled in the letters. 'We've got a pick up and drop off first. Then a visit to an old friend.' He folded the paper, finished his coffee, and started the car.

'An old friend?' asked Nash.

'You'll see,' said White.

They joined the ceaseless traffic crawling slowly along the choked arteries of the city. Glass and concrete and steel, a sky like oil and soot. White began a monologue about what he had watched on the TV the night before, but Nash paid him no attention. He felt melancholy, and in no mood for banter.

They arrived at their first destination. Nash left the car and entered the lobby of a large office block. A man in a suit was waiting for him. 'Nash?' he asked, and Nash nodded. The man handed him a plastic carrier bag with something heavy in it. Nash did not look to see what it was. 'Any papers?' he asked. But the man had already turned away.

Nash got back in the car, placing the bag at his feet, and they started driving again. An hour later they arrived at their destination and Nash took the bag, still without looking in it, and knocked on an unmarked door. The door opened a few inches and someone inside reached out. Nash passed the bag in, and the door snapped shut. *What is this?* he asked himself, for the hundredth time. *What are we fucking doing? What the hell is it all about? The greater good? What is the greater fucking good?*

'Coffee,' said White. They parked up and got lattes from a café. It was busy with workers from the offices that filled that part of the city and Nash watched the ebb and flow of people with a sense of confusion, of being outside of everything. He wondered what it was that they did all day long, and how, if at all, he fitted into it. He didn't, he concluded.

'Right, this next one should be interesting,' said White.

They drove out into the suburbs. White parked up and they walked a couple of blocks, stopping at the entrance to a narrow alleyway. Nash remembered. It was Hauser's place. He felt the slow creep of nausea.

'Is he here?' asked Nash.

'No, he's not.'

Thank God, thought Nash.

He followed White down the alley to the door where they had confronted Hauser on their previous visit. White produced a bunch of keys, and after trying several he unlocked the door and let them in.

'What happened to him?'

'He had to go away.'

'What do you mean?'

'Just that. He had to go away. Far away.'

'Why?'

'Let's say that his services were no longer required. Let's say that his continued presence here became a risk.'

'A risk?'

'Yes, a risk.'

They entered what looked like a large storeroom. It was a big space, long and with high walls and strip lights. The air was dry and dusty. There were piles of cardboard boxes, a stack of white plastic barrels with bright blue lids, and a row of what looked like industrial freezers. Something large under a wide black tarp.

'What are we here for?' asked Nash.

'We've been sent to retrieve something important.'

White walked slowly through the storeroom. At the end was an office space. There was a door and a large window in the dividing wall. Inside, Nash could see a desk, chairs, filing cabinets, shelves filled with files, and a bookcase. White rattled the keys and tried several. The door opened.

In the office the air was stale. Amongst a jumble of papers on the desk by the computer was an ashtray with a single cigarette butt in it. White took out a piece of paper from his pocket, unfolded it and read carefully.

'Our instructions,' he said to Nash, waving it.

He went to the bookcase, counted the spines down from the top and then across from the left, and selected a volume, *The Secret Agent* by Joseph Conrad. 'Nice touch,' he said, showing Nash.

He flicked through the pages of the book and a white envelope fell out.

'Perfect,' he said, picking it up and laying the book on the desk. 'Right, we're almost done. Just one more thing. Wait here, will you? I just need to get something from the car.'

He left the office, walked back through the storeroom and went outside, closing the door behind him.

Nash inspected the bookcase. The books it held were a seemingly random selection, of all types and genres, and they all seemed to be brand new and unread. He looked about the room, trying to discern some trace of Hauser that might tell him what kind of a man he was, or what it was he did (or had done) for The Grey Man. There was nothing. He considered opening some of the files but thought better of it.

White reappeared at the door and gestured for him to come over. He had a jerry can. He offered it to Nash. 'This is your bit,' he said. 'I don't want to get any on my suit. Over there.' He gestured to the nearest stack of cardboard boxes. 'Empty it.'

Nash did as he was told. He unscrewed the cap from the jerry can and smelled petrol. He sloshed it over the boxes, soaking them. The smell was strong.

'Leave the can,' said White. 'Stand back.' He had a box of matches. He lit one and tossed it and for a moment it seemed that nothing would happen. There was a slow blue flame and then it caught.

'Come on,' said White. He pulled Nash towards the door. It was amazing how quickly smoke was filling the space. They stepped outside and White locked the door behind them. They walked quickly back down the alleyway. Nash looked back and was surprised that, for now, there was nothing to be seen, perhaps just a few wisps of grey smoke. Inside, he knew, it would already be an inferno.

In the car, as they drove away, Nash said, 'White, can I ask you something?'

'Sure,' said White.

'It's just that I have' – he hesitated – 'I have doubts.'

'Doubts?'

'I can't help but think that it's all a mistake. That I was recruited by mistake. That I'm not the person they think I am.'

'But Nash, old man, surely you've realised by now that these people – *our people* – don't make mistakes. If you're here, it's because you are *meant* to be here. It's like a vocation, a calling, even. Yes? You've been *called*.'

'I don't know,' said Nash.

'You'll be okay. Don't overthink it.'

'But what if I want to, you know, get out? What if I've had enough?'

'Like I said, Nash, don't overthink it.'

But Nash did overthink it. He lay awake at night overthinking it. He thought about it all day long. Where had Hauser gone? Nash had the distinct impression that Hauser had not simply upped sticks. Something had happened to him. Something had been *done* to him. He remembered the look on Hauser's face when White had shown him the gun. Worse still, he remembered the look on White's face.

And what they had done at Hauser's place was arson.

Eventually, he resolved to quit. It was the only way. He'd long since let go of the hope that it was some sort of government secret service thing he'd been recruited for. That would have been okay, exciting, maybe even inspiring, but he was pretty sure that was not the game. There was a crazy end-of-days agenda they were pushing, and he was increasingly sure that it was funded by some sort of criminal activity. What it was, exactly, he wasn't sure. Drugs, perhaps. He had always thought that he was, essentially, a *good person*. It was impossible.

When he again raised the possibility of quitting with White, he was once again rebuffed.

'It was a mistake,' said Nash.

'If you say so,' said White.

'I need to get out.'

'No, you don't.'

'But it was a mistake. I shouldn't be here.'

'Look, Nash,' said White. 'This isn't the kind of gig where you can just come and go as you please. You saw how tricky it is to get in. It's just as tricky to get out.'

'So, I *can* get out?'

'I'm not saying you can't, let's put it that way. But I don't recommend it.'

'Why?'

'Because you'd be throwing away a wonderful opportunity.'

'But it doesn't feel like an opportunity. It feels like a mistake.'

'It's still early days, Nash. You're still *on probation*.'

'But surely, if I'm going to get out, it would be better to do it sooner rather than later? You know, before I'm in too deep?'

'In too deep?' White chuckled evilly. 'In too *deep*. That's a good one.'

'What do you mean?'

'Well, it's relative, isn't it? You might say you're already in pretty fucking deep. But then again, how deep is deep?'

They drove in silence for some time.

'They don't make mistakes,' said White, after a while.

'But what if they do?'

'They don't.'

Nash continued to overthink it, obsessing over his predicament. He went back over the conversations he'd had, right at the start, with The Grey Man. He speculated on what exactly he had signed. Was it a contract? A pact? He thought that perhaps the next time they were assigned to accompany one of their senior colleagues, someone with influence, he should say something. Ask some questions. It was getting to the point where each night, as he went to bed, exhausted with worry, he dreaded the coming day and what it might bring. He was certain that, sooner or later, they would be asked – no, *compelled* – to do something really awful.

With that possibility in mind, Nash asked White, 'What's the worst job you've ever had to do for them?'

'The worst?'

'Yeah, the worst. I imagine they've had you do some pretty dodgy stuff, no?'

White considered. He grinned, and then leaned in towards Nash.

'There was this one time,' he said quietly. 'Quite early on. I was still learning the ropes. I was paired with Spink.' He chuckled at the memory. 'They sent us to a place, an empty house, with instructions to clear up.' He gathered his thoughts and Nash had a kind of lurching sensation deep in his stomach. 'It was a big place,' continued White, 'quite fancy. But it had been emptied out. No furniture, carpets, anything. And I remember it was sort of dry and dusty, the air I mean, like no one had been in there for years. We got in through a window at the back and went through all the rooms, but they were empty. Clear up, they said, but there was nothing to clear up. Finally, we realised there was a cellar and went down there, and that's where we found what it was we'd been sent to clear up.'

'What was it? Drugs?'

'A headless corpse.' White paused and watched Nash, to see the effect his words would have.

'What the fuck do you mean?' said Nash, aghast.

'It was a corpse and it didn't have a head,' said White, quietly.

'Fucking hell.'

'Yes. Exactly.'

'Who was it?'

'No idea. Like I said, there was no head. Anyway, I couldn't believe it, but Spink just took it in his stride. Like it's the kind of thing that happens every other day. Run-of-the-mill stuff. All in a day's work. My god, Spink was a real pro. Fucking unbelievable. He said, "Stay here and watch it" (I mean, it wasn't going anywhere, was it, without a fucking head?) and went back to the car. He came back with some bin bags and a hacksaw. "Normally," he explained to me (*normally*, can you believe that?), "normally, we'd roll it in a carpet to get it out to the car, but as we don't have a carpet we'll have to improvise. Get its clothes off."'

Nash groaned.

'Yeah,' agreed White. 'So, I got the clothes off (not an easy task, given how stiff it was) and then Spink went to work. It was wearing quite a nice suit, if I remember rightly.'

'What did he do?'

'He took the arms and legs off, with the saw. There was no blood at all. Isn't that strange? No blood at all. I confess, I puked my guts up. It was the noise of it, more than anything. Horrible. And you know what? Spink whistled a show tune while he did it. *Singing in the Rain* or something like that.'

Nash felt very cold. This was not what he had expected when he asked White about the worst job he'd had to do. This terrible story cast everything in a very different light.

'We bagged up the clothes and then we bagged up the limbs – separately, of course – and then we carried it all out to the car. And we spent the rest of the day driving across the city, dropping the bags – weighed down – into different canals. Honestly, sometimes I wonder what you'd find if they drained the canals. A fucking horror show.'

Nash felt faint. White chuckled.

'Yes, that was probably the worst one. Quite unpleasant, really. Still, at least we didn't have to kill anyone!'

After that, Nash entered a dense funk. The tale of the headless corpse had utterly unnerved him. He couldn't speak. The rest of the day passed in a vague way, and when White got out of the car to go and deal with their next assignment, Nash stayed in the passenger seat, biting his nails, staring blankly at the passing traffic, the blinking lights in the gloom, the heavy clouds slowly crawling across a greasy sky.

That evening, when he got home, he stood in front of his bathroom mirror for a very long time, examining the troubled-looking person in the reflection. This person looked very tired and very very worried. His face was pale, his blue eyes were watery. His suit was cheap and nasty and his tie, shiny. The person in the mirror looked like he had not had a good night's sleep in ages. He looked like he was haunted.

What the fuck are you doing? he said to himself.

What the fuck are you doing? he repeated.

You have got to get out of this.

Yes, he thought, agreeing with himself. *I've got to get out. It's not good. It's not what I thought it was. But what the fuck did I actually think it was anyway? Secret service? You fucking idiot. But maybe it's not too late. Not too late to sort everything out. Find Dad, make it right, maybe even take up that place at university at last.*

For a moment another reality swam in front of his mind's eye. Possibility. A different path. A new start. Everything in its right place. Family. A regular job. Maybe even a relationship. Wasn't that how it was supposed to be?

He rubbed his eyes, making them even more bloodshot. He felt like crying, but no tears came.

Nash's work phone – the one that The Grey Man had given him – rang only once.

When it rang, he jumped. The phone was in his jacket pocket. He extracted it and stared at it for a second with a kind of horror – *number withheld* – before answering.

'Good morning, Mr Nash,' said a voice.

'Mr Gray, how are you?'

'Very well, Mr Nash, despite the blind indifference of the universe – or perhaps because of it – I am thriving. And you?'

'I'm fine,' he lied. 'What can I do for you, sir?'

'Just checking in, Mr Nash. How are you finding the work?'

'It's good, thanks. I think.'

'Well, I hear you've been expressing some doubt about the work. About its legality. Your suitability. Et cetera.'

'No, no, not at all,' he blustered, cursing himself. White had ratted. Of course he had. It was his job to rat.

'You know you wouldn't be working *with* us' – (Gray emphasised the *with*) – 'if we didn't think you were right for the job?'

'Yes, I know. And I'm very grateful. For the opportunity.'

'Well, then, what are you worried about?'

'I'm sorry, I suppose I thought it would be different. You see, I wasn't really told what the job involved. I should have asked more questions. When I was recruited.'

'*Called.*'

'Yes, called. And I'm still unsure, if I'm honest.'

'Unsure?'

'Yes, of what the job actually involves. What it is we're doing.'

'It's still early days, Mr Nash. It'll all become clear in due course.'

'I hope so,' said Nash, forlornly. He heard a soft click on the line and then silence.

After, considering the conversation, he cursed himself again for not asking more questions. He pressed redial and waited, hopefully, but nothing happened. *Number withheld.*

(13)

Nash was chopping wood when Brigid arrived. Unseen, she watched him for a while from behind a tree where the valley track emerged from the woods. It was a cold but clear morning and he had taken off his coat and hung it on the door to the shed. Clouds of steam rose off him, catching the low angled sunlight filtering through the trees. She saw that he was strong and his technique was good. Beside him was a pile of thick logs that he had sawn into shorter lengths, their ends glowing with orange light, bright against the drab browns of bark and the dull grey of the shed. He would bend to select a log and set it on the chopping block, sometimes adjusting the orientation. Then he would carefully offer the blade of the axe to the wood, assessing the angle of cut, before bringing it back over his head and swinging it down. Most times the log split at the first blow, but sometimes the blade lodged in the wood and he would then lift it again, not so high this time, and bring it back down against the block with force. When this happened, he sometimes muttered to himself. Around the chopping block was a scattering of golden chips and splinters. Each time,

Nash gathered up the split logs and tossed them into the basket he had positioned nearby. When the basket was full, Brigid called out.

'Nice chopping!'

He turned to her, surprised and smiling.

'How long have you been there?'

'Long enough.'

'Sneak!'

He leaned the axe against the chopping block, pulled his coat on and blew into his cupped hands.

'Here, give me a hand, would you?' The basket was full and heavy, and he lifted it awkwardly and began to lurch with it over to the house. Brigid gathered up an armful of split logs and followed him.

He emptied the basket by the pile at the back door. 'Could you stack them?' he asked. 'I'll get the rest.'

Obediently, she lifted the tarp and stacked the logs. Nash took the empty basket back to the chopping block and gathered up the remaining wood. When the job was done, they went inside, and Nash put the kettle on.

'How's it going?'

She nodded. 'Okay, I guess.'

He made tea.

'So, what can I do for you, young lady?'

He felt foolishly happy that she was there. It was only the morning but already her visit had lifted his day.

'Well, it's a nice day, and as Ma is off, I thought we could go to the barrow.'

'Pay a visit on King Arthur?'

'Exactly that.'

'Splendid. Will we need supplies? I have biscuits.'

'Then we're all sorted. It's not so far.'

They set out. Brigid explained that the barrow was high up on the mountain – a lofty place, elevated and isolated, as befitting the burial site of a king. She led him through the gate and along the path that contoured across the hillside, before climbing down through the trees into a narrow valley. They then followed this up, and as they walked Brigid pointed out places where, she said, the ground would soon be carpeted with bluebells (*'witches' thimbles, cuckoo's boots'*) and wood anemones. She showed him some very small yellow flowers which, it was said, only grew where the blood of Roman soldiers had once been spilled.

'How do you know all this stuff?' he asked.

'I just do, from growing up here. But I read books too. It's nice to know what things are, don't you think?'

'I do,' he replied. 'It's something I'm finding out for myself.'

The hillside began to level off, and they came to a clearing. In the centre of it was a low mound from which protruded rounded grey boulders mottled with moss and lichen. They skirted the mound and Nash saw that on the side facing down the valley was an opening. A cut led in and down, lined with long stones lying on their sides. A doorway was formed, with a huge stone laid across it like a lintel, framing a darkness.

'A king was buried here?' he asked. 'I thought it would be bigger.'

'No, it's just that round here pretty much any old stone or burial chamber or so on gets associated with Arthur or Merlin and that lot. What I read is that originally it was a stone circle. Then the mound was built over it, using the stones, and the chamber was constructed. This type of structure is called a Passage Tomb. Who was put in there, no one knows. Or how many. They found human bones when they excavated it, but that was ages ago. Arthur's Door is just a popular name. It's marked on the maps as *Bryn Celli Ddu*, which means something like The Mound in the Dark Wood.' She took off her rucksack and set it down on a stone. 'You know, I think it would be brilliant to be an archaeologist.'

'Those maps,' said Nash. 'Could I get a look?'

She took her head. 'They'd kill me,' she said, simply, and Nash was not sure if she was joking. She looked serious. He said no more.

Nash took in the scene. The trees ringed a circle of sky, bluer now, and looking up he felt disorientated. The harsh call of a pheasant sounded in the woods, answered by an echoing shriek from somewhere far off in the distance. The mound was not that impressive, he thought, but there was *something* to the place. He slowly circled it, and when he came back round to the opening, he saw that Brigid had disappeared. He called her name and she answered from within the chamber.

'In here,' she shouted. 'Come on.'

He stooped and went into the darkness, feeling the chill in the air inside. The floor was uneven and he stumbled, putting one hand out to steady himself against the wall of the passage. The darkness was very quickly absolute. He felt the space open out. The air smelt of the earth. Turning, he could see light coming from the passage he had followed.

'Here,' said Brigid. He couldn't see her but felt her put her hand on his arm.

'You know, they found finger bones in here,' she said. 'Lots of them. Isn't that weird? What do you suppose happened?'

'I couldn't possibly say,' said Nash. He was thinking, sacrifice, *human sacrifice*.

They came back out into the light, blinking, and sat on the boulders by the entrance. Nash offered Brigid a biscuit.

'Tell me about the city,' she said.

'What do you want to know?'

'Is it very exciting?'

'Yes and no.' He thought about it. 'I mean, if you live there, it's just what you know, it's your reality, your everyday, so it just is what it is. But I guess it *is* exciting. There's so much going on. It's really alive, if you know what I mean.' He paused and thought about it. 'But also, you know, it's pretty terrible. The air is thick with pollution. The traffic barely moves. Everyone's in a hurry and angry on top of it. And the birds, my god, you should see the birds.'

'What birds?'

'It's not like here. There, there's something wrong with them, with all of them. The pigeons are everywhere and they're disgusting. None of them have feet.'

'What?' She looked aghast.

'All rotted off. And then there are the seagulls. Terrifying. Rats, stray dogs. Flies everywhere.'

'It sounds lovely!' she said sarcastically. And then, 'Do you have lots of friends? They must be missing you. Do you meet up with them in bars and cafes? Do you go nightclubbing?'

He shook his head. 'The truth is, Bee, I'm a bit of a loner. Always have been. Only child, see?'

'Me too.'

He looked at her and she smiled, sheepishly. 'We're alike then.'

'Are we?' The thought had not occurred to him that he might be *alike* another person. He thought of himself as alone, sequestered, unique, isolated (a tree on an empty moor, leaning into unrelenting winds). He nodded slowly.

'Even so, it must be amazing to be able to go and see a movie any time you want.'

He nodded.

'And shops, shopping, restaurants. And museums and galleries!'

'If that's your thing.'

'Oh, it is my thing. I'm sure of it. I know I'd love it. There's nothing here, see?'

She took another biscuit.

'Have you got a girlfriend at home?'

'No.'

'Why not?'

'I don't know. I guess for the last couple of years my mind has been on other things.'

'Like what?'

'It's hard to say. Something happened and I sort of lost my focus. Lost any sense of direction.'

'What happened?'

'It's complicated.'

'Go on.'

'Well, my mum died. And then things seemed to fall apart. Well, things *did* fall apart. I lost my way.'

'I'm so sorry. What happened, was she ill?'

'No, it was an accident. A car crash.'

'Oh my god, that's awful.'

'I was in the car with her.

'No!'

She sat in silence, her face creased in thought, as if trying to imagine the scene. He waited.

'What happened?' she asked.

'It's a long story. We were on our way home and a car coming in the opposite direction veered across into our lane. It hit us, head on. Mum was hurt really badly. The doctors couldn't save her. I was pretty smashed up.'

'So awful! I can't believe it. I'm so sorry.'

'I know. I can't either, even now. It's strange, but so much of it just isn't there anymore. I remember getting into the car. And I remember the lights coming across at us. I don't remember the crash itself.' Nash paused, watching the images unspool in his mind's eye in slow motion, as they had done every day and night of his life since.

'What happened?' asked Brigid, quietly.

'The world stopped the moment the car hit us. When I woke up, I was in hospital. I knew straight away that quite a lot of time had passed.'

'Were you badly hurt?'

'Broken ribs, broken collar bone, broken nose, cuts and bruises all over, two black eyes. The shattered glass had gone in me all over. They got almost all of it out, but for weeks after I'd pick at the scabs and find weird little shards of glass inside, like horrible little gemstones.'

'What about the other driver?'

'He was killed instantly, they said. I was the only one who survived. Anyway, the thing was, Dad blamed me for it. At first, he was terribly sad. He came and sat by my bed at the hospital in silence. Horrible silence. But then he got angrier and angrier, more and more bitter, and then he stopped coming. By the time I got home, he couldn't really bear to look at me even. I felt I didn't have a choice. I had to get out, for his sake as much as mine.'

'What happened then?'

'By the time I was better the summer was over, and I'd missed the chance to take the place at university I'd been offered. So, I deferred. It was always my intention to go, just a year later. In the meantime, I had to get away, but I didn't have any money. Someone told me about fruit picking, and I got a job on a farm in Kent, living in a static caravan with a couple of other guys. It was okay. I kept myself to myself. I did that for a couple of months. And that was the start of the time when I drifted. I didn't know what to do with myself. I was drinking, trying to lose myself, trying to blank it all out, I guess. Or trying to lose the guilt. Because Dad made me think perhaps it really *was* my fault, that it was because of me that she had died.

'When the season ended, I went back to the city and worked on some building sites, in warehouses, that kind of thing. Rubbish jobs, really, but I didn't have to think too much or deal with people. At first, I still thought I would eventually go to university, get back on track, just a year later. But by the time I needed to make a decision about it, it was clear to me that it wasn't going to happen. It's hard to explain why. And somehow a couple of years went by, just like that.' He clicked his fingers. 'Eventually I ended up with this lot. The people I work for, whoever they are. That's a whole other story, really. But the point is, when they approached me, for the first time since the accident it seemed that something was happening, was going to happen. Something good.'

'Do you regret it?'

'The crash?'

'No, not going to university.'

'Maybe. I don't know. Look, it's important to say I never intended it to turn out this way. I didn't have a plan. I don't have an excuse. I was just trying to find a way of living, of being in the world, after what happened. And it was really hard. It really did turn my world upside down. And before I knew it so much time had just gone and I hadn't made any progress at all. And then this *opportunity* came along and it felt like I didn't have a choice.'

Brigid nodded sympathetically. 'I understand, I think,' she said. 'What were you going to study?'

'Maths. Can you believe it? It seems so odd now, the idea of spending three years studying a subject like that. It seems so pointless.'

'I want to go. But I don't know what I'll study yet. I just can't wait to get away.'

They sat in silence for a few minutes. Nash had the uncomfortable feeling that maybe he'd said too much. But it also felt good to have revealed something of himself. It was the first he'd talked of it in a long time. Somehow Brigid made it possible. He felt he had never spoken so openly before.

'What about your Da? Did you try to talk to him?'

'Of course. But he blamed me. It was impossible. The more time passed, the more he blamed me.'

'And what about you? Did you really think it was your fault?

'No, not really. I mean, I knew it wasn't. But after a while, with Dad being the way he was, it started to get to me. I did feel guilty. I did feel responsible.'

'It's awful. It's an awful thing.'

'It is. Really awful.'

Nash got up and then sat down again.

'What about you?' he asked.

'There's not much to tell. I live here.' It was as if that summed everything up.

'Boyfriend?'

'Nope. There's a boy at school who likes me, but I don't like him. I mean, I don't like him like that.'

'Fair enough. What about your father? Your mum said it's just you and her.'

'Yes, he passed away too. So, I do sort of know what you mean when you said you were lost. I mean, it's not the same, of course, it was a long time ago.'

'I'm sorry.'

'It's okay. He was ill for a long time – at least it seemed like a long time to me – and then he was gone.'

'Were you very close to him?'

'I don't know if that's the right word. I loved him, he was my Da. I miss him. I suppose Ma misses him too. It leaves a hole.' She smiled, sheepishly. 'It's something we've got in common, isn't it? We're both only children and we've both lost a parent.'

She was warm and her eyes were bright. Nash smiled too.

'Yes, it's a bit of a coincidence,' he said.

'It is,' she agreed, and her face coloured.

Nash got up and made a circuit of the mound. It wasn't particularly impressive. It was smaller than he'd expected.

But on the other hand, there *was* something to it. Something indefinable. A presence.

'What's the village like?' he said.

'Small.'

'I walked to the end of the track once,' he said. 'Right to the edge of the village.'

'I saw you. I waved and you waved back.'

Nash grinned. 'I know.'

They walked slowly back down the mountain, threading their way through the trees, chatting as they went.

'Are you getting used to Paradise?' Brigid asked him.

'It does my head in,' said Nash.

'What do you mean?'

'I mean, I can't get my head around it. It's too much. All the animals and insects and trees and dirt and everything. It's too much for me to be able to have any perspective.'

'But it's just... *nature*?'

'No, it's chaos. It defies understanding. Or anyway, it defies my understanding.'

'I don't know what you mean.' She thought about it. 'It's easy to understand. In fact, it's simple really. Start with a tree. The tree grows and makes fruit or nuts or pinecones or whatever. The fruit falls off the tree and insects eat it. The insects get eaten by birds. And the bird gets eaten by a fox, let's say. Or he steals the eggs. When the fox dies, his body rots down, consumed by grubs and bacteria and so on, and the rain washes all the nutrients back into the soil where they feed the trees and plants and the whole things starts over again. And that's life. It's quite beautiful really, don't you think?'

He nodded. 'I know that. I get it. It's the sheer variety that's too much for me. It feels like madness, pure anarchy.

All the hundreds of different bugs and beetles and flies, and worms and slugs and crawling things, the thousands of mosses and ferns, mushrooms, moulds, creeping vines and stinging things. All the poisonous things. All the things trying to kill each other, feeding on each other. All the trees, each one home to an entire universe. All the birds. And then I think of the small stuff, the micro stuff, and it's just too much. It's overwhelming. I read in one of the books in the house that a single teaspoon of soil can contain ten thousand organisms. It's a morass of life, curdling, swarming, writhing. It's revolting. Ugh! It does my head in.'

'But the city's like that too, isn't it?'

'In a way, yes. All the people and so on. But underlying it is order. Straight lines. It makes sense to me.'

'But there's order in the woods too. It's just a different kind of order.'

'I can't see it. All I can see is excess, confusion, turmoil.'

She laughed at him. 'God, Nash, don't overthink! It's just nature!'

'Sometimes I feel like I overthink everything.'

They walked in silence for a bit, Brigid leading the way, and then Nash said, 'But what about you? We never really talk about you. What do you want to do, when you finish school?'

'I don't know. Maybe I'll be an artist.' She grinned, sheepishly, as if ashamed to admit to such an absurd idea. 'I know I want to get away from here, but I don't really know yet what I might do. I do love it here. But it's all I've known. And that's why I want to get away. To see things. To see the world, as they say.'

'And do you think you'll come back. Once you've seen the world?'

'Who knows. Ma doesn't want me to go. She hates it when I talk about it.'

'She doesn't want to lose you.'

'I know.'

'Here's a question. You said there's nothing to do, so how do you fill your days, when you're not at school or creeping about in the woods?'

'My hobbies?'

'Yeah, I guess.'

'I like birdwatching. I like drawing and painting. Here, I can show you.'

She stopped walking, took a sketchbook from her bag and handed it to him. Inside were pencil sketches of leaves and flowers and some quick portraits of a woman he took to be her mother; yes, it was definitely Owen. She had captured something of her quite well. There was a careful drawing of a cat and some landscapes. Some had delicate washes of pale colour on them.

'I take it everywhere,' she said. 'You never know when you might see something worth drawing.'

He turned the pages and there were some very detailed watercolours of birds; a robin, an owl of some kind, others that he couldn't identify. They were beautiful.

'I cheated with those,' she said. 'I copied them out of a book.'

'I don't know anything about art but even I can tell you're really good.'

'Thanks.' She looked pleased and that pleased him.

'But how do you become an artist? I've got no idea how you would do that.'

'I don't think you do around here. You'd have to get away and go to art school. You have to study.'

'Where would you go, if you could?'

'The capital, if I could. But Ma won't let me. At least that's what she says now. Too dangerous, apparently. Also, she says I should stay on the farm. Apparently, it's my duty.' She pulled a face.

'But you said yourself, you don't do everything your mum says.'

'I know, but going away to study is a big deal, especially as she'd be left on her own. I'd only be able to do it if she was really behind me.' She stopped and seemed about to say something.

'What is it?'

'Can I draw you? Do you mind?'

'I don't know, Brigid. Really?'

'Yes. Please.'

'I don't even like having my photo taken.'

'It's only for me to practise. It's called life drawing. No one will ever see it. Please!'

'Well…'

'Brilliant, thank you! Okay, why don't you sit here.' She gestured to a fallen tree.

Nash sat, awkwardly, and Brigid straddled the tree trunk about three feet away from him, rested her sketchbook against the bark and began to draw his profile.

'Don't move,' she said. There was silence for a few minutes and then she exclaimed, 'Damn, that's no good.' She turned the page and started again. 'I definitely need more practice.'

Nash squirmed in her gaze. He was self-conscious, unused to being looked at like this, *scrutinized*, unnerved by the quick movement of the pencil on the paper, somehow pinning him down. Whenever he turned to look over at what she was doing, she told him off. 'Are you not done yet?' he kept asking,

'No! Keep still!' she commanded.

When she had finished, she showed it to him. It was a sketch, quick and light, an accumulation of wispy marks just beginning to cohere into a person. It was him.

'Amazing,' he said, shaking his head.

'We can do some more, at the house,' she said. 'If you don't mind?'

'Okay,' he said. 'For you.'

They resumed walking.

'What about you?' asked Brigid.

'What do you mean?'

'What are you into?'

'Do you know,' said Nash, 'I seem to have lost the knack of having a hobby, of interests, if I ever had it. I mean, what is a hobby? A diversion, a way to pass the time. I used to do all sorts of stuff, sports, I even read books. Yes, it's true! But somewhere along the line it all fell away.'

'When your ma passed?'

'Yes, I think so. I'm only beginning to realise just how much that derailed me.' He paused and then went on. 'I feel like an old man, but I'm barely alive. I mean, I've barely begun to live. I'm young, still, but I don't feel it. The accident happened at pretty much the exact moment I left school, just as I was about to start living my life, and it changed everything. I mean, I never even got started. Now, I'm not sure I've ever really lived. I'm still waiting.'

'What for?'

'I don't know. For someone to give me permission to start.'

(14)

As the trees came into bud and the woods were slowly transformed from a dreary monochrome into something brighter, a new world inflected with vivid moments of almost luminous green, Nash saw Brigid about once a week, usually at the weekends. They would walk together in the woods or play cards at the kitchen table. Once, when she had told her mother she was doing a birdwatching project, she came to see him three days in a row. When she did not appear on the fourth day, he experienced an unfamiliar sense of loss. He missed her, he realised. Sometimes she bought him newspapers and they would do sudoku or the crosswords together.

After, he would go through the papers carefully, looking anxiously for signs of the organisation's activities. Sometimes he perceived them – just hints and glimpses – in between the lines of stories about unsolved murders, suspected arsons, missing persons and the appalling litany of environmental collapse. Something would tell him that it was the work of The Grey Man and his colleagues, but he could never be certain. Yet he felt them, intuited them. On one occasion, reading about an incident where a corpse had been found lying in the middle of a suburban street, he thought he saw him. The story was accompanied by a photograph of the scene – an empty stretch of road, taped off, something indistinct, like a stain, where the body had been lying – and in the background a crowd of onlookers had gathered at the barrier. Amongst them, Nash was sure, stood Gray. He examined the grainy image carefully for some time. Yes, it was The Grey Man. As always, something in his expression suggested he found the scene before him somehow amusing. His thin lips made a half-smile. Nash pored over the image, trying to see if Black was there too, but he could not pick him out. Why was Gray there? Returning to the scene of the crime, to check that all was in order?

When he complained about the books in the house, Brigid started to bring him selections from her own collection. He had so much time that, even though he was a slow reader, he would go through several volumes a week. Brigid's favourites were fantasy, especially Tolkien, who, she told him earnestly, had created an entire, completely believable world, with its own complex flora and fauna, a detailed history and even new languages. He vaguely remembered reading *The Hobbit* when he was younger, but *The Lord of the Rings* defeated him. He couldn't get on with it, finding it completely unbelievable, ridiculous even. Brigid was disappointed and he felt that this was somehow a failing, a flaw in his character. He made excuses and asked her to bring him stories set in the *real* world.

He wondered at her interest in him. He enjoyed her company, and looked forward to her visits, but he wondered why she came. He concluded that she regarded him as a curiosity, an unusual species to be studied. Coming from the capital, he was unlike anyone she knew in the valley. The valley which, he learned, she had only left a handful of times, and then only to go to Aber for the shops, or to Cardiff for school visits to the museums. As such, she loved to quiz him about city life, which she regarded as exotic and extraordinarily glamorous, inflected with a sense of magic. Sometimes her questions surprised him. What does the Underground smell like? What can you hear when you lie in bed at night? What colour is the river?

Sometimes they discussed his situation, and he picked her brains, trying to work out what his options might be, when they finally did come for him.

'Bee,' he said, 'if you needed to get away from here, if someone was coming who wanted to... *hurt you*, what would you do, where would you go?'

'I've been thinking about it. I know what you're taking about. Before, I said that you'd need to get to the train at Aber, but I've changed my mind. It's too obvious. I'd go up.'

'What do you mean?'

'I'd go up the hill, over the mountain. I don't think they'd expect that. They'd be thinking you'd go down the valley, to the village and then to the road, wouldn't they?'

He nodded.

'How many are there? Coming for you?'

'I don't know. Three, four, maybe? Look, I'm just speaking hypothetically.'

'I know. It's all speculation, isn't it? Maybe they won't come at all. Maybe they've forgotten all about you. Let's hope so.' She smiled. 'The valley is like a funnel. If they were waiting for you, and they knew where to wait, it would be hard to get past them if you go down.'

'So, you'd go over the mountain?'

'Yes. I'd do the unexpected.'

'What's on the other side?'

'Of the mountain? Not much. There's a wide valley, not as wooded as this one, it's more fields. And more mountains beyond that. There's a couple of farms. And a road leading down and out.'

Nash generally only shaved once or twice a week, and he avoided the mirror. One day, Brigid told him that he was beginning to look like a hippy and announced that on her next visit she was going to cut his hair. He began to protest but she shut him down with a gesture. 'I'm doing it,' she said, firmly. She could be bossy sometimes and he liked it.

The next time she came, she brought comb, brush and scissors. She placed a chair in the centre of the kitchen and told him to sit.

'You're starting to look like a wild man, a werewolf. When was the last time you washed your hair? It's filthy.'

'Ages,' he said. 'Sorry.' He was embarrassed. 'I ran out of shampoo but forgot to ask your mum for more.'

She grimaced. 'No wonder it's so tangled. Right, go and wet it and then we can brush it through.'

He did what he was told. When he came back, she told him to take his top off and sit. He did. She draped a towel around his shoulders and began to brush his hair. When she touched the nape of his neck for the first time, he flinched.

She felt it. 'Are you okay?'

Nash felt strangely alive. 'I'm just nervous. Try not to cut me.'

'Well, keep still or I'll take an ear off.'

She ran her fingers through her hair and his scalp tingled.

His mother cutting his hair. Combing it out again and again so that he becomes drowsy, running her fingers across his scalp, carefully cutting his fringe – straight across and over the ears – leaning in close so he can feel the warmth of her and see the golden down on her skin where it catches the light, inhale the complex sweetness of her perfume. She finally wakes him, or rather, brings him back to the present by ruffling his hair and kissing his forehead. There you are, darling. So handsome! *Her voice. He looks down and is surprised to see just how much she has cut off, the curls lying in a ring about where he perches on a stool, his bare toes gripping the crossbar.*

'Have you done this before?' he asked.

'Only Ma. Don't worry, I know what I'm doing. And anyway, if I do make a mess of it, no one's going to see it, are they?'

'Yeah, but don't make a mess of it, okay?'

'You've got nothing to worry about,' she said. 'I'm making it up as I go along.'

She began to cut his hair and he closed his eyes.

Later, he asked Brigid, 'The people who have stayed here before, did you meet any of them?'

'No, when I was younger I didn't dare come up here. But the year before last I started spending more time in the woods, exploring. That was when I got the birding bug. I used to sometimes come by the house to see if anyone was here. There was one last year, an older guy, but I never spoke to him. I watched him though.'

'How long was he here for?'

'Not as long as you. Probably only about a week or so. Most of them only come for a week or so. Never as long as you.'

'And is it empty the rest of the time?'

'I guess so. Ma comes up once a month or so, just to check everything's okay. She'll come after a storm too. Just in case. Check the weather hasn't got in. In spring and summer she drives up, but in the winter the track is too bad.'

'It seems strange that it's just empty.'

'Bit of a waste, isn't it?'

Nash nodded.

'Once or twice, Ma asked me to come up with her to help with the cleaning.'

He thought about this.

'Was there ever anything strange, when you were cleaning?'

'What do you mean?'

'I don't know, anything out of the ordinary. Signs of a struggle.'

'God, no.' She shook her head. 'Just dusting and cleaning. And bagging up the rubbish.'

'I'm just trying to work out what's going to happen when they come for me. When they come to tell me what has been decided.'

'They'll take you back, won't they?'

'That's my expectation. But there's a chance they might be told to do something more... definitive.'

'But you said they would exonerate you?'

'They will. I'm sure of it. But there is always another possibility.' He made a face.

She knew what he meant and tried to reassure him. 'It won't come to that, I'm sure.' After a while, she asked, 'Why do you work for them?'

'When they asked me to join, I didn't have anything else. It felt like there was nothing to lose.'

'Why did they want you? Don't take this the wrong way, but you don't seem like the type.'

'Well, that's where you're wrong, Bee. Apparently, I *am* the type. I have within me a great capacity for... *action*. That's what Gray said. I don't know where it comes from. It's not anger, it's something else. Sometimes I think I have a demon inside me. I didn't know I could do it until I was attacked.'

'What happened?'

Nash described the incident in the pub, playing down the whole thing. He didn't want Brigid to think he was some kind of *thug*. 'The weirdest thing was that it didn't hurt, you know, when he hit me. And I was calm. Can you believe that?'

Nodding, she said, 'I think we're all capable of extraordinary things.'

'Gray was there,' he said. 'He saw it all and that's how all this started.'

Once, she asked him what he actually *did* for them.

'To be honest,' he said, 'I'm not really sure. That must sound crazy. It *is* crazy. I thought I was getting into one sort of thing – something good – but it's clear to me now that it's something else completely. What exactly, I still couldn't say. It started as one thing but it seems to have turned into another. Sometimes I get the feeling that it's all a terrible mistake. That I've been recruited – if that's even the right word for it – by mistake.'

He paused and thought about it.

'What do you know about them?'

'Not much. Ma doesn't tell me. She says it's best I don't know. It's funny, sometimes she's quite busy with their stuff and then there'll be long times when nothing happens, when Paradise is just empty and we forget all about it, about *them*. Or at least I do, I don't know about Ma.'

She thought about it. 'So why *are* you here,' she asked, 'at Paradise? Did you do something wrong? As far as I can tell, people usually come here when they've done something wrong.'

'No,' he replied firmly. 'Someone else screwed up and I dealt with it.'

(15)

Their instructions were simple. They were to go to the hotel at the stated time. It was important they be punctual. Without a key card, they would not be able to use the lift, so they were to take the stairs to the sixth floor. They would go to room 606. Rana would be waiting. But Rana would not actually be waiting for them, White explained, he would be waiting for Cardoso. He would have an envelope that he was expecting to hand over to Cardoso. 'We're not sure,' White said, 'if Rana and Cardoso have met before, so there's a possibility that Rana will think that one of us is Cardoso and will simply hand the envelope over. This is the *best-case scenario*. However, if Rana knows that neither of us is Cardoso – if they *have* in fact met before – we will have to make him hand over the envelope.'

Nash nodded.

'That's why we're giving you this,' said White. They were sitting in the car. He leaned across, opened the glove compartment and took out a plastic carrier bag. Inside were a compact black pistol and a box of ammunition.

Nash watched as White loaded the gun and then showed him how the safety catch worked. He handed it over and

Nash weighed it in his hand. Then he gripped it and put his finger to the trigger.

'White, I'm really not sure.'

'Look,' said White, 'you shouldn't have to use it. If he doesn't want to hand over the envelope to us, it should be enough to just show it to him.'

'And if it's not?'

'Not what?'

'If it's not enough to just show it to him?'

'We'll lean on him. Put him under a bit of pressure. Hit him with it, if necessary. But you shouldn't have to actually fire it.'

'Then why load it?'

'Oh, come on, Nash. You have to be prepared for the *worst-case scenario*.'

'Which is?'

'Rana actively resists giving us the envelope. He leans on *you*.'

'Will he be armed too?'

'I very much doubt it. He thinks he's going to a simple handover. At least that what we think he thinks.'

'But he might be?'

'It's a very slim possibility. Negligible, I'd say. But he's a pro. You'd think he would also be prepared for the *worst-case scenario*. So, yes, it is possible. Listen, don't overthink it. It'll be fine. You'll be fine. Just remember, the most important thing is to get the envelope.'

'What's in it?'

'That doesn't concern you. Or me, for that matter.'

'How will we know it's the right envelope? I mean, what if there's more than one envelope? What if there are lots of envelopes?'

'Then we just take all the envelopes. We can sort that out later.'

White looked at his watch. 'Okay, we've got an hour or so. I'll park up close by.'

It was a bright morning. They drove through the city and Nash thought through what White had told him. It was some kind of test, he supposed. The next rung on the ladder. Progression. He felt strangely calm and clear, considering he had a loaded gun resting in his jacket pocket. He touched it and found that the metal was cold.

White parked the car in a side street.

'Okay, we've got some time. The hotel is just round the corner. We can check it out before going in. Once we're done, we should split up. I'll come back to the car, you head to your place. You'll take the envelope, okay? They're more likely to follow me. Take a roundabout route, go along the canal. Go slow, don't rush. That's important. Don't draw attention to yourself. Get the Underground but switch trains. You know the kind of thing.'

Nash nodded. 'What then?' he asked.

'Some colleagues will come to you to pick up the envelope. They'll come to your place later. They'll tell you what to do. If all goes well, we'll be back on the beat tomorrow morning.'

'How will I know it's them? I mean, how will I know it's not another interception? Tit for tat?'

'You'll know.'

They started walking. It was bright and Nash put sunglasses on. The air was cold but the sunlight on his face was warm.

'Listen, this is important,' said White. 'The gun. Drop it in the canal, even if you haven't used it. Understand?'

Nash nodded.

'Understand?' White asked again, insistently, and Nash nodded again.

The hotel was new and shiny, a blocky construction of glass and steel, its name – NEST – above the entrance in blue neon. White checked his watch and said they were ten minutes early. The hotel was located on a small square with a grassy area centred on an ornate fountain. They crossed the road and found a bench. Nash sat and took in his surroundings, working out which way he would have to go when he left the hotel. A handful of abject pigeons – footless, mangy – alighted around them, cooing and strutting absurdly. White shooed them away.

This is ridiculous, Nash thought. *What am I even doing here? With a gun in my pocket? Should I call the police, end it all?*

Two minutes before the hour, they walked back across the road and pushed through the doors into the hotel lobby. The reception desk was to the right and a member of staff was dealing with a guest who was either checking in or out, suitcases stacked beside him. The lifts were straight ahead, and to the left Nash saw a door with a sign for the stairs above it. They quickly crossed the lobby and went through the door. Nash took his sunglasses off as they climbed the stairs. On the sixth floor they came out onto a landing. The lift doors were there, and signs pointed left for rooms 601–610 and right for rooms 611–620. The carpet was a swirling pattern of nauseating burgundy and dark grey. The walls were a deep blue. Colourful abstract prints hung in rows. Nash checked himself. He took the gun from his pocket and clicked the safety off and then back on again. Deep breath. White nodded and smiled a horrible smile. *He's nervous but trying not to show it*, thought Nash.

Strangely, Nash was not nervous. He felt perfectly calm.

They followed the corridor past a series of identical doors and around a corner. Before room 606, Nash again checked himself. White whispered, 'You knock. I'll hang back.'

Nash held his breath and listened but could hear nothing from inside. He put his right hand in his pocket, on the gun, and knocked twice, hard, with his left. He felt calm, ready. White was against the wall, a few feet to his left.

After what seemed like an age, he heard sounds and the door opened to reveal a man in a light grey suit. He was perhaps sixty years old, slim, his skin and eyes pale, his hair grey and slicked back. The texture of his skin was unnaturally pasty, chalky, and he seemed to be wearing make-up, eyeliner, rouge, even a hint of lipstick.

'Rana?' said Nash.

'Yes.'

'Have you got it?'

Rana seemed confused. Nash looked over his shoulder into the room and saw an envelope on the bedside table.

White pushed past him and forced Rana up against the wall. 'The envelope,' he said to Nash. 'Get it.'

There was a short passageway into the room, off which a toilet and bathroom opened. Nash squeezed past and went into the main part of the room and saw that Rana was not alone. A second man in a pale blue suit was in an armchair by the window, which spanned from floor to ceiling, and which was dazzlingly bright. For a moment, Nash thought they had come to the wrong room, had stumbled upon a completely different kind of tryst. Seeing Nash, the second man – that was Cardoso, he supposed, but what was he doing here in the room, had he come early, or had they arrived late, or been given incorrect information? – rose to his feet and reached inside his jacket pocket. Nash went to reveal his gun – to *show* it – but the sight snagged on the lip of his pocket. He fumbled and it tumbled from his hand, falling to the floor at his feet, and he stumbled as he bent to retrieve it. Rana was behind him, and Nash was aware, as he crouched and reached for his pistol, that Cardoso had taken out a gun and made a step forward. Rana said something from behind him, which Nash did not understand. Nash's hand was on his gun. Cardoso said something indistinct. His gun was pointing at Nash.

Nash stood, and as he did, Cardoso fired. It was astonishingly loud in such a small space and the bullet went into the wall behind Nash's head. It seemed like it took hours for Nash to raise his gun so that it was pointing at Cardoso's face. He was about to say something.

What is he going to say? Nash wondered.

He squeezed the trigger and as he did White came past him, knocking him off balance. The gun bucked against his hand as he fired and more explosions filled the small space, from Cardoso's gun and then White's. And then another. Cardoso's face disappeared and a dark red flower painted from blood appeared on the wall behind him as his body collapsed. A table lamp on the small writing desk disintegrated, fragments of glass and metal ricocheting across the room.

The light from the window was too bright, fiery.

White was falling, slowly.

Rana came from behind, shouldering Nash so that he lost his balance and they toppled together onto the bed. Nash was on his front and Rana was on top of him, trying to pinion him. He had an arm around Nash's neck, choking him. With a huge effort, Nash twisted and freed his arm and brought the gun around, but fired straight into the wall. White was on the floor beside the bed, below them, turning over, bringing his gun across. Nash pushed Rana back and White fired. Another blood flower bloomed improbably on the ceiling above them and Rana instantly became slack and heavy. Nash rolled over, pushing Rana away from him, so that he slipped to the floor at the foot of the bed, leaving a smear of blood across the sheets, and lay beside White.

Silence and stillness. After the gunshots, the hush seemed to pulse. Nash's ears were ringing, whining, whistling. He was breathing hard but felt steady. White was on the floor. He had dropped his gun. He tried to get to his feet, failed, tried again and pitched backwards. He lay on his back groaning and gurgling, and Nash saw that he had been shot in the neck, that there was in fact a massive hole in his neck, a black hole, and an obscene amount of blood was coming out, slicking his shirt and suit. White brought his hands up to try to stem the tide – it looked like he was strangling himself – but it was futile, the blood just kept coming, flowing, pooling, thick and oily. Nash watched with horrified fascination. White was trying to say something, gesturing to Nash, his eyes wide and panicked, so Nash went to the bathroom and took a towel from the rack, thinking to staunch that awful hole in White's neck, knowing it was little more than a gesture. By the time he came back White's eyes were closed.

He picked up the envelope and sat on the bed, avoiding the blood smear. The paper was heavy and textured and, on the front was a single word:

ACCELERATION

He briefly considered opening it. Instead, he pocketed it and then went into the bathroom and ran the cold tap. He washed his hands and splashed water on his face and tried to collect his thoughts. He was surprised by how calm he felt.

He went through what had happened in his mind. Rana had opened the door. He, Nash, had not touched anything but the bathroom door handle and the tap. He took the towel and wiped them both down. He went back into the room and looked again. They were all dead. The blood on the wall was beginning to run. Three men were dead. Where Cardoso lay, a dark stain was spreading through the pale grey carpet pile. He was covered in blood. No, he was *drenched* in blood. There was blood everywhere. Outside the high windows the city shone and sparkled in the winter sunlight. A wall of white clouds like a mountain range waited on the horizon. Spots of blood on the glass, hanging in space, caught the light and gleamed like tiny ruby lenses.

I should call the police, he thought.

I should not *call the police*, he countered.

I can't call the police, he decided. *What am I thinking?*

Nash looked around the room again. It seemed futile to attempt to tidy up. He wondered if he should go through the men's pockets, if he should take the guns with him, but in the end decided he should just leave everything as it was. He had the envelope. He should leave, and quickly. If anyone had heard the shots, then the police would be coming. It was impossible that someone had *not* heard the shots. So, the police must be coming. He listened. Nothing. Yet. He used the sleeve of his jacket to turn the handle and open the door to the room. The corridor was empty. He quietly closed the door and walked quickly back to the landing, through the door and down the stairs. The lobby was busy, a large group was in the process of bringing luggage in from a coach parked outside. He put his sunglasses back on, quickly exited the hotel and crossed the square, heading for the canal as he had been instructed. He walked slowly, carefully monitoring his fellow pedestrians, watching the flow of traffic, looking back over his shoulder often to see if he was being followed.

As he walked, he again went over what had happened. Cardoso was not supposed to have been there. What had he been doing there? He was supposed to be coming later. Had he come early? Had they been late? No, they had been on time. On the dot. Had the time of the handover been changed without their knowledge? Had it been a trap, an ambush? He saw Cardoso again, in his mind's eye, the gun levelled at him. He was sure that if he had not fired then Cardoso would have shot him, killed him. It had been a matter of life or death. And yet.

How many shots had been fired?

He went over it all again. More than four shots. Was it five? Six? Seven?

A mistake. He was beginning to feel that it had all been a terrible mistake.

At the canal he lingered. There were some ducks. The sunlight on the water. When he was sure he was not being observed, he took the gun from his pocket and dropped it into the dark water. As it sank into the shadows he had the feeling again. It had all been a terrible mistake. Not just the events of this hellish day, but all of it.

PART 2

(16)

Lying in bed in darkness, he hears something scuttling about somewhere above him. *Scuttling* is the right word. It is not scrabbling or scratching, words which would bring to mind mice or rats, but *scuttling*, which summons nightmares: spiny crabs and furred spiders and other such abominations. He climbs from the bed and turns on the light. Standing on the bed, he tries to work out where the noise is coming from. It is definitely above. As he listens, it moves away. He follows it down the passageway, watching the ceiling and listening, and there, above the stairs, he sees a hatch that somehow he has not noticed before. It is cold and his breath clouds the air in front of his face. He can hear the wind in the trees outside the house. The noise stops. It is most likely a mouse, or perhaps a rat or squirrel, he thinks. Maybe even some kind of large insect. But it cannot be a crab, he reassures himself. It cannot be a crab, the kind of creature that has haunted his sleep since he was little.

He takes the chair from the second bedroom and, standing on it, presses his ear against the trapdoor and listens. There is only the groaning and creaking of the old house. Sometimes, in the night, he could swear he hears it breathing. Very slowly, he pushes the hatch up – half expecting something to lunge down at him from the darkness – and pushes it to one side. There is nothing.

He goes back to the fireplace and retrieves matches. Standing on the chair, his eyes are just level with the frame of the opening, and he strikes a match. The brief flare of light reveals the roof void, blackened timbers like the ribcage of some awful old beast, a fog of cobwebs. No creature is revealed. No eyes reflect the dying flame. He lights a second match and sees an old biscuit tin just back from the edge of the opening. *Family Selection*. Instinctively, he grabs it.

He replaces the trapdoor and listens again. Nothing.

The biscuit tin is dusty. With some difficulty he gets the lid off. Inside is a piece of paper, folded many times. He spreads it out on the bed. It is a large sheet, made of many smaller sheets struck together with brittle yellow Sellotape. It is covered by an intricate drawing of a spider's web. But no, it is not the ordered concentric weaving of a spider's web, but something more eccentric. Spindly lines, quavering and hesitant, radiate from a single point. Some zig and zag, cutting across the others. There is something about it. It is familiar, somehow, though he cannot pinpoint how.

He pins it up in the spare bedroom and in the following days keeps coming back to examine it, to try to make sense of it. He decides it is not a drawing of a spider's web, or an explosion, but a map. It is a map of Paradise. Nonetheless, he cannot make sense of it.

Whoever made this map, if that is what it is, and concealed it in the attic, had grappled with it over a long period of time, that much is clear; the patchwork paper, the many erasures, reworkings, corrections. The lines – paths? – often peter out as they reach the edge of the paper, as if ink or pencil had given up the will to describe the world.

After this discovery, in the long nights, as he lies in bed trying to make sense of what has happened, what is happening, what *will* happen, he is haunted by the thought of the empty space above him, the darkness and whatever it is that lives there and *scuttles*. It is another thing to worry about. Another thing to get under his skin, into his dreams, to unsettle and unnerve.

The map, he decides after a few days, with growing disappointment, is no help at all. Something tells him that since it was made (who knows how long ago, the paper is brittle, like parchment) the woods have shifted. Though he knows it is impossible, he feels it, somehow. *The forest is sentient.* Of this, he is certain. It considers him. He feels it weighing him.

He traces a line with his finger. The map may once have been accurate, but it no longer is. It is a map of a past reality.

The wind in the trees in the night. It seems to be telling him something.
Shhhhh, shhhhh, it says.
Or shoo, shoo.
Or even, she, she, she.
It is insistent.

(17)

He told Brigid about a dream he kept having, with small variations, which had made a powerful impression on him. In the dream he was in the capital again. It was late afternoon, and the light was beginning to fade. A pale pink glow was upon the sky, which was piled high with mountains of cloud. Lights were on in all the buildings, but the city was deserted. He had walked slowly down the street, peering into the windows of the shops – and could see neat racks of clothes, displays of shoes, homewares, banks of TV screens, hi-fi equipment – but no people, no one.

In the dream, he studies his reflection, faint in the glass, and keeps walking. It doesn't seem strange that he is all alone in the city, but he is curious, where is everyone? It is not a place he recognises and so he keeps walking, passing a church, its pale stone washed with late light. Its doors are closed.

He stops and looks down at his feet and sees that weeds are pushing up between the cracks in the pavement, proliferating, rapidly covering the ground, even curling up over his feet and curling around his ankles. Looking up, he sees that vines are quickly scaling the walls around him, wrapping the buildings in foliage. The streetlights are sprouting branches, becoming trees. As Nash keeps walking, picking through the dense vegetation springing up around him, he sees that the sky is suddenly filled with flocks of birds, not the awful pigeons but crows (wheeling), swifts (darting and plunging), starlings (flocking), and high above great birds of prey describing wide loops on the thermals. Turning a corner, he comes upon a herd of small deer, who regard him quizzically but without fear.

Then it is dusk and the city is no more. The ground beneath his feet is mud and stone, run through with busy roots. Great and ancient trees arch over him. The air is filled with the rich scent of soil and pollen, of new growth. The wind in the trees is like the sound of the sea.

He had, at first, been pleased to find himself back in that familiar world, amongst concrete and glass, the hard straight surfaces, the sense of order. But as the city disappeared to be replaced by the forest, he was delighted. He was filled with a kind of ecstasy. When he woke, finding himself back in the cold dark room, breathing the smoky scent of the dead fire, he felt bereft. He had got out of bed and gone to the window, with the feeling of the dream clinging to him. Out there the forest was dark and dense, impenetrable, as it always is. It continues. He knew then that it will go on forever, long after mankind has vanished. And high above, high in the sky, a bright silver moon had ridden triumphantly upon banks of cloud.

When he finished telling her about the dream, she smiled.

'It's obvious, isn't it?' she said.

He shook his head. 'What?'

'You're growing into the woods. And finally, the woods are growing into you.'

(18)

'Would you say this is now spring?' asked Nash. He and Brigid had been walking together in the woods. Brigid had spotted a woodpecker – a flash of black and white and red – and insisted they stop and watch it. She was standing, her binoculars to her face, staring up into the trees. Every now and again a drumroll of sharp knocks reverberated above them. Nash was seated on a fallen tree, poking the ground at his feet with a stick. Leaves were coming on the trees. The grasses were greening. New bracken shoots were pushing through. Banks of waxy leaves flourished where bluebells would soon come.

'I guess so. You can see it, can't you? The green shoots. The daffs are coming. Sometimes I think I can smell it.'

'I know what you mean. Something in the air has changed, hasn't it? It's funny. Like God flicked a switch. I never noticed the seasons before, in the city. There, they don't really mean anything. They blend one into the other.'

'Spring is my favourite,' said Brigid. 'I love the feeling of possibility. Everything is new again.'

Nash nodded in agreement.

Some days later, Nash was sitting outside the back door of the house in bright sunshine when a shower came on quickly. Bright rain, like quicksilver, flashed in the shafts of sunlight and a rainbow formed over the house. Normally, he would have run for cover, but on this occasion, for some unknown reason, he stayed sitting and raised his face to the sky, letting the rain wash over him, letting it trickle into his mouth, cold and clean.

The shower lasted no more than two minutes, and by the time it passed Nash's clothes were wet through. He could feel the dampness against the skin of his arms, his shoulders, his back, and a chill had gone deep into him for the air was still cold, despite the brightness of the sun. But there was something else, something wonderful. He felt clean for the first time in ages. And the light seemed to have entered him, to have penetrated his being, that bright silvery radiance of rain falling through sunlight, like diamonds.

He felt new. It was just as Brigid had said. Newness.

Time passed. Hours, days, weeks. And as the time passed, Nash had started to lose track of it. In Paradise, it became abstract, meaningless. At first, he had kept a tally, making marks on the back of the kitchen door, measuring, counting; but at some point he forgot, lost count, and soon after gave up. In this vague flow from day to day he was sometimes even able to forget the reason he was there. The worry, the fear, the dreadful anticipation, the endless going over of what had happened at the hotel, would fall away from him and he was left only in the moment, admiring the sunlight slanting through the kitchen window, the slow play of dust in the brightness, taking simple pleasure in the chopping of wood, a hot mug of tea on a cold day, the preparation of food. He studied the field guides and found it intensely satisfying.

Once, he and Brigid were walking in the woods and stopped and pointed at a tiny blue flower nestled amongst dark green leaves. 'Look at that,' he said. 'Isn't it beautiful?'

She looked at him with surprise and made a question with her eyes.

Bending down, she asked, 'What is it?'

'Sweet violet,' he said, cautiously, crouching beside her and using two fingers to gently angle the flower towards them. 'It's a sweet violet, isn't it?'

'Mr Nash!' she exclaimed happily. 'I do believe we'll make a naturalist of you yet!'

Nash smiled. He felt unaccountably pleased with himself. It was like he had discovered the key to a secret space.

Time flowed, gently, like a stream tumbling down from the mountains above, and Nash realised with surprise that he was starting to think of the house as 'home'. It still repelled him, with its unexpected angles, its unknown creaking and groaning, the weird charms and signs nailed into the pitch-dark wood of the ancient beams, the dust and the spiderwebs, but it was where he lived. Yes, he lived in Paradise.

His life was stripped back. He prepared simple meals. He kept the log piles well stocked. He walked in the woods. He read. In a way, it was wonderful, to have no schedule, to take each day as it came. Yet Gray, Black and the whole blind network lurked somewhere, just offstage. He could not forget them. He sometimes wondered, hopefully, if they might have forgotten about him, but knew that at some point a reckoning would come.

(19)

The first time he saw the fox, Nash was standing in the kitchen, absently looking out at the entangled world that surrounded the house. In the corner of his eye, he registered movement by the log pile and looked closer. It was carefully sniffing at the large lump of wood he used as a chopping block. It was a handsome creature, an extraordinary rust-red with the bushiest tail he had ever seen. In the city, the foxes were abject creatures: diseased and malnourished, with matted, patchy fur and rat-like tails, if they even had tails. Scavengers. He associated them with death and decay. When he was a boy, their cat, a tabby called Bobbin, had become ill and died. Nash had been heartbroken. At that time, they had a small garden, a mean square of thin grass edged with ragged shrubs. His father had taken the dead cat, wrapped in newspaper, and buried it in the far corner of the garden, beneath a bush. But the next day, when he looked out of his bedroom window, Nash saw that the poor creature had been exhumed, beheaded and eviscerated. Its guts, which were a horrible blue-grey colour that he never forgot, were spread across the lawn. Its head lay on the back doorstep, like an offering, or a threat. A *fox* had dug it up, his father explained. That was the kind of animal *foxes* were. Nash gagged as his father gathered Bobbin's limbs and organs and stuffed them into a plastic carrier bag, which he unceremoniously dumped into the dustbin. After, when he heard the foxes calling in the night, those weird noises so much like a child being tortured, he shuddered and tried to banish the sound from his consciousness, covering his ears or turning on the radio to mask the unholy wailing.

But *this* fox by the log pile was not such a creature. For a start, he was confident. The urban foxes slunk from shadow to shadow fearfully, but this one almost swaggered as he appraised the chopping block and then sniffed around the shed. He was taking his time. His brush was full and high. His chin and throat were a brilliant pure white. He looked towards the house and Nash had the curious sensation that he was seeking him out. Nash watched, fascinated, as he cocked a leg against the chopping block and pissed all over it. By this time Nash had seen many creatures in the woods, but this fox seemed somehow special. He gave the impression that this place, these woods, were *his*. His domain, his home, his kingdom.

Something moved in the horse chestnut tree and the fox paused and looked up. He settled on his haunches, patiently. The crows were there, watching. Crowley was there, intent, his head cocked.

Eventually, the fox had seen enough and confidently trotted off between the trees. Nash went inside and took a field guide from the bookcase and read about the curious habits and characteristics of foxes. The Red Fox, *Vulpes vulpes*, he read, is mostly nocturnal. They are solitary creatures, but a family group is known as a *skulk*. A fox's hearing is so good it can hear rodents moving around underground, or the ticking of a watch forty paces away. In most cultures foxes are regarded as opportunistic, cunning and wily. All over the world the fox is regarded as a trickster.

The next time he saw this particular fox, they were deep in the forest. It seemed impossible, but he was sure it was the same one. He was following a wide path when something made him stop and look back. It was there, a hundred yards behind him. They stood, watching each other for a long minute. In the city, he thought, he had had similar encounters, usually late at night, returning home. A brief face-off on a dark street, usually beneath a yellow streetlight. The animal would wait carefully for a few seconds and then race off, keeping low, furtively seeking cover between parked cars or ducking into a garden, disappearing. But this fox did not flee. He sat and watched Nash. Eventually Nash resumed his walk and, glancing over his shoulder, saw that the fox was following him. He thought about shooing it away but didn't. Sometime later, when the path inexplicably came to an abrupt end beneath an enormous oak tree, he turned back to retrace his steps and there was no sign of it.

When the fox spoke to him for the first time, Nash felt – as he had begun to suspect for some time – that Paradise was affecting him more profoundly than he had previously realised, that his grasp of reality was becoming tenuous. That he might even be *losing his reason*.

It was a bright morning, almost warm, and Nash had brought a chair from the kitchen and set it by the back door. He was sitting in a pool of sunshine, a cup of tea cradled in his lap, with his eyes closed. He could hear the gentle susurrations of the soft wind in the trees and enjoyed the roseate glow through his eyelids filling his head with warmth. Did he fall asleep? Later, when he thought about it, he could not say for certain that he had not.

When he opened his eyes, he saw that the fox, almost orange in the sunshine, iridescent against the dun-coloured wood, was by the log pile. It didn't seem to have seen him and was, as before, sniffing inquisitively around the shed. Nash stood, to get a better view of it, and it turned and looked directly at him. But instead of fleeing into the undergrowth, it regarded him, cocked its head at an angle, and then, as if making its mind up about something, came trotting over.

Nash was taken aback but didn't move. The fox stopped about six feet from him and spoke.

'Good morning,' it said.

Nash could only think that he was dreaming.

'Good morning, Nash,' the fox said again.

'How do you know my name?' he somehow managed to say.

'I know everything about you,' said the fox.

'How?'

'Because I *am* you.' The foxed paused, as if to let that alarming revelation sink in. And Nash thought, *I should turn around, go back inside and then come out again, and it won't be here*. He rubbed his eyes, like a character in a carton who can't believe what he is seeing. The fox was still there, sitting on its haunches, waiting.

'So, you're not real?' Nash asked, anxiously.

'Oh, I'm real alright. You made me.'

'Why? Why would I do that? *How* would I do that?'

The fox shifted and carefully scratched behind its ear with a hind paw.

'This is crazy,' said Nash.

The fox nodded. 'Maybe *you're* crazy.' It paused and then went on. 'They're coming for you, you know?'

'I know, but when?'

'Soon, I think.' The fox raised his snout and sniffed the air, closing his eyes. He turned back to Nash. 'You should prepare.'

'I know, I'm going to.'

'But you never do, do you? You keep putting it off. When they come, it'll be nasty.'

'You think? I don't know,' said Nash. 'I'm pretty sure they'll come to tell me that everything's okay.'

'No, I don't think so,' said the fox. 'I've got a hunch that when they come, it'll be nasty. And if it is, what are you going to do? Roll over?'

'Do you think I should get out?'

'I'm not sure that's an option. They'd know. And they'll come after you.'

'Then what should I do?'

'Prepare yourself. Be ready. Have a plan.'

'But how can I be prepared if I don't know what I'm preparing for?'

The fox looked at him steadily. 'Be ready for anything. *Anything.*'

Nash nodded.

'Look, Nash, I don't know why, but you seem very slow on the uptake here. I think the woods have addled your brains. You need to get your shit together. Seriously. Yes?'

Nash nodded. He knew it. And it was true, the woods had done something to him. He was not the same as he had once been. He was no longer the person who had been brought to Paradise in the depths of winter. That person was another Nash, one he could no longer be sure even existed. It was true, he thought; somehow everything had changed. The world had changed and he had changed with it.

'What's the worst-case scenario?' asked the fox.

Nash thought about it before answering, even though he already knew what the answer was.

'Bad news,' he said. 'They've considered what happened, they've reviewed the evidence, and they've decided that I'm at fault. Or, worse, that what happened was a deliberate attempt to compromise the network.'

'So, they take you back, to face the music,' said the fox, 'or...'

'They do it here. They end it here.'

'An execution.'

Nash grimaced. 'That's not a nice word.'

'Which is more likely?'

'They'd do it here.'

'I think you're right. Dig a shallow grave somewhere in the woods where no one goes. You just disappear. Easier to get rid of the body out here. Easier than in the middle of a city.'

Nash thought about White's story, Spink and the headless corpse.

'Right palaver getting rid of a body in a city,' said the fox, showing sharp teeth. 'No one knows you're here, do they? If you don't turn up, will anyone try to find you?'

Nash thought of his father, Mooney. There was no one. He shook his head.

'But look, you know you didn't fuck up, don't you?'

Nash agreed, doubtfully. 'It was a mistake. A terrible mistake. But not *my* mistake.'

'So, if they come back and we're looking at a worst-case scenario, are you just going to go along with it?'

'No, of course not.'

'But if they turn up and The Grey Man is like, *ah Mr Nash, we're here to do you in, on account of your awful complicity, duplicity, whatever,* and you're like, *but Mr Gray, no thanks, I'm an innocent man*, what's going to happen?'

'It will kick off. They'll do it anyway.'

'Of course they will. You resist at all, and it *will* kick off. Unless they take you out from a distance, sniper-style, and if that's the case then there's nothing you can do. You won't even know you're dead. Though something tells me that's just not their way. But otherwise, you are going to need to push back.'

The fox caught a scent and was silent as he sniffed the air and concentrated. Satisfied, he resumed.

'Let's say two guys come, Gray and that fat fuck, Black, for example. And they've got orders just to finish you right there and then. You've got to be able to read the room, to know which direction it's going in. Anticipate. And you need to get the jump on them. Of course, Gray being such a talker, he's probably going to tell you what's going to happen before it happens.'

It scratched itself behind the ear and yawned.

'So, you need to be ready to fight. What've you got?'

'Just the axe.'

'The axe. Beautiful. Old fashioned, but effective. Wielded with guile, with a nice sharp blade, the axe can be a deadly weapon. Especially in the hands of a killer. Keep it keen, yes? What else.'

'A hammer.'

'Lovely. Proper thug weapon that. Old school. Ronnie Kray did some of his best work with a hammer. Nice hard blow to the head and your man's a goner. Messy though.'

The fox considered. 'Look, an axe and hammer are all very well, but as the saying goes, you don't bring a knife to a gunfight. You bring a gun to a gunfight. A *gun*. You need a gun, Nash. They're going to have guns.'

Nash groaned. He didn't want to hear it.

'Why don't you ask Brigid?'

'She won't have one.'

'No, *she* won't have a gun, but she may know where to get one. She likes you. She cares about you. I think she'd help. She doesn't want anything bad to happen to you.'

'I don't want to get her involved.'

'She's already involved. You should ask her.'

'I don't know.'

'Ask her, Nash. Your life could depend on it.'

'I'll think about it.'

'Really?'

Nash nodded.

'Okay, now, let's say they come, and you read the room, and you somehow get the better of them and you're the last man standing. What next?'

'Get out.'

'Get out. Precisely. I do believe you're starting to get it, Nash.'

'They'll come after me.'

'Almost certainly. So, you'll need to throw them off the

scent. Make them think you've gone one way, when in fact you've gone another.'

Nash considered this. It was all too much. 'You know,' he said, 'I'm not so sure I want to go back after all.'

The fox regarded him quizzically. 'What do you mean?'

'The city, the organisation, those people, all that, that life. I don't think I want it anymore. I'm not even sure it was my life. It feels like it happened to someone else. I think I might be better off staying here, in this place. There's something about it. It doesn't want to destroy me. These woods, this place, it took a long time for me to realise but – I know this sounds crazy – it's healing me. It wants me to be a part of it. To be integrated.'

'What the fuck are you talking about?' said the fox. 'You a hippy now, or what? Look, when you signed up, Nash,' said the fox, 'you didn't sign up for work experience. With this lot, once you're in, you're in.'

'But no one explained that,' said Nash whiningly, knowing that he sounded pathetic. The sinking feeling was becoming a plunging, a descent, a headlong hurtle into a bottomless abyss. There would be no end. Not only would he have to get away, but he would have to disappear. He could never have a normal life, not now. He would have to find his way to a place where they would not find him. He would have to erase himself all over again.

'Cheer up, old chap,' said the fox, regarding Nash quizzically. 'It might *just* be okay.'

'Thanks,' said Nash, sarcastically. And then, 'I guess I'll take okay.'

'Look, Nash, this isn't like one of those movies, *Rambo* or whatever, where you can sharpen some sticks and rig up some booby traps in the woods. This is real, yes? No sharpened sticks. When I say you've got to be prepared, what I mean is that you've got to be prepared mentally. You've got to be ready to do what you need to do. Which might just mean killing one or two or more men. But they are men who will kill you if you don't kill them. It's as simple as that. So, you must have your arsenal, minimal as it is, in good order and to hand, so that you're ready to act.'

'We haven't talked about the best-case scenario,' Nash said hopefully.

'Ah, yes, best-case scenario. That's a good one. That's where they come and Mr Gray shakes your hand and is like, *congratulations, old friend, and welcome back into the fold, allow me to drive you back to the city where we'll line up a series of unpleasant and highly illegal tasks for you to perform on our behalf at great personal risk to your well-being.* Yep, that sounds brilliant, Nash. Best-fucking-case scenario, that one. Seems to me, Nash, that we're not talking best- and worst-case but frying pan and fire.'

After that, Nash would see the fox most days. It was as if it was keeping an eye on him. If he was walking in the woods, he would see a flash of orange and rust amongst the trees and know it was there. Or he would see it from the kitchen window, sunning itself in the clearing by the log pile. Sometimes when he was chopping wood it would appear and watch him.

Later, when he saw Brigid, he told her. 'There's a fox,' he said, 'and it's following me.'

She laughed. 'No way. A fox wouldn't follow you. Foxes are scared of people. And anyway, there must be dozens of foxes in this valley. You're seeing different foxes.'

'No, it's definitely the same fox. I know because he…' Nash hesitated, and then was quiet.

She grinned at him, shaking her head. 'What's his name?'

'I don't know. I'll ask him next time I see him.'

(20)

Some days later, they were walking together in the woods. Brigid was watching a bird through her binoculars when he noticed something glinting, something shiny, high up in one of the trees that lined the track they were on. Unable to work out what it was, he borrowed her binoculars and searched amongst the branches until he found it: a camera. A surveillance camera, much like the type one sees in car parks and malls, trained back along the track in the direction they had come from.

'What. The. Fuck,' he said, slowly.

'What is it?' Brigid asked.

'A camera. A fucking camera.'

'Where?'

She took the glasses and searched the tree until she too located it.

'Yeah, it's a camera,' she confirmed.

'What's a camera doing in a tree in the fucking woods?' he asked, angrily.

'I think it probably belongs to the conservation organisation – the Woodland Fund or the Wildlife Fund or whatever it is. The one that does projects here.'

'Who?'

'They do projects in the woods. They monitor the various animal populations and so on. This is a Site of Special Scientific Interest. Once a year they come and download the files from the cameras. It's important work.'

Nash shook his head. He contemplated climbing up into the tree and tearing the camera down. He didn't believe for a second that it was being used to monitor animal populations. How would that even work?

After that, as he wandered amongst the trees, he would often see the shiny little boxes with their cyclopean black eyes, always high up and inaccessible. He couldn't believe he had not seen them before. Sometimes he threw stones at them.

(21)

'Better late than never,' said Mary Owen. She produced a plastic carrier bag from the boot of her car and handed it to him. It was heavy with records. 'Not much of a choice, I'm afraid,' she said. 'Oxfam only had classical. Well, go on, see if it works. I'll unpack and make tea.'

Nash carried the bag of records through to the sitting room and sat cross-legged before the ancient hi-fi system. He switched it on and pulled the records from the bag. They were old. He knew the names – Beethoven, Mozart, Bach and so on – but did not know the music. To him, classical music, orchestral music – *old* music – all sounded pretty much the same. It was either heavy and sonorous and melancholy and slow or sweet and silly. The record on the top of the pile was of solo piano pieces by Bach. He carefully drew the record from the inner sleeve, lifted the cover of the record player and located the vinyl on the turntable. He lifted the arm and carefully brought it across and dropped it into the outer groove.

Music filled the room, crisp piano notes sprinkled into the air, chasing each other, describing a descending melody, rushing and slowing. And then a second melody, entwined, coiling around and through the first. It was like a circle and an ellipse, abstract forms rotating in space, passing each through the other, the whole within a sphere that itself turned slowly with implacable logic. Nash closed his eyes.

His mother sitting at a piano. A house he can barely remember. The carpet is burnt orange, and the furniture is dark leather It is a modern house. One wall is filled with French windows and beyond them is a garden, bright with sunshine. There is a picture of an owl. The owl watches him, its huge eyes like fiery orbs, but he isn't afraid of it, even though he is only three or four years old. Somehow, he has forgotten all of this, and now it is present again. There is an upright piano and his mother sits with her back to him, and plays, beautifully. Her long hair shines in the sunlight. It is the same music.

He was brought out of his reverie by Mary Owen setting two mugs of tea on the little coffee table and settling back onto the lumpy sofa.

'Sounds good,' she said, smiling.

'It does, doesn't it?'

They sat sipping their teas, listening to the music. When one piece ended and there was a silence, Mary said, 'It sounds like flocks of birds.'

'It reminds me of my mum,' he said. Mary smiled and nodded.

When the record finished there was a thumping noise, and the arm lifted from the vinyl and swung back to its resting place.

'Amazing,' said Nash. 'Thank you. I thought classical music was all old-fashioned rubbish.'

'Don't suppose it would've lasted so long if it was,' said Mary. 'Must be something to it.'

She got up and carried their mugs back through into the kitchen and put them in the sink. He followed her.

'So, how are you?' she asked.

'I don't know. Okay, I suppose. You know, sometimes it feels like I've been here a lifetime.'

She nodded. 'Time in the woods moves differently to time without the woods. I've felt that myself. They say a day under the trees is worth two in the fields.'

He wanted to say that, in a funny way, after all, he wasn't lonely or unhappy. That he was even what might be described as content. That he was getting to grips with living in this wreck of a house in these strange woods and that it pleased him; the daily routine, the basic tasks: chopping wood, lighting fires, cooking food. Yes, if it wasn't for the fact that he didn't know what the hell was going on, how long he was to stay here and what was to happen when they eventually came for him, he would say that he was content. But he didn't say anything, only shrugged.

'I see you've got water mint,' she said, gesturing to the bunch of leaves he had picked earlier that day, propped in a jam-jar with water. She looked at him slyly. 'Where did you get it?'

'From the stream. There's lots of it.'

'Yes, but how do you know to pick it? How do you know what to do with it? It's not the sort of thing a type like you would know, is it?'

He hesitated. 'It's for tea.' She nodded. 'I read about it,' he said carefully. 'In one of the books I found here.'

'Is that so? Which book was that then?'

'The Shell one, I think. It has a section on edible plants. I thought I'd try it.'

'Well, well, is that so. Whatever next?'

'I just thought I'd try it. It's good.'

'Oh, I know it's good.' She watched him. 'I'm just a little surprised.'

Nash shrugged. 'Me too.'

When Mary Owen left, he went back and sat again before the hi-fi. There were three Bach records in the bag. He listed to them each in turn, marvelling at the music. One was solo piano, one solo cello, and the other orchestral. He liked the solo pieces best. Their apparent simplicity revealed an astonishing complexity.

He didn't listen closely to the music, not really. He didn't have to. It wasn't necessary to pay close attention to it. It was better to let it wash over you, like the tides, the passing of the hours, the slipping of day into night and back again, the seasons, a slow and steady pulsing, an inexorable rhythm.

Sometimes the music seemed like the product of a machine – cogs, gears and wheels turning with carefully calibrated loops and spirals of sound – but at the same time it was overwhelmingly human. His mother had played that music once.

(22)

Nash was lolling on the sofa before the fire. He had put down the book he had been reading, a slim volume entitled *Heart of Darkness*, and was daydreaming, drawing out a line from the cursed African forests of the book to the haunted woods around the house. His reverie was interrupted by a loud hammering at the front door. The first barrage of blows brought him upright with a shock. The second, which followed the first after just a few seconds, brought him to his feet. He opened the door and was confronted by Brigid. A different Brigid. Her usual calm stillness, her assuredness, had vanished, replaced by a wild energy. There was fear in her eyes and she was out of breath.

'You've got to come,' she said. 'Can you come?'

'What is it?' He could see that something was wrong and he wondered if they were coming, if this was it, finally.

'I need your help. Come quickly.'

She started off and Nash grabbed his coat and followed her.

They went quickly down the track, Nash trying to get his coat on and catch up. The sky was low and it felt like it was about to rain. She took the path they had previously followed up to the stones, but after a few minutes turned off onto a smaller track. He caught up with her and stopped her with a hand on her shoulder.

'Bee, what is it? What's the matter?'

She turned and he saw there were tears in her eyes.

'You've got to help,' she said. '*We've* got to help her.'

Something must have happened to her mother.

'It's not far,' she said. 'Quick, come on.'

She was off again and he was struggling to keep up, slipping and sliding in the mud and tripping over stones and roots. Rain began to fall.

The path took them through trees and over a stretch of hillside thick with bracken. They climbed a stile over a crumbling stone wall and went through a stand of pine trees. Then they left the path and climbed up the hillside where the trees were further apart. Brigid was going fast, and once again Nash saw the ease with which she navigated the terrain, her sure-footedness, her certainty.

She slowed to a walking pace, and they emerged from the trees at a rocky gully. An old fence of rusted barbed wire crossed it and held in the wires was a deer. When it saw them, it began to struggle.

Brigid sobbed and turned to Nash.

'I found her like that,' she said. 'I don't know how long she's been there for.'

They went closer and the animal bucked and struggled against the wire which was tangled about its back legs and tight around its neck. Its hind quarters were covered in terrible cuts and crusted with dried blood.

'Maybe you can hold it still and I can free the wire,' said Brigid.

But as they moved closer the animal went into a frenzy of kicking and pushing, only succeeding in binding itself in the wire even tighter. It let out a horrible scream and then fell back, which held it hanging limply. It panted hard, its snout flecked with white foam, its dark eyes staring wildly. It's terrified, he thought, and in pain. It will never let us help it. He held out a hand, in a gesture of calm, and the animal rolled its eyes and tried to turn about. Blood was flowing freely from where the barbs were cutting into its chest.

'Hang on,' he said. 'Let's think about this. We don't want to make it worse.'

He tried to work out what it would take to free the deer. Each hind leg was secured by loops of wire, and several went around its neck and across its chest. They were fixed to a rotted fencepost that had snapped off. The next post was thirty or forty feet away and looked secure. If he could somehow hold the deer still and it didn't struggle too much, it would still be an impossible task to carefully extricate it from the grip of the barbs. And it would struggle. And while she was not a stag, she was still a big animal and he knew that in her terror it would be too much for him to hold.

'I don't know how we can do it,' he said.

'We've got to try,' pleaded Brigid. 'I can't bear it.'

'I know. If we could cut the wire...' He was thinking out loud.

Brigid pulled off her rucksack and reached inside. 'I've got my knife,' she said hopefully, holding it towards him.

He took it. It was a single-bladed pocketknife. Wooden handle, the blade perhaps four inches long. It was well looked after, and the blade was clean and sharp. He took a piece of the wire in his hand and tested it. The metal was old and rusty, but it was still thick and strong. The knife would never cut it.

'I don't know what we can do,' he said. 'If we had wire cutters, we might be able to do something.'

The animal lay still, breathing heavily. It closed its eyes.

'We've got to do something,' said Brigid. She was crying.

Nash looked up at the sky, which was a vast shadow, and let the rain run over his face. He was filled with helplessness. Brigid walked away and stood beneath a tree, facing away from him. He could see little shudders shaking her shoulders.

He crouched down beside the deer. This time it did not buck and kick. It opened its eyes and contemplated him with surprising stillness. Perhaps it had no more energy to fight. Its eyes were beautiful, deep wells. There was sadness there.

He stood and walked over to where Brigid waited beneath the tree. She turned to face him.

'Even if we could free her, how long would she last? She's badly injured and she's lost a lot of blood.'

'Look,' she said, and now there was anger in her voice. 'If we can't free her, then we must do something else. We can't just leave her like that. We should stop her suffering.'

Nash knew what she meant and nodded. He weighed the knife in his hand.

How hard can it be? he asked himself. And yet. The idea of it filled him with dread. He had looked into those dark eyes and seen something there. And it had seen him.

He went back across to where the deer lay amongst the coils of wire and crouched down beside it once more. Again, it was still. He looked back over his shoulder and saw that Brigid was watching him intently.

He reached out and rested his hand on the animal's nose, feeling its breath hot against his skin. The hair on its snout was soft.

'I want to help,' he said, softly. 'But I can't get you out.'

The deer let out a long sigh. It looked past Nash into the distance.

He could not do it. He stood and took a step back.

'I'm sorry,' he said to the deer. He rubbed the water from his eyes and walked slowly in a small circle. He avoided eye contact with Brigid. Again, he weighed the knife in his hand and considered what it was he had to do. It would only take a moment. And there was no doubt that it was the right thing to do. The animal was in a terrible way. If they left it, a slow and painful end awaited it.

And yet.

Again, he crouched beside the deer. It opened its eyes and shifted slightly.

And yet.

He stood up again and Brigid was beside him. 'Give it to me,' she said angrily and seized the knife from his hand. She crouched beside the animal, said something quietly, and in a single smooth motion drew the knife across its throat. The cut was deep, and a slick of hot blood was released, pouring over the rocks at their feet. The deer made a sound like a cough and closed its eyes. It seemed to settle back against the barbed wire, as if all tension had slipped from its muscles.

Brigid stood up and spat at him, 'You coward.' She pressed the bloody knife back into his hand and walked back to the tree. She stood sobbing, her forehead pressed against the coarse bark of the trunk.

Nash looked down and saw that the rain was washing the blood away already.

Brigid stood with her forehead pressed against the tree trunk, her hands at her sides, sobbing silently, for what felt like a very long time. Nash sat on a rock and watched her. He had let her down. The rain fell steadily and soon there was almost no sign of the blood that had gushed forth so freely. He began to feel very cold.

Eventually she roused herself and came over and sat beside him. Her long hair was plastered against her cheeks, making her look even thinner than usual. Her eyes were red. There was something defeated about her, so different from her usual confidence.

'I'm sorry,' he said.

'It's okay,' she replied. 'I was just angry that we couldn't help. I felt helpless.'

'I know.'

He wondered if he should take her hand or put his arm around her shoulders, but he didn't dare to.

They sat in silence for a few minutes and then Brigid stood up. 'I want to cover her,' she said. She took her knife back from him and began to cut bracken, laying the fronds over the dead animal. As the body was concealed, she took branches and laid them against it too, to pin the bracken in place.

'It doesn't seem right to just leave her like that,' she explained. 'The carrion crows will come, and that's okay, that's nature's way, but it just doesn't seem dignified to leave her like that.'

He nodded and helped pull some large branches over and position them across the pile of bracken. When it was done, they sat a while in silence. Something seemed to be holding them back, preventing them from leaving that place.

When Nash realised that Brigid was shivering, he stood up. 'Come on,' he said. 'We're both cold and soaked through. Let's get back to the house and get a hot brew on.' He offered his hand. She took it and he pulled her up. 'You lead the way,' he said.

Brigid took them slowly back down the hillside, through the trees. For the first time she seemed to be hesitant. All her confidence and energy had ebbed away. Nonetheless, she found the way. Nash would quickly have become hopelessly lost, for he had not paid attention on their panicked way up the hill. Lower down the mountain, the forest seemed even more gloomy than usual.

At the house, Nash piled logs onto the fire in the sitting room and told Brigid to sit before it and warm herself. She did as she was told, and he wrapped a blanket about her shoulders before going back into the kitchen. He made them mugs of tea – putting a spoonful of sugar in each – and they sat before the fire and drank them in silence.

After a long time, she spoke. 'I hate this place,' she said quietly.

'No, you don't.'

'I do. I hate it.' She was angry again. 'I can't wait to get away.'

'But you always say how much you love it.'

'It's just talk. There's nothing to do here, is there? There's all that out there – the woods, the mountains, the valley – but there's nothing to *do*. I can't go to the cinema, can I? Or even the library. I can't go to see a band play. I can't even go to a café. I can't even just walk to a shop, to go shopping for clothes or something, just for the hell of it. It's rubbish!'

'You're upset because of what just happened. But you know, don't you, that all *that* stuff is rubbish, really. It's all fake, artificial, plastic. This is *real*.'

She shook her head. She was holding back tears. Finally, she stood up. 'I should go,' she said quietly.

Nash got up too. He wanted to comfort her but didn't know how. 'You know,' he said, 'it was the right thing to do.'

'I know. But that doesn't stop it being sad. I love the deer. In the summer I like to watch the fawns playing in the woods. Some of them will even come and eat from your hand. It's because they haven't learnt to fear us yet.'

Nash felt again that he had let her down and wondered how he could make it better. At the front door he said, 'Brigid, I'm so sorry.'

'It's okay,' she said and turned to go.

He was going to ask when she would come back, but she walked away down the track before he could say anything.

(23)

When Brigid asked him about his parents, Nash told her that they were odd. But he also said that he thought, on reflection, that all children find their parents odd to a greater or lesser extent. Do they not? Brigid was not sure. She didn't find Mary odd. No, it was true, he did not really know what to make of them. They were odd. He loved them, obviously, meaning he felt for them something that seemed to equate with what he understood love to be, but, at the same time, he found them perplexing, a mystery. Sometimes, especially when he was older, he looked at them and wondered what the connection was between them, between himself and this man and woman he did not really know. He felt himself to have come from somewhere else entirely. He had wondered on many occasions if he might be an orphan.

His father, Richard Nash, known as 'Dick', worked in insurance and hated it. Sometimes, it seemed that he hated everything. He sweated anger, bitterness, resentment, a sense of somehow having been *wronged*.

He had been in the army before his son was born. But unlike other ex-servicemen Nash had met, who referred to their time in the forces proudly, as if it was something that defined who they were, his father's time in uniform was almost never mentioned. Sometimes, his father made oblique references to his *service* or might mention to his mother a person they had known at that time. But he never talked about it to his son. Nash knew about it – he had even seen his father's medals, wrapped carefully in cloth and placed in a shoebox at the bottom of his parents' wardrobe – but did not understand why it was seemingly a secret. This was a source of confusion for him. The medals must mean his father had distinguished himself in some way. Yet Nash sensed some vague disgrace, distant, that could never be talked about, but which he nonetheless intuited in the interstices of his parent's conversations.

One Christmas, when he was small, Dick Nash got into a terrible argument with an uncle, also an ex-soldier, who was staying with them. It started with a card game and escalated with extraordinary speed. Within moments his father and uncle were on their feet and screaming accusations and counter-accusations at each other across the table. He had seen (and felt) his father's anger many times before, but this was something different, something ferocious, volcanic, carrying with it the terrific possibility of violence. Nash shrank into his seat and put his hands over his ears, but still heard his uncle call his father an *assassin*, a *murderer*, a *terrorist*. The boy ran from the room in tears.

At first, he assumed they were just insults intended to wound, words used in the heat of argument, but gradually, the more he thought about it, the more they began to colour the way he saw his father. He became scared of him.

Another time, they had an unexpected visit from one of his father's old comrades. They were just finishing their supper, the three of them seated at the kitchen table in silence, when the doorbell rang. His father went to answer it and Nash followed him, curious, for the doorbell never rang in the evenings. His father opened the door to reveal a huge man, seemingly as broad as he was tall, with a massive beard. As the door opened, he snapped to attention and saluted.

'Jesus,' his father groaned, but he was smiling. The two men hugged; the only time Nash ever saw his father do such a thing.

'Who's this then?' asked the newcomer, gesturing to Nash. 'Is it John? Going to be a warrior like your father, are you?' He rubbed a massive hand in Nash's hair. 'When we were in the desert together, your father was a beast. Absolutely unstoppable. A machine.'

'Quiet, Joe, we don't talk about that stuff anymore.'

The words the man called Joe used to describe his father seemed, to Nash, to be utterly fantastic. He couldn't reconcile them with the man he knew, who wore suits and ties and worked in an office. It was impossible. For the first time, the realisation dawned that his father had had another life, before he, Nash, had entered the world. That he was, in essence, two different people. It was a difficult notion for his young mind to accommodate.

The two men sat at the kitchen table, talking late into the night. When Nash went to say goodnight, his father explained, 'Joe's going to stay the night.'

Joe stood and rather formally offered his huge hand to Nash. He shook it vigorously. Joe was grinning.

'Good man,' he said.

In the morning, he was gone.

His father had once been in the *desert*.

Dick Nash was a military man but seemed to go to pains to hide it. Out of uniform, in ordinary clothes – in the *nondescript* clothes he favoured – he looked like a solder in hiding. His carefully trimmed moustache caused Nash agonies of shame if he ever appeared at school. As he grew older, the son came to resent the father's harsh and dictatorial way in the house, his expectation that things be done just as he liked them to be done, and promptly too.

Once, Nash dared to ask his father about his hidden history, his concealed past.

'What did you do in the army?' he said.

His father scowled. 'I don't like to talk about it.'

'Why not?' He was disappointed. 'I know you've got medals. How did you get them?'

'How do you know about them?'

'I've seen them. Mum was cleaning one time and the box was out. I had a look.'

'You shouldn't have done that. Those are from a different time. From when things were better.'

'How do you mean?'

'That's enough said now.'

'But you must have done something brave to get those medals.'

'That's enough, son. Hear me?'

Nash had let it go.

Yes, his father was a mystery. He wondered at which parts of himself came from his father, at the ways in which his father's DNA defined him.

Where his father was heavy, his mother was light, sweetness and light. Sheila (known as 'She') was gentleness personified. He thought she was beautiful, of course, but he knew others saw it too. He saw the way men looked at her when they were in the street. She was tall and thin with long blonde hair that she normally wore in a braid that fell down her back. She had a narrow face with small mouth, perfect teeth, green eyes. In contrast to his father's dour suits, she wore brightly coloured clothes: blouses with fantastic patterns in sky blue, burnt orange and glorious magenta, neck scarves of turquoise with lemon yellow polka dots, checks, stripes, paisley. She was a teaching assistant at the local comp (the same one he went to, another source of shame and embarrassment) and in the summer holidays taught English to international students at a big language school in the centre of town.

Their house was small and neat and exceptionally tidy. When he was young, Nash did not dare leave his toys lying around anywhere, for fear of his father's wrath.

He was happy enough at school for the most part. His results were average. But when he was sixteen, they took him out of the comp and he was sent to Thrift House, a second-rate public school in a once-grand Victorian building with dragons on the gateposts, so he could get the 'best start'. His parents had saved so that he could go. His mother patched his clothes when they were worn out. They drove an old car scarred with rust. They never went to the cinema or restaurants. Nash was not allowed to buy books (except when he was given tokens for birthdays) but must always have them from the library. Of course, he hated the school and wondered why they had sacrificed the chance of decent summer holidays (they only ever rented a small apartment or cottage somewhere on the south coast, while friends boasted of the sunny paradise that was the South of France) to pay the fees. He never felt he belonged at Thrift House, where other boys were dropped off in the mornings from shining BMWs and Volvos, had new trainers and cash to buy clothes and records, to get fried chicken after school. But, Nash reflected, he had never felt he belonged anywhere. It was just how it was. He got on with it. He was bright enough and worked reasonably hard. His grades were okay. He was not part of any cliques, but was broadly popular. He even had friends.

When Brigid asked him why he had 'joined up' (I was 'called', he corrected her, automatically) he thought about it a long time before replying.

'The thing is,' he said, 'nobody wanted me. My father didn't want me. All through my childhood I had the sense that he didn't want me, that he resented me in some way. Mum wanted me, of course. She doted on me when I was little. But after the accident she wasn't there anymore. And Dad hated me then. And then they came along, and they *did* want me. This guy, Gray, The Grey Man, said *we want you*. It was enough for me. I suppose I didn't think it through, didn't ask enough questions. It was just that he said they wanted me.'

He became aware of how pathetic this sounded and gave her a sheepish smile.

'Oh, poor Nash,' she said quietly, and he wasn't sure if she was sympathising with his predicament or teasing him for a perceived weakness or sentimentality.

For a long time after the accident, Nash had felt that something was very wrong. Something had gone wrong with his being, with himself. There was an absence. He'd always felt like that, more or less, but now it became an overwhelming sensation, something he felt from the moment he awoke to the moment he fell into sleep. And it was there in his dreams too, which were filled with holes and voids. Something was missing. *He* was missing. It was as if some vital element of his being had been erased. He pictured himself as a drawing on a chalkboard that has been rubbed out. You can still see it, beneath the wash of chalk dust, but it's almost gone. A ghost, essentially. Yes, he was a ghost in his own life.

And then, he thought, there was the thing with the deer. His failure, as he thought of it. What did it mean, he asked, that he had not been able to bring himself to do it?

When he had hit Amis, his mind had been clear. He had been an empty vessel. No thoughts, no emotions. He had not even thought about what he had to do, he had just acted.

How could it be like that?

On the mountainside, in the rain, his head had been filled with a tangle of thoughts, with *why* and *how* and *what if*. It had been impossible to act.

Did it mean there was something wrong with him – that some vital quality (call it something like humanity) was lacking – or did it perhaps mean he was getting better? He could not say.

Perhaps, he now considered, Paradise was some sort of holding room, a place he had to pass through in order to find himself again. It was possible it had been necessary to be *called* in order to find his way to Paradise. And from here, he might emerge, as a butterfly emerges from the chrysalis, renewed.

(24)

For a long time after the accident, Nash drifted. For a while he stayed at home, recovering. His physical wounds healed but the psychic ones did not. They only became deeper. There was a kind of emotional paralysis, a painful solitude. His father lived in his own world, remote and enraged, and it soon became clear to him that he would have to get out. His father's barely contained hostility and resentment made life in the little house intolerable. He missed the deadline for registering at university, but when he called and explained the circumstances they were very understanding and sympathetic and told him he could defer his place until the following year. This seemed a good idea. It was clear that he wasn't ready. He asked them to send him the paperwork, and when it came he dutifully filled out the forms and returned them. Soon after, a letter arrived confirming that he could take up his place in the following academic year.

Someone told him about the fruit picking in Kent and he said to his father he would go there for a couple of weeks – the farm had accommodation for the workers in caravans and old Scout tents. It would be good for them to have some space. He needed to get out of the house. He could see the relief in his father's eyes, and it was like a punch in the gut.

When the season ended, he went back but did not go home. One of the guys he had shared a caravan with on the farm had something lined up on a building site, and Nash went with him. They had rooms in a cheap hostel. The accommodation was nasty but that was fine. He worked hard, harder than anyone else. His diet was atrocious. The only thing he spent money on was beer. Beer and the bottles of whisky he kept by his bed seemed to dull the ache he felt whenever he stopped to think, when he lay there, unable to sleep, brooding, self-loathing. He thought constantly about what had happened.

After the building site, he did various jobs. They were rubbish jobs, simple jobs, mindless jobs – the kind of jobs you can do with a hangover – and before he knew it, a year had gone by. He forgot to contact the university. When he finally remembered, he assumed a letter had been delivered to his father's house (he now thought of it as his father's house, not 'our home'), and was sitting unopened in a pile of mail.

He resolved to do something about it, to get back on track. He kept on writing letters to his father but never posted them, for he felt they did not adequately express the depths of his despair and he couldn't risk the possibility of misunderstanding. He could not call him and dared not visit, for he could not bear to hear (or see) his disappointment (or even hatred). He needed a sign from him. He needed some kind of permission but knew, at the same time, that it was something his father – in his bitterness, in his anger – would never offer.

And then, to his amazement, another year had gone. It was incredible how the time raced away when you did not pay attention to it, the days blurring one into another, weeks into months, all lost.

He moved every few months. It was easy enough to get a job, he discovered, wherever you happened to be. You just had to be willing to do the jobs no one else wanted to do. Someone had to wield the STOP/GO sign and endure the abuse of enraged motorists as they crawled past the never-ending roadworks on the bypass. Someone had to wield the machine – essentially a powerful vacuum cleaner – that sucks the guts from the carcasses of chickens at the processing plant. There were building sites up and down the land that needed barrow-wheelers and shit-shovelers. There were shelves to be stacked, litter to be picked, mountains of leaflets (advertising the restaurants that deep-fried the chickens) to be stuffed through letterboxes.

But, somehow, it wasn't all bad. There was a season in France, working the grape harvest, shitfaced every night on the ridiculously cheap local wine. That, he had to admit, was even fun. He lived in a small encampment of tents in a field. He even had a girlfriend, a sweet Spanish girl called Gabrielle, who called him *carino* and came to his tent every night. But it didn't last. It was really only a half-hearted attempt at a relationship for he didn't think he deserved to be loved. Gabrielle once said to him, in her charming English, that he was *too alone*. Pathologically alone. 'Why be this alone?' she said. 'Why be broken? We can mend him.' When the harvest was done, he headed back to England.

There was, too, the job as a municipal gardener in a small town on the south coast. Days spent mowing and raking, mulching, planting and pruning. That was pleasant. But when the weather turned, it wasn't.

Three years had slipped away.

Back in the capital, he got on the night shifts, the night shifts which turned your life upside down. The night shifts which were perfect for the misanthropes, the loners, the damaged ones. You worked under artificial lights while the rest of the population slept, and you slept while everyone else worked and played. He liked it, more or less, for he didn't have to talk to anyone. He was hardening, withdrawing, building a shell about himself. He worked in a vast warehouse, from where the orders of supermarkets were fulfilled. On arrival he was allocated a sort of motorised platform, to which was affixed a train of cages on wheels. He was a given a list of products and would wind his way through the enormous labyrinth tracking down boxes of toilet paper, crates of orange juice, tins of this and that, and loading them into the cages. No communication with anyone else was required. When the cages were full, the correct numbers of every item ordered piled in, he would drop them off at the allocated loading bay and begin the whole process again. During the breaks, no one spoke to each other, everyone in their own world: dissociated, alienated, disconnected. That's what the night shift did to you. It closed you down. When the shift was over, they would gather silently outside the warehouse entrance in the dawning light, waiting for the minibus that would ferry them back into the centre of town, and there was something anaesthetizing about the whole thing.

It was at the warehouse that he met Mooney. At first it was a question of drinking. They kept such odd hours it was inevitable they would fall into step. The weekends were exercises in erasure. When a room came up at Mooney's place, he moved in. It was a shithole, but that was fine. He didn't care.

One Sunday he took a train back to the part of the city he had grown up in, determined to finally talk to his father. He wandered through the shopping centre, peering into the windows of the shops. This was where he had hung out with friends as a teenager . Everything was so familiar yet so changed. He had thought it might be comforting to be back there, but it was not. He wore a hoodie pulled up around his face, and watched the crowds warily, for the last thing he wanted was to be recognised or, worse still, to be engaged in conversation by some old friend or contemporary from school. He was not ready for that.

He bought a coffee, crossed the railway line, and followed a path along the edge of a ragged park. Turning down a side street, he came to the row of small, terraced houses where he had once lived. He saw the familiar blue front door and his bedroom window, and at that moment he was unaccountably terrified. Fear gripped him. He lingered on the opposite side of the road, trying to summon the courage to ring the bell. But then, as he watched, the door opened, and an unknown young couple emerged. They locked the door behind them and set off up the street, hand in hand. Nash looked again and saw now that the curtains in his bedroom window had changed. The small garden had been tidied; the bushes cut back.

An hour later the couple returned, carrying shopping bags, and went back in. From across the street, through the window of the sitting room, he saw them moving about inside, and at one point the man came to the window and made a point of staring straight at him. Unnerved, Nash moved off. He wandered the streets for a while, trying to make sense of what he had seen, and then returned to the station.

On the train he picked up one of the free newspapers which were always left behind by the morning commuters. The front page proclaimed war and disease, flood and storm, the collapse of certainty. Inside were vacuous tales of celebrities and sportspeople. However, one short piece caught his attention, about insurance scams. As he read it, a thought came to him. His mother would have had life insurance. There would have been a payout after the accident. Had his father taken the money, sold up and moved away? But so quickly? And without consulting him? But of course, he thought, he had no means of contacting him, even if he had wanted to. He had lost his phone in France, and when he got a new one he had a different number. At the time, he hadn't thought about what that meant. Perhaps, he thought, sadly, he'd tried calling that old number, again and again, hopeful, time after time, in mounting desperation? He dismissed the notion. It was years now since the accident. It was a long time now since he had seen him. When he left, he had been so sure that his father wanted no more to do with him, he had not told him where he was going.

That was what *estranged* meant.

(25)

Nash didn't want a gun. If he had a gun, he would likely have to use it, and the thought filled him with horror. He never wanted to fire a gun again. But eventually the fox's exhortations to *be prepared* convinced him. He gave in and asked Brigid, and she reluctantly agreed to bring him her father's shotgun.

Two days later, when Nash was sitting outside on one of the kitchen chairs, contemplating the ruined garden and the wall of trees beyond it, Brigid came through the gate at the side of the house. As well as the little rucksack she always had with her, she had something in a dark green canvas bag slung over her shoulder. From the shape of it, Nash's first thought was that it was a tennis racquet or perhaps a musical instrument, a trombone or guitar, though it was too long and thin.

'Are you going to play for me?'

She looked puzzled and he gestured to the bag.

'Oh no,' she said and lifted it from her shoulder and offered it to him. It was heavier than he had expected. He set the wider end on the ground at his feet and unzipped it. Inside was the shotgun.

'Oh, Jesus,' he said.

'It was Da's,' said Brigid. 'He used it for pheasants, rabbits. It's been stored away for years, hidden in the back of the cupboard. I don't think Ma will miss it. She's probably forgotten it's even there.'

Nash nodded. 'My god, Bee,' he said. 'I don't know. I'm pretty sure everything's going to be okay.' Now he had the gun in his hands, he felt even less sure.

'I know, but what if it isn't? What if something bad happens?'

He took the gun from the canvas bag. Standing, he weighed it and then took it to his shoulder and sighted along the barrel, pointing past the tangled garden into the thickness of the forest.

'I've never fired a shotgun before.'

She looked at him with surprise.

'It kicks.'

'I know.' He examined it, cautiously.

'You know how it works?' she asked.

'Yes!'

'It's not like a rifle.'

'What do you mean?'

'It doesn't fire a bullet.'

Nash looked blank. 'What does it fire?'

'It sprays. The cartridge is packed full of pellets, little ball bearings, and they're like a cloud. When they hit something, especially at close range, they can go in all over the place. It's not tidy. Look, it's break action.'

She took it and showed him the lever to break the stock. He looked down the barrels, two tiny of circles of light like distant moons.

'That's the safety,' she said, pointing.

'I know,' he said, though he didn't.

'There's just one problem,' she said, rummaging in the bag. She took out a box. 'We don't have much ammunition.'

She opened the box and held it out for him to see. There were only three cartridges.

'When they come,' she said, 'how many will there be?'

'Two, probably.' In his mind's eye, he saw The Grey Man and Black. 'Maybe more. I don't know.'

She nodded. 'I'll have a think about where I can get some more. But in the meantime, you'll have to make do with those.'

She watched him weighing the weapon, clicking the safety on and off. Sunlight bounced off it. 'I wish I'd brought you more cartridges,' she said sadly. 'Then you could practise.'

He shook his head. 'Two barrels,' he said, 'but just one trigger.'

'I think you pull the trigger twice. I don't think they both go at once.'

He nodded and examined the weapon. The wooden stock was finely grained and the colour of treacle. It was marked and scuffed – had been very well used – and was polished to a dark and lustrous patina. In contrast, the barrels were dull grey, almost black. Around the body of the gun and the brass trigger guard engraved tendrils coiled. He ran his finger over them. He put the stock to his shoulder again and sighted along the barrel. Surprisingly, it felt good, natural. He squeezed the trigger cautiously.

'I don't know, Brigid,' he said. 'Maybe you should take it back.'

'I just think,' she said, earnestly, 'that you should be prepared. Hopefully you won't need to use it. But it may be, perhaps, that just having it, and showing it, is enough, you know, if things look like they're going to get sticky.'

He nodded. White had once said something similar. 'Okay,' he agreed. 'Thanks, Bee. I really appreciate it. Tea?'

She nodded, smiling, pleased. He leant the gun against the chair and went into the kitchen.

When he came back out, she was aiming the gun at various points in the trees.

'Oof, it's heavy,' she exclaimed, setting it down.

'Listen, when you came, you didn't come from the track. How did you get up here?'

'No, I almost never come up the track. There's a much quicker way that follows the bottom of the valley and then climbs up quickly through the wood. I thought you knew. It's steep and it's easy to lose the way, but if you know it, it's much quicker. You've walked the cart track, so you know how it meanders and keeps on switching back on itself to keep the gradient easy. The lower track is way quicker but much steeper. I can show you it, if you like?'

'How about I walk you back down? Then you can show me.'

She nodded and took their mugs back inside. He zipped the gun and cartridges back into the canvas bag and thought about where to hide it. It would need to be somewhere accessible. As a temporary measure, he pushed it under the sofa. He would find a better spot later.

Brigid led the way through the gate and onto a narrow path, little more than a deer track, really, that Nash would never have seen. It dropped quickly down, slippery and precipitous, through dense undergrowth, and then kept alongside a narrow stream that tumbled over rocks and sometimes formed pretty little pools and made small waterfalls. Eventually, the way began to level out and Nash could see, from a break in the trees, above and to the left, high up on the ridge of the valley they were descending, the cart track. When the church steeple came into view, he told Brigid that he should turn back.

'Thanks, Bee,' he said. And before she could duck away, he gave her a clumsy hug. 'Thanks for looking out for me.'

'It's nothing,' she said, blushing. 'Take care. I'll see you soon.'

He nodded and she was off. He slowly retraced their steps back up the head of the valley. There were daffodils and bluebells and tiny yellow flowers like stars that he did not know the name of. Birdsong and the wash of a breeze through the budding leaves of the trees. Pheasants calling. Crows and rooks.

Back at the house, he retrieved the gun from beneath the sofa and sat with it. It puzzled him. It was an evil thing for sure, a killing thing, yet holding it was reassuring, somehow, and when he brought it up and sighted along the barrel it felt right, *good*, even. He ran his fingers along the cold, smooth metal of the barrels, and stroked the satisfyingly curved wood of the stock.

Where to hide it? He must think through the possible scenarios that would play out if – when – they came.

Paradise is waiting. The house settles its old bones. It is patient. Around it the trees sway in the breeze. They sense the coming of Ostara, the equinox, the turning of the wheel and the beginning of the new year. They sense that change is coming. A shiver runs through the woods. It is a pulse.

A flock of birds takes flight and circles against the sky before returning cautiously to the roosts.

(26)

When Nash arrived at the party, he was nervous. Gaia King had taken the unprecedented step of inviting their entire year to her house to celebrate the end of the exams, the end of school, the new life. Nash knew Gaia a little. He was friends with some of her friends. She was generally accepted as the coolest, most desirable, the alpha female of the year. Her parents were rumoured to be fabulously wealthy. Nash would normally have been surprised to get such an invitation, but the fact that Gaia had asked everyone eliminated the usual invite anxiety. Gaia said she wanted everyone to be together one last time. It was to be a celebration.

'Which is kind of fucked up,' said Rob Frame, 'given she only ever hangs out with her clique. I'd be surprised if she even knows our names.' He gestured at their little group.

'Speak for yourself,' said Nash. 'I know Gaia, she's okay.'

'Apparently, she said the party is a *gift*,' Rob said, sarcastically, and rolled his eyes.

'Don't be mean,' said Nash. 'I think it's a sweet thing to do.'

'It's just PR,' said Rob.

'Maybe. But you'll drink her booze, won't you?'

Rob nodded enthusiastically and took a long swig from the bottle in his hand.

They were on the Common with Smithy and John Fallow, drinking cold beers and passing around a joint, killing time and getting loaded ahead of the appointed hour. The party was supposed to be fancy dress but none of them had made the effort. Talk was of their expected exam results and plans for the summer. They were all excited, optimistic. Holidays, jobs, university. All this was coming. Life awaited them. When Nash half-closed his eyes against the brightness of the summer day, it was as if they were bathed in a golden glow, a holy light of possibility, of becoming. *I'll hold this moment*, he thought.

When they arrived at the house, he was stunned by the size of it. It sat in the centre of a parade of mansions like elaborate wedding cakes. The path to the front door was through a formal garden festooned with balloons and strings of lights.

The front door was wide open. Music and the sound of many people came from within. As they approached, a figure in a gorilla suit exited, rummaged in its pockets, and took out a packet of cigarettes. The gorilla head was removed, revealing Andrew Major, head boy, Gaia's boyfriend. Hot and flushed, his face slick with sweat, he grinned at them. 'Welcome, chaps,' he said, as if he owned the place and this was his party. He exuded confidence, entitlement. He hugged Nash, clumsily, and shook hands with the others with exaggerated formality. 'The bar's in the garden.'

'Fucking prick,' said Rob, under his breath.

They pushed their way in to the crush of people. High fives, hugs, fist-bumps. Down the cavernous hallway, hung with streamers, past doorways opening into large rooms filled with people, some in fancy dress, where the light bulbs had been switched for blue, purple, red and green, into the kitchen, a huge room with a concrete floor, deafening dance music, a massive table laden with bowls of nuts and crisps, plates of sandwiches and cocktail sausages, and out into the garden, lit with strings of festoon lights, where the bar was manned by young men and women in black tie and seemingly any drink you might want was on offer.

He could not believe how many people were there. There were adults – Gaia's parents, presumably, and their friends – as well as his classmates. Nash had never had more than one or two friends to visit. He was, frankly, ashamed of his small home. It seemed mean and cramped. He had never had a party; it was simply an impossibility.

He moved through the rooms, a beer in his hands, sometimes stopping to talk. Conversations were shouted. The atmosphere was maniacal. The music was loud and soon his voice was hoarse from yelling.

One room was where the dancing was. He leant against the wall and watched Alice Bird for a long time. He felt that he had been watching her all year, and, in a way, he had. There was something wonderfully free and unselfconscious about her that drew him. Reading aloud a passage from *Gatsby* in an English class, sketching a skull in the art room, boiling a test tube of liquid in the lab, and now dancing, whirling and moving with a fluidity and ease that he knew was beyond him. She did everything well.

She was dancing as part of a group of girls. He knew some of their names. *I should ask her to dance,* he thought. But it was impossible. Something held him back. It always did. He was leaning against the wall and Rob Frame was there too. 'Go on,' said, Rob. 'Ask her.' But Nash could not move. Instead, he drank his beer, too fast. Rob moved away, disappointed. Nash continued to watch her, marvelling at her beauty, and for a moment they made eye contact and she smiled at him. He looked away. Gulped down the last of his beer. Fled to the bar to get more. Cursed himself.

In the garden he found somewhere to sit and watch. He thought to himself, *Are these my friends? Do I even know these people?* Yes, he knew them, but only in the most superficial sense. He had sat next to some of them in classes for the last five years, they had played games of football, rugby and cricket. They had been on field trips for geography. There had been parties. But he did not know them. And, more importantly, they did not know him. How could they?

I am at the party, he thought, *but I am not of the party.*

He could feel himself becoming melancholy. But then Alice was there.

'Can I sit?' she asked. He nodded and shuffled up to make space for her. She sat, too close to him. He could feel her there.

'You're not dancing?' she asked.

'I might later. I'm no good.'

'It doesn't matter if you're good or not. It's how it makes you feel.' She had a glass of white wine and brought it to her lips and Nash saw how long and fine her fingers were.

'Maybe,' he said. 'But if everyone is laughing at you, it's hard to feel good.'

She laughed. 'I'm sure you're not that bad.'

'No, I am. Really. It's actually offensive.'

She laughed and leaned against him.

'But *you* were amazing,' he said, feeling brave.

At that moment he sensed something pass between them. It was a connection, and somehow, he thought, somehow the universe had slipped, tilted, adjusted, and had angled itself in his favour for once. They talked and the party – swirling and shouting, leaping and screaming – receded into the distance. It was easy, after all. When she finished her wine, he went to get her some more, and when he came back she was still there, waiting for him. It was amazing.

He asked her if she would like to meet up, maybe see a movie or something, and to his astonishment she agreed. They exchanged numbers.

'I should find Gaia,' she said, standing. 'I haven't talked to her yet.' He stood up too.

'Call me,' she said.

She kissed him. First on his cheek, and then on his lips, very softly. It was gentle and *almost* chaste, but it seemed to him that it was also charged with a mysterious form of energy. As she walked away, he felt lightheaded. It was too much. Anything that came after would be a disappointment; his night had peaked. He resolved to leave. *Hold the feeling*, he thought. In the house, the first casualties were slumped on sofas or against the walls. The air was thick with vape. The front step was splattered with vomit. He did not say goodbye to anyone but slipped away, unnoticed.

Outside, the air was fresh. He felt happy, ecstatic even, and a little unsteady. Thinking he would walk home – it would be about forty minutes and would clear his head – he set off. He walked for a while, taking deep breaths of cool air, then realised he was lost. He had somehow taken a wrong turn. Worse still, his phone had died. He saw the lights of a parade of shops along a main road and thought he would get a taxi. But when he reached the road and padded his pockets, he realised he did not have his wallet. He had either dropped it or left it on the counter of the shop where he had bought the beers he had drunk – so many hours ago – on the common with Rob and the others.

He had change in his pocket and called home from a phone box. His mother answered.

'I'm so sorry,' he said quickly. 'I know it's late, but can Dad come and get me? I don't have money for a taxi and I'm not sure where I am. And my phone's dead.'

'Are you drunk?'

'No, no. Just tired.'

'Hang on.' Her voice was muffled. He heard talking, distant, angry, and waited nervously. She came back on. 'He can't come. He's had too many. Says you should find your own way home. But don't worry, I'll come. How will I find you?'

He peered out through the dirty glass and named the streets. 'I'm here,' he said, 'in the phone box.'

'Okay, wait there, love. Be careful.'

Nash perched on a low wall and waited. He felt remote from everything. The traffic, the people making their way home after nights out, in pairs and groups. He was alone, but not lonely. He thought of Alice. It was as if a miracle had occurred. His head clearing, he wondered now why he had left the party.

Eventually he saw the car coming. It pulled over and he climbed in.

'Are you drunk?' asked his mother.

'No, no,' he said. 'Just tired. I'm so sorry, Mum. My phone's dead so I thought I'd get a taxi home. But I've misplaced my wallet.'

His mother sighed, wearily. 'Well, these things do happen. More to some than to others, it seems. I really don't appreciate it, having to come out at this time.'

'I know. I'm so sorry. Thanks for coming.'

'You're supposed to be an adult now. Looking after yourself.'

'I know. I know.'

'How was the party?'

'It was okay. Biggest house I've ever been in. Going to be a mess in the morning. But I suppose they'll just get cleaners in.'

'Have you been smoking?'

'No, but there were people there who were.'

'You stink of it.'

They pulled out into the traffic and drove in silence. His mother was quiet. She made it clear that the conversation was over, rolled down her window, letting cold air rush around the car, and kept yawning and rubbing her eyes. Nash had the feeling of being in a cocoon, insulated and sealed off from the world, from the party and all the people there, the sense of past or future.

Along Hobbe's Marsh the road widened, a single carriageway on their side but double coming in the other direction. To the right, a wide expanse of darkness, the lights of houses and cars small and distant on the other side. To the left, rows of houses, parked cars, concrete, metal and glass, a proliferation of light, reflections, refractions; Nash was lulled, hypnotised almost, by the streaming, flickering flow as they sped past.

He looked over at his mother. She was beautiful still, of course, but tonight, he thought, she looked old for perhaps the first time. It surprised him, to see her in that way. Washed with orange light from the streetlamps and streaked with whiteness from the headlights of the oncoming cars, she did not seem quite real.

A steady stream of traffic was coming past in the opposite direction. From the river of brightness, he saw two lights detach themselves and move across, a car shifting lanes into the central carriageway. It moved slowly, hesitantly, as if it were not a deliberate manoeuvre, and Nash looked again at his mother who, at that moment, yawned, closing her eyes. The lights continued to drift left, into the central carriageway and then slowly, reluctantly, further across, into the lane in which they were travelling. The car was coming straight at them.

'Mum,' said Nash. And then again, louder.

The lights of the car coming at them became very bright, and Nash involuntarily threw his arm up across his face as his mother, too late, braked and hauled the wheel to the left.

But later, when he tries to remember what happened, there is nothing. He remembers the party and Alice Bird and waiting to be picked up and that feeling of being distant. He remembers the illuminations across the dark emptiness of Hobbe's Marsh and the river of lights coming in the other direction, the way the other car – almost in slow motion – detached itself from the steady procession of traffic and drifted across into their lane. But then there is nothing. It is as if a door has slammed shut, as if all the lights have been instantly flicked off, as if the world had ended. And he wonders if he imagined it all.

He woke up in a hospital room. Everything hurt. He was connected to a machine. A drip went into his arm. His hand was bandaged, two fingers splinted. It felt as if someone had dug a sharp object into his head, through his eye socket, and left it there. He tried to sit up but couldn't, not without sending pain shooting through his chest and back. He lay still and surveyed the room. Pale light came from the window. The blinds were drawn.

After some time, a nurse came in.

'Mr Nash,' she said, her voice gentle, 'you're awake, that's wonderful.' She picked up the clipboard that hung at the foot of the bed and made a note on it. 'How do you feel?'

'Terrible,' he groaned. It hurt to speak. His jaw ached. 'Really awful. What happened to me?'

'Car accident. Bad one. You've been here two days.'

'Can I get some water? I'm so thirsty.' His mouth felt sandpaper-raw, desiccated.

She poured water from a jug into a plastic cup and offered it to him. He took it with his unbandaged hand and gulped it down. Gestured to her for a refill. And then another.

There had been an accident. A crash. A splintering of reality. A coming apart.

'My mum?' he asked.

She shook her head. 'I'll get the doctor to come and take a look at you. He can tell you what happened.' She smiled at him. 'Don't go anywhere, okay? He won't be long.'

She closed the door behind her as she left.

Nash inspected himself. There was padding on his ribs, held in place with bandages. He tentatively moved his legs and wriggled his toes. His face was sore and tender all over and there were bandages around his forehead.

After some time, a young man in a white coat came in. 'I'm your doctor,' he said. 'You've been banged up pretty badly, Mr Nash. Bruising all over. But you're lucky. You've only a broken collar bone, a cracked rib and a broken finger. A fair amount of glass embedded in you still, though we got most of it out. Two black eyes – we thought initially there might be a fracture of the left socket – and a nasty bump on your head. We thought that might be more serious – especially when you didn't wake up – but the scans look okay. Amazing really, given the circumstances.'

'The circumstances?'

'The crash. Do you remember it?'

Nash remembered lights, pinpoints of brightness, shards of crystal, gemstones scattered across an ink-black sky, fragments of the universe, but it was all abstract. It didn't coalesce into anything concrete. 'I don't know,' he said.

'I'm afraid the police will want to speak to you. I'll let them know you're awake but will ask them to hold off coming until tomorrow, to give you time to get your thoughts in order.'

'Why the police?'

'Because it was a fatal accident. Oh, I'm so sorry Mr Nash, you don't know.'

'What happened?'

'I'm so sorry. Your mother…' He trailed off. 'I was under the impression you had been informed.'

'What happened?'

'She was brought into the hospital and went straight into emergency surgery, but I'm afraid she didn't make it. We did everything we could, but ultimately her injuries were too severe.'

This didn't seem to make sense, but Nash nodded slowly.

'A fatal accident?'

'I'm so, so sorry.'

The doctor stood over him, looking concerned. After a while, Nash asked, 'What about the other one? The other car?'

'The driver of the other vehicle was killed instantly.'

Fragments of the universe in motion.

Cracks, fissures, breaks. Wreckage. Black holes. Ruin.

'I'm so sorry, Mr Nash. Shall I ask for the bereavement counsellor to come and see you, or a priest?'

Nash shook his head, wonderingly.

The doctor laid his hand gently on Nash's arm in a consoling gesture. 'Look, I'll be back later and we'll run another series of tests, just to be sure everything really is as it should be. If the pain gets too much ask the nurse for another dose, yes?'

A policeman came. 'What do you remember?' he asked solemnly. Nash told him. His mother picking him up. Hobbe's Marsh. The car drifting into their lane.

'Did your mother seem intoxicated?'

'What do you mean?'

'Slurring her speech, anything like that?'

'No, she was just tired. She wasn't happy to be out at that time. It was late and she was tired.'

'The toxicology report shows she had alcohol in her system. Though I should say, she wasn't over the limit or anything like that.'

'No, she was just tired. I shouldn't have asked her to get me. I should have walked.'

The policeman made notes.

'What will happen?' asked Nash. 'Will there be an inquest?'

'I don't think so. It seems straightforward. We've checked both vehicles and can rule out mechanical failure of some kind. There are witnesses. Chap in the car behind you saw the other car coming across into your lane. Said he was surprised you didn't swerve until it was too late. I can't say for sure, but from what you've told me, it's probable the driver of the other car fell asleep. And your mother just wasn't quick enough to get out of his way. As you said, she was tired and was just too slow. It was an accident. A terrible accident. You were lucky to survive.'

'Lucky?' repeated Nash, wondering what *lucky* was.

The next day a different policeman came and asked the same questions. Just double-checking everything, he said. Nash told it all again. Every time he told it, he felt less and less that he was recounting a real memory, and instead that he was telling a story he had read or seen in a movie. He felt his purchase on it diminishing. *Had it really happened?* he asked himself, when he was alone. *Or did I dream it?*

Finally, his father came. He looked exhausted, hollowed out. He sat in a chair next to the bed and began to cry. It was the first time Nash had seen his father do this and it was terrifying. At first it was quiet. He closed his eyes and shuddered gently. But then deep, wet sobs and groans shook him. He leaned forward and cradled his head in his hands, crying and rocking. Nash did not know what to do. When he arrived, he had not said anything. He had stood by the bed and looked at him – stared at him, in fact – but had not said anything.

'Dad?' he asked. He needed him.

Nash knew he had been sitting beside his bed while he had been – what was it, asleep, unconscious? – the nurses had told him so. He had held his hand, they said. But now he seemed reluctant to touch him, or even look at him. He avoided his eyes.

Nash knew then that his father blamed him for what had happened. If he hadn't got his mother to come and get him, she would still be alive. He didn't say it, he didn't say anything, but Nash knew.

(27)

In the first weeks at Paradise, especially at night, Nash sometimes sensed that the woods were inside. Not just surrounding the house for miles in every direction but *within* it, permeating it, as if the walls had dissolved, removing any boundary between inside and outside.

And sometimes too, after time had passed, he felt the woods were *in* him. That he was also without boundaries and permeated by that teeming vegetal world: blood, nerves, bones, thoughts and sensations mingled with leaves, sap, bark, microbes and bacteria, a terrible and wonderful commingling of atoms and molecules, systems and networks.

At first, he found these sensations profoundly disturbing (he felt that his grip on the fact of his physical being, his identity as Nash, *a human being*, was tenuous) and would try to shrug them off, turning on lights and pacing the rooms, searching for signs that the house had been breached (half expecting to see tendrils curling under doors or prising open windows, leaves and petals drifting into the corners, the air misty with pollen and spores). He would rub the skin on his arms and legs vigorously, pinch his neck and face, blow his nose and run his hands through his hair (expecting to find it matted with earth and seeds). It was as if the house had been *invaded*. As if he himself had been *infected*.

But, after some time, the horror had receded. Rather than invasion, it began to feel more like equilibrium, that a strange kind of balance had been achieved between inner and outer realities. The house was still permeable, as was he, but it was no longer a takeover.

Moreover, he began to feel that the woods had become benign towards him. They were no longer hostile. He stopped feeling that he was an imposter, a foreign body, an unwelcome intruder. He did not feel welcome exactly, but rather *accepted*. His daily walks through the woods, along the tracks and paths, began to take on a different character; they were less fearful attempts to know his surroundings (and understand the possible ways out, the means of escape) and more amiable wanderings, during which he enjoyed visiting certain familiar places (the spring, the barrow) and greeting certain trees and plants, and seeing how, from day to day and week to week, they changed as they came into bud and then leaf.

He picked bright yellow daffodils and, back at the house, stood them on the table in a jar filled with water. He gazed at them wonderingly. They seemed to exude light. It was a hopeful light. It was the light of spring.

The revelation was simple, when it came, yet almost overwhelming. *It's all connected*, he thought with wonder. The water, the air, the soil. The worms and insects and birds and beasts. All of it. Entwined. Entangled. And me too.

The woods are life. All the extraordinary beings that call this place home: microbes, bacteria, lichens, fungi, mosses, worms, beetles, crawling things, hedgehogs and stoats, badgers and foxes, deer, all the birds and flying insects, all the unbelievable variety of plant life. Paradise is a singularity. It is a single being, made of many parts.

The woods are timeless. They are the end of time. For in the woods, it is always the present.

(28)

Mary Owen came in her car, as she often did now, but this time Nash knew immediately that something had changed. She had brought more supplies than she usually did, which was strange, but what disturbed him was that she was surly and uncommunicative. It had taken a while, but over time he felt that Mary had warmed to him as he had warmed to her. He had formed the impression that she had actually become fond of him; she brought him little treats and was always careful to ask how he was getting on, keen to give him advice, recipes and so on. He looked forward to her visits, to the games of Rummy they sometimes played. Now she worked in silence and emanated an aura of annoyance, even hostility. She shushed him away brusquely when he tried to chat. Normally, she didn't venture beyond the kitchen during her visits; but now, after unpacking everything, she went upstairs without saying a word. He heard her moving about in the bedroom at the top of the stairs, at the other end of the house to the one he slept in, and he wondered what she was doing.

When she came back down, she said, 'I've made up a bed in the other room.'

'Why?' he asked.

'Someone's coming.'

'What the hell. So, they've made a decision?'

'No, someone's coming to stay.'

'What? Who?'

'I have no idea.'

'How long for?'

'I don't know, Nash. You know I don't. I don't know why you keep asking so many questions.'

'I'm sorry. But when? When are they coming?'

She shrugged and, without saying goodbye, went quickly to her car.

Nash stood on the doorstep for a long time afterwards, feeling disturbed. Eventually, he took the gun from where it lay behind the sofa and carried it to the shed beside the woodpile, concealing it beneath some old sacking.

The next day, he walked in the woods for a long time, eventually coming out on the hillside below where the standing stone pointed towards the notch in the ridge. Above him, everything was clear – a ghost moon hung there, pale in the morning sky – and below the hills and valleys ran away from him into the far distance, eventually fading into a bluish haze.

It was dusk when he returned to the house, a blush in the sky, the air chilling. Approaching the house, he saw that lights were on. A figure, silhouetted against the light, was sitting at the table in the kitchen. He didn't risk a look in through the window but went stealthily to the front door.

The axe was there, and he took it up and carefully and quietly opened the door and went in.

The kitchen door was open. White was sitting at the table. He wore smart black trousers, a grey sweater and immaculate white sneakers. His neck was bandaged. Hearing the door open, he turned.

'Nash, old chap,' he said cheerfully, rising. 'I was wondering when you'd appear.'

Nash was astonished. He had seen the hole in White's neck. He had seen him lying still and lifeless in a spreading pool of blood. White had been dead for a long time.

'White,' he said. 'How?'

'Good to see you too!' White grinned.

'But how?'

'How did I get out after you left me for dead?' White smiled.

'You *were* dead.'

'Evidently not, old man. No thanks to you. Look, I don't *really* hold it against you. I'd have done the same.'

'What happened?'

'I lost a lot of blood, for sure.' White gestured to the bandage about his neck. 'Took a pretty major operation and a couple of blood transfusions to get me right again.'

'You had a *hole* in your neck,' said Nash, quietly.

White nodded. 'I was out for an age. But you know, even with all that shooting, no one came. Isn't that incredible? I thought the police would have been in there almost immediately. But no. I came round perhaps twenty minutes later. I was very weak. God, there was so much blood. It was a hell of a scene. I saw you'd gone and the envelope too, and I somehow got out of the room and into the fire escape at the end of the corridor.

Smeared a lot of blood on the carpet on the corridor, but with that pattern I don't suppose anyone would have noticed. I made a call and waited in there, and about forty minutes later they came and got me. Just in time, it seems.'

'Jesus,' said Nash. 'I can't believe it. What do you think happened? Why was Cardoso there?'

'Who knows. Maybe he just turned up early.'

'You don't think it was a setup?'

'No. But if it was, our people will find out. Listen, tell me what happened. I'm missing some of it.'

Nash hesitated. He tried to parse White's intention. 'What do you remember?' he asked, cautiously.

'I remember the hotel. The carpet, do you remember the carpet?' He made a face. 'I remember going into the room. You went first and I got Rana up against the wall and told you to get the envelope. I was trying to hold him but he got free. And then there were shots. That's all.'

'To be honest, it's not that clear to me either. Cardoso was there. In the room already, waiting. There was a lot of shooting. I couldn't tell you who shot who. It was chaos, a complete fucking mess. I don't know who it was who shot you.'

'Really?'

'Really. It was chaos.'

'And you?'

'What do you mean?'

'You didn't get hit? In all the *chaos*?

'No.' Nash shrugged. 'No, somehow I didn't get hit.'

'And you took the envelope?'

Nash nodded. 'I followed the instructions. They came much later and brought me here.'

White nodded. 'To be fair, I would have done the same thing, if it had been you lying there with a hole in your neck, bleeding out.'

'I don't doubt it.' Nash was quiet, watching White. 'What happened next?' he asked. 'How is it you're here? How did you get here?'

'I've been shut away in a private hospital ever since. Gray came yesterday and said I was passed to leave. Black drove me. He's not much of a talker, is he?'

'Gray told you to come?'

'Your old friend.'

'I thought you didn't know Gray.'

'Everyone knows Gray.'

White sat down again. 'So here I am. I'm to keep an eye on you. Apparently, it's not for long, just a week or two at most. I'm to rest and recuperate and,' he said, self-importantly, 'I'm to keep an eye on you. They're worried that the longer this all goes on, the bigger the flight risk you are.'

'So, you're guarding me?'

'Just keeping an eye on things.'

'Have you got a gun?'

White shook his head.

'Why haven't you got a gun if you're supposed to be guarding me?'

Nash put the axe down in the hall and took off his jacket. He poured himself a glass of water and drank it.

'So, are you going to show me around this dump?' White said.

Nash took White around the house. It took less than two minutes. He couldn't believe there was no television. On

White's bed (which had been made up by Mary Owen and dressed with a colourful quilt she must have brought with her) was a Gucci leather holdall. *A short break in the country*, thought Nash. *Lovely*.

He took White outside and showed him the chopping block. Next, he explained the log piles and the need to keep the fire going. White just wasn't interested. 'Whatever, whatever,' he kept on saying.

'Listen,' said Nash. 'It gets fucking cold, especially at night. Though spring is coming so hopefully it's getting better. Let's hope you've brought some warm weather with you.'

'Whatever,' said White.

As they came back in, White stopped and gestured at the grass cross hanging above the front door. 'What's this?' he asked.

'Peasant charm,' said Nash. 'To bring us good luck and ward off evil.'

'Jesus Christ.'

'Exactly.'

White laughed. 'At this point you need more than a funky cross made of grass, a lot more.'

That evening, Nash made a simple supper and they sat at the kitchen table to eat together. It was awkward. Nash had a bottle of Mary's homemade cider in a recycled plastic bottle and White grimaced when he offered it.

'What is it? Owen's piss?'

'Cider. It's good. You should try it. It might help you relax.'

'Yeah, right. Look, firstly I don't drink. And secondly, if I did drink, I wouldn't drink that. That shit makes you blind.'

'No.' Nash grinned. 'It makes you see.'

At Paradise, in the woods, White was nervous. He was afraid. He tried to hide it, but Nash could see it. His air of confidence, his belief in his own invulnerability, had vanished. It reminded him of when he had first arrived, the feeling of strangeness, of being in an alien, hostile place. Every sound grating against his nerves. The unknown. It made White voluble. He needed to talk. He didn't like the silence and so he tried to fill it. He talked, incessantly. Now, finally, he was going to talk about the people they worked with, the people they worked *for*, their *mission*. 'Tell me about it,' said Nash. 'Now we're here together, you may as well. Come on, tell me what you know about them. I'm still trying to figure it out. Tell me about Gray.'

'Gray is a devil,' said White. 'Gray is a nihilist and – moreover – an extremist. If you gave him an atomic bomb, he'd use it.'

'Why?'

'Because he thinks mankind has had its day. He thinks it's time. He *hates* everything. He hates *everyone*. He is, in his own way, an environmentalist, albeit one with some extreme ideas. He thinks that the planet should be cleansed. He wants to restore the earth to its original state, *untainted*, free of the disease of man. That will happen anyway, eventually, of its own accord, of course. It's human nature, isn't it, to destroy everything we touch, to *shit in the garden*? But Gray believes we should speed the whole thing up, rush it along. The quicker the better, as far as he's concerned.'

'I don't understand.'

'He wants to end it all.'

'But what's in it for him.'

'Nothing. It's a philosophical position. A moral position.'

'How is he going to do it? He, they, the organisation, they can't do it on their own, can they?'

'But it's not just him, you know. He's part of a wider network, a much wider network. Worldwide, in fact. Their fingers are everywhere, in everything. And the time is coming. You've got the Accelerators in the US, the Anti-Natalists, the Eschatologists, the Neo-Templars, New Luddites, the Anarcho-Primitivists, the Ultra-Darwinians. In Italy there are the Neo-Futurists, in France there's the Phare group. Eco-Anarchists in China and Indonesia, Sun First in Japan. Others, too. Those are just the serious ones. Then there are the crazies, the religious nuts, the UFO freaks, the comet-watchers. Of course, they all have different agendas. Some are nihilists, pure and simple, some are for regeneration, a new start. But they're united in one key thing: the desire to force a reckoning.'

Nash shook his head.

White pointed a finger at Nash. 'I can't believe it. You don't know any of this do you? You literally have no idea what's going on.'

Nash shrugged. 'How could I?'

White made a face and then went on. 'Will he do it? Will they do it? *Can* they do it? I honestly don't know. It's probably impossible. Almost certainly impossible. The odds are stacked against them. Gray works for this government and that corporation, this agency and that syndicate, doing the jobs no one else wants to do. But just as many are against him, are against all this, actively trying to shut it all down. But he'll keep trying. They'll all keep trying. As I said, it's a philosophical position.'

'But if it's impossible, what's the point of any of it?'

'You know, you and Gray are not so dissimilar. You both overthink things. Listen, I get paid well, you get paid well. Gray believes he's doing something for the greater good. The rich – those who are invested, those who have a stake – get even richer. It is always so.'

'So, is Gray is actually in charge?'

'Only of his circle. There are others holding the purse strings, so to speak. A board, if you like. The millionaires, billionaires, trillionaires – they see the network as a way to disrupt the markets, make money. But they don't really believe Gray will succeed. They use him.'

'And you, what do you believe?'

'What does it matter? I get paid well.'

'There's got to be more than that, surely?'

'Look, I think he has a point. Who's going to clear it up? Who's going to sort it out, fix it? The politicians? Don't make me laugh. They're too busy lining their pockets and pursuing their petty agendas, scheming and plotting to cling on to what little power they have. The tech guys? The tech bros? For all their liberal credentials, their handwringing, they don't care. Of course not. They don't give a shit. Basically, they're the same as the politicians. The Church? That's a joke. The Church is dying. And honestly, I don't think anyone cares. No one. Everyone's locked into their own little bubble: chasing, scrabbling, grafting and grifting, burning coal and gas and oil, shitting in the garden. There are microplastics in the fish and the birds, all the way through the food chain, rivers filled with sewage, plagues and pandemics, cancers, tumours, genetic mutation. Wars, everywhere. Literally *everywhere*. How many wars? I've lost count. And the worst of it? No one gives a shit. We've fucked it all up. We've had our moment. And if that's the case, perhaps the right thing to do is admit it, and get on with bringing it to its conclusion. Endgame. But while we're at it' – he grinned at Nash – 'so what if we make some money?'

'But what's the point of making money if it's all going to hell?' Nash trailed off. He shook his head. It was too much.

'You know,' White continued, 'Spink once told me that Gray used to be a priest. What do you think about that?'

White rarely left the house. He didn't want to get his sneakers dirty. And he was terrified of the darkness within the woods, just as Nash had once been. If the sun was shining, he might sit on a chair by the back door, in the place where Nash had enjoyed letting time slide by. But he never ventured beyond the ruined garden.

Nash could not bear to be with him. White's presence drove him out of the house, into the woods, where he spent more and more time wandering and wondering.

'Where do you go?' asked White.

'I walk,' said Nash.

'Why? What for?'

'I find it comforting.'

White shook his head in disbelief.

Three days after White's arrival, Nash was lying on his bed reading when he heard voices below him in the kitchen. He went down and found White at the front door, leaning against the doorframe. Brigid stood beyond him on the gravel. She looked worried, scared. It unnerved him.

Seeing him appear behind White, she said quickly, 'Well, I'll be going. I'm sorry to have disturbed you.'

She walked away and White turned to face Nash, a vicious grin on his face.

'Owen's girl, isn't it? She didn't even knock. She came straight in, brazen, as happy as you like. She had a hell of a shock when she saw me.'

He moved through into the kitchen and Nash followed him.

'Has she been coming here much?' He regarded Nash, slyly. 'Oh my god, she has, hasn't she?'

Nash had to resist the urge to punch White's grinning face.

'Does Owen know? She doesn't, does she? Shit.' White whistled through his teeth, grinning.

'Don't tell them, for fuck's sake. She's done nothing.'

'Oh no, I'm looking forward to seeing you explain this to Gray. My god, Nash. How old is she?'

Nash shook his head and turned his back. He needed to think. As he climbed the stairs to his room, White whistled again. White knew about Brigid and was going to tell Gray. It changed everything. Even if they were coming to absolve him – them – of what had happened at the hotel, it changed everything.

(29)

The next day, he went to the spring. He needed to get away from White, from the house. He needed to think. It was a place that felt special. He drank the water that came from the mountain, that was said to heal, and sat on a tree stump. Soon after, as if he had summoned her, Brigid appeared.

'I thought I might find you here,' she said, sheepishly. 'I skipped school. Listen, I'm sorry. I didn't know he was there.'

'I was going to tell you.'

'Who is he?'

'He's called White.'

'But what does it mean?'

'Nothing, Bee. Don't worry. It's nothing. You'll be okay.'

'But what about you? Will you be in trouble?'

'I'm in enough trouble already. It won't make any difference. And look,' he took her hand, 'I promise that nothing will happen to you or Mary.'

She disentangled her fingers from his. 'Who is he?' she asked. There was fear in her voice, but also defiance.

'He's called White. I used to work with him. He was with me when it all went wrong. I thought he had been killed.'

'Killed? Oh my god. Who by?'

'Don't worry. Like I said, it was a fuckup. I did the only thing I could do. The right thing.'

'Did you kill someone?'

'No.'

'Do you promise?' She looked at him carefully.

'No, I didn't.' He considered. 'Obviously, White wasn't killed, as I thought he was. He's been in hospital all this time. He says they've sent him here to watch me or guard me. But I think he's here so they can deliver a double verdict. Kill two birds with one stone, as they say.'

'I don't like the sound of that.'

'I know.'

'Is he your friend?'

'White? No. He's an arsehole. It seems strange to me now that there was actually a time when I almost enjoyed his company, a time when I thought that working with those people was the answer to my problems.'

'How long will he be here for?'

'He says it's not for long.'

'Then we're almost at the end?'

'Yes, I suppose so.'

'Is that good or bad?'

'Good. It's got to be good, hasn't it?'

'Yes, it's got to be good.' She smiled, brightly. He knew she was trying to comfort him.

They sat together in companiable silence for a while and then Brigid's mood seemed to shift. 'Nash,' she said, 'I've got some news.'

'Oh, yes?'

'It's spring.'

'So it is.'

'Seriously, winter has passed, finally. The wheel of the year is turning. And that means it's almost time for the Lent fair.'

'What's that?'

'It's our spring celebration, in the valley. There's a procession, singing and dancing. A feast. The biggest bonfire, bigger even than Bonfire Night. It's to welcome the new season.'

'It sounds good. When is it?'

'In a week. On the day of the equinox.' She paused. 'But that's not all.'

'Go on.'

'Every year at the fair, a boy and a girl from the valley are crowned the Spring King and Queen. It's a great honour.'

He looked at her. She was bursting with excitement now, with the effort of holding back her news.

'And this year?' he asked.

'It's me!' She stood and did a little pirouette. 'Can you believe it?'

He clapped her.

'Congratulations, Bee.'

'Thanks! I'm so excited. I never thought it would be me, never. When Ma told me, I thought she was teasing. The only thing is, I'll have to wear a dress.' She made a face.

'Have you even got a dress?'

'No, but Ma says she'll make one up for me. She's already got the material.'

'No offence, but I don't really see you in a dress, Bee.'

'I know. It's not really my style.'

'You're what they used to call a tomboy.'

'Yeah, yeah, yeah.' She did another pirouette. 'Be that as it may, on the day of the fair I'm going to be a queen. And I'm going to make the most of it.'

'It's wonderful, Bee.'

'Will you come?' she said, suddenly very serious.

He shook his head. 'I can't.'

'Please come,' she said, plaintively. 'I really want you to be there.'

'It's too risky, you know that. Especially now that White is here.'

'But the thing is, everyone wears masks, at least for the ceremonial bit of the day, even the king and queen. If you wear a mask, no one will know it's you. And lots of people come from all over to watch the procession and the crowning ceremony – it's quite famous, you know – so there'll be lots of strangers and no one will notice you. I know they won't.'

'Even if I thought a mask would be enough of a disguise, I haven't got one.'

'You can make one. Or I can make one for you.'

He shook his head again.

'It's too dangerous, Bee. What if White realises I've gone? What if they find out that I've violated the terms and conditions and left the woods?'

She frowned and he thought she was going to stamp her feet like a little girl, but she contained herself and walked away, prodding at the ground with a stick. She stood with her back to him, and he had the uncomfortable notion that she might be crying.

'Maybe I can come down to the edge of the woods, to the end of the track, and watch from there.'

She shook her head but didn't turn to face him.

'I'd still see you in your dress, Bee.'

'It's not the same,' she said quietly.

The next day she called to him from the woods as he was chopping wood. White was inside. He followed her between the trees until the house was out of sight.

'I've got it,' she said. She put her rucksack down and pulled from it an object wrapped in cloth. She carefully unfolded it and revealed an extraordinary mask.

She handed it to him. At first, he had thought it was made of leaves, but he saw then that it was made from felt, cut into leaf shapes and layered onto a card template, which was in turn attached to an old baseball cap that the peak had been cut off; it was not so much a mask as a headpiece. Woven through the felt leaves were too-bright tendrils of plastic ivy, and long feathers which splayed outwards dramatically. He held it to his face and found that it fit perfectly. It was as if it had been moulded to the contours of his brow, to the bridge of his nose. Brigid clapped her hands with glee.

'It's a good fit,' he said.

'I had to guess it,' she said happily. 'It looks brilliant. Do you like it?'

'I love the feathers,' he said.

'They're mostly pheasant. But I wove some crow and owl feathers in too, for luck.'

'I love it,' he said.

'Then you'll come?'

'We'll see.'

In the house, he stood before the mirror in the bathroom. The mask was very striking. It covered almost all his face; only his mouth and chin were visible. Brigid had carefully arranged her materials so that the whole construction was precisely symmetrical, seemingly flowing from a single point between the eyes. The leaves swirled around the eyeholes, and then spread outwards; the feathers flared away from the eyes, forming two sprays, like horns. It reminded him of the painting of an eagle owl in one of the field guides.

It was remarkably well-made and there was something powerful about it, even when the eyeholes were empty. Although it was new, it was also ancient, somehow. Feral, pagan, it was a being of the woods: part man, part plant, part bird. He knew if he was to wear it, it would change him. He placed it on the mantle in his room. It watched him, balefully. Lord of the Woods. King of Paradise. He hid it from White, concealing it amongst his clothes.

In the following days, Nash would often take the mask out and contemplate it as he considered the possibility of visiting the fair. He was torn. He wanted to go for Brigid. She wanted him there and he did not want to let her down. It was to be a big day for her, and, for whatever reason, she had decided that it was important that her new friend be there to bear witness to her moment of glory. He was also curious; the fair sounded like it would be an unusual spectacle. He liked the sound of the masked procession and the crowning of the King and Queen of Spring. But the prospect of mingling with strangers was daunting. He had neither seen nor talked to anyone else (apart from with Brigid and Mary Owen, and latterly White) in what felt like months, years, even.

If he did go, White would just assume he had taken himself into the woods on one of his walks, what White disparagingly called his 'rambles'.

If what Brigid said was true, he thought, that as well as the villagers and people from up and down the valley the fair would be filled with visitors and sightseers, perhaps he really would be anonymous. Perhaps he need not speak to anyone but might just observe all the goings on from the periphery. Might that not be possible? Especially if he were to wear the mask.

The mask considered him back. It dared him to wear it.

But Nash would not go to the fair. Two days before, that decision was made for him. Brigid came to the house. White was in the sitting room, dozing before the fire, and she whistled and beckoned from the trackway. It was early evening, and she was out of breath, her hair wilder than usual, having run much of the way. He went to her and saw immediately that something was wrong. He knew what she was going to say before she spoke.

'They're coming,' she said, gasping for air. 'I had to let you know. They're coming.'

A chill came upon him, ice against the skin on the back of his neck. A cold pressure from temple to temple, across his forehead, as if his head was gripped by a huge frozen hand.

'Get your breath, Bee,' he said.

She stood with her hands on her hips, breathing deeply.

'How do you know?'

'Ma got in cleaning stuff. Lots of it. Bottles of bleach, bin bags, and so on. It's what she always does when the house is to have a deep clean.'

'This house?'

She nodded.

'Did she say anything?'

'No, but I know what it's for. They're coming. And maybe they'll take you away, maybe not. Either way, Ma will come up here and clean the house just like she always does. She'll remove any trace that you were ever here.'

'Are you sure?'

Brigid nodded, solemnly.

'Do you know when?'

She shook her head. 'Soon, I think. Really soon.'

'Will it be before the fair?'

She shrugged and looked like she would cry.

Disordered thoughts crowded Nash's mind. Should he run? Prepare to fight? Prepare to defend his case? How could you prepare if you didn't know what you were preparing for? Should he warn White?

'Look, I've got to go,' said Brigid. 'I just had to let you know. Be careful, okay?'

'Thanks, Bee,' he said. 'Thanks for looking out for me.'

'That's okay.'

'Take care.'

'You too.'

They hugged, awkwardly, and then she turned and plunged back into the trees, following the steep track down into the lower valley.

For some time, Nash remained standing at the edge of the woods, gazing out into the gnarled chaos that surrounded the house. The sky was pale blue, but over the hills, above the mountain, dark storm clouds were forming. *You couldn't make it up*, he thought, bitterly. *A storm is coming. At last, a storm is coming.*

Should he tell White? No, he would not tell White. He was on his own.

Soon the blue was gone and rainclouds the colour of ash hung low over the woods. The birds were disturbed. The crows called harshly to each other, cries of protest. A wind began to blow, moving the piles of dead leaves before the house into strange little dances.

When the rain started, he went back inside and sat in the dusky gloom of his room holding the mask, waiting for it to give him a sign.

I'll decide in the morning, he thought, knowing that he would not decide in the morning, that he would not make a decision until the moment was upon him. He would prepare, he would have his speeches rehearsed, his weapons ready, his bag packed, but he would not know how it would play out – how *he* would play it out – until they arrived. Then he would know.

Ostara, the Equinox.
The Wheel turns.
Just for a moment, light and darkness are in balance.
The Wheel turns.

(30)

From his vantage point amongst the trees below the house, Nash watched the black car make its way up the pitted track, rolling and bucking with the uneven ground, sometimes slowing and moving at a crawl, sometimes lurching forward, its wheels spinning in the mud. He recognised it immediately as the same one he had arrived in. In the front, as the car moved slowly past his position, in silhouette he could see just two figures: Gray and Black, he assumed.

What did that signify, that it was just the two? Had they come to take him back?

It was the day of the fair. He had woken early that morning, feeling sure that this was the day. He had risen, washed and prepared breakfast. He had chopped and stacked logs, as he always did. He had cleaned the kitchen and made sure the house was in order. He had made his bed. It was a fine morning, bright sunshine sparkling on the wet grass, and shining on the new leaves of the trees (and backlit, the new growth was luminous, like stained glass, dappled). There was a fresh bite in the air. However, he noted, there were also dark clouds in the distance again, waiting. He assumed that whoever was coming would come in the afternoon. It had taken hours to get there when they brought him, and he thought it would be the same again, even if they left the capital early.

White's door was still closed. He seemed to sleep a little later every day.

Nash's few things were packed in the small rucksack he had arrived with. He placed it out of sight behind the kitchen door.

He sharpened the axe and placed it carefully in the hallway.

At midday he weighed the hammer in his hand, feeling the heft of it, and wrapped it in a tea towel and placed it on the windowsill in the sitting room. He took the small paring knife and placed it in one of the kitchen drawers, making sure it was not amidst a jumble of spoons and forks.

He took the shotgun and walked down the track for half an hour, to where there was a clearing and a view down the valley. In the distance, he could see the church spire and, from somewhere nearby, a plume of smoke rising steadily into the still air. A bonfire. A celebration. He longed to go down there but knew he could not.

He returned to the house and stoked the fire in the sitting room. White, lolling on the sofa, ignored him, sulking. He built the fire up so it would burn slow and long, and then, taking up the shotgun again, made his way to the place where he would wait. It was below the house on the steep hillside, amongst thick undergrowth, close by the last turn the track made before its final climb up to the house. He had a good long view down the track and could see how many cars came. As they slowed to make the turn, he would see who was in them. He would then be one step closer to knowing what his course of action would be.

The black car went by and carried on up the hill, and Nash waited to see if there were any other vehicles coming up behind. He waited as long as he dared but none came.

So, it was just The Grey Man and Black.

He approached the house cautiously, coming from the opposite direction to the cart track. About a hundred yards off, he crouched amongst the roots of an impossibly gnarled old oak and watched.

Black was making a round of the house. He was wearing his dark suit and Nash was struck by how incongruous he looked. *Lost in the woods*, thought Nash. *He's so out of place.*

He shifted his position and leaned behind a spray of ferns as Black approached the little gate at the edge of the so-called 'garden' and squinted into the darkness of the woods. For the briefest moment, Nash considered raising the shotgun and firing (in his mind's eye he saw Black reeling from the blast, clutching at his guts, and collapsing into the undergrowth) but he hesitated. *No, let's see what they have to say first*, he thought, and watched as Black turned and made his way back to the house, pausing to awkwardly wipe something from his shoe. *Fox shit*, thought Nash, with relish. Black passed around the front of the house, out of sight, and Nash guessed that he was going to report to Gray. He pictured him, The Grey Man, seated at his kitchen table, waiting. He would be smoking, wreathed in a blue fog.

Nash settled back against the oak tree, feeling its mass at his back, and gazed into the wilderness. Birdsong sounded encouragingly all about him, also the soft drip of water, and the ssshhhing of the breeze high in the trees. Away to his right, a small patch of blue sky was like a solid object, and as he watched, a large bird of prey (*buzzard*, he thought immediately) passed across it in a graceful arc. At his feet, the earth was alive, teeming with insects and burrowing creatures, worms, microbes, bacterium. He could sense it all. He was alive, too. It all was.

He waited, absorbed by the thronging about him, and then moved smoothly and silently to the gate, through it and into the lee of the house. He could smell the woodsmoke from the fire he had set earlier. Keeping low, he passed to the front of the house, the way Black had gone before him, and looked carefully in at the window of the sitting room. It was empty. They would be in the kitchen, then.

At the front door he gently placed the shotgun – barrel down, stock up – against the wall where it was partially concealed by ivy. He paused and listened but could hear nothing from inside the house. Soundlessly, he went in.

From the hallway, he could see into the kitchen. The Grey Man, grey-suited, was seated, smoking and picking at a fingernail. He had taken a saucer and placed it on the table. Beside the saucer was a gun, a small pistol like a fist. Did the gun signify intent, was it a sign? No, standard procedure. How could they know what state they would find him in? They might expect him to have anticipated a negative verdict and be ready to take the initiative.

White also sat at the table but he seemed somehow vague. He was lost in thought. Nash thought he was much changed. He no longer had about him an aura of capability. *He is diminished by everything that has happened*, thought

Nash. Some are diminished, some are eclipsed, some are transformed, become something else, made anew – *pass over*, one might say, to a new state. For some reason he thought of a butterfly.

The air in the room was hazy with blue smoke, and sunlight from the windows created diagonal bars of light and darkness. Gray seemed to have aged. There had always been something attenuated about him – too tall, too thin, almost translucent, so that the blood shone through his skin from beneath – but now he looked even greyer and more creased than before. He looked tired. Even so, he exuded threat.

Black stood behind him, leaning against the sink, looking out towards the log pile and the woods beyond. His hair was cropped close to his pink scalp, like suede. His suit was still too tight, and his beefy neck still bulged like sausage meat over the collar. He rocked gently from one foot to the other, a tightly wound coil of energy, waiting to explode.

They had not heard him enter and Nash observed them for what seemed like an age. Looking in through the door like that, the view framed, he thought it was a like a scene in a play, frozen.

He coughed, gently, and they all turned to look at him.

'Mr Nash!' said The Grey Man, standing. White also stood, pushing his chair back with a screech. Black's hand went quickly to his jacket, but Nash stepped into the room, his hands open, to show that he carried no weapon, and Black relaxed.

'Mr Nash!' repeated Gray. He seemed genuinely pleased to see him. 'We were just wondering where you might have got to.' He stepped forward and offered his hand. Nash hesitated, and then shook it, weakly.

Now he was in the room, he was aware of the profound psychic distance between himself and the newcomers. They were businesslike, as per Gray's injunction to him at the beginning. They wore smart suits, white shirts, sombre ties. They were clean shaven, well groomed. Gray's black shoes shone. Even White had managed to keep his sneakers pristine. Nash felt acutely how unkempt he was, and was – just for a moment – ashamed. He could not remember how long it was since he had shaved, and it was weeks since Brigid had cut his hair. His clothes were shabby, grimy. There were crescents of dirt beneath his nails.

'How are you, old chap? How have you been?' The Grey Man no longer seemed old and decayed. He was now energised, demonic.

Nash nodded. 'Still here.'

'Indeed, and thriving, by the look of things,' said Gray, grinning. 'Doesn't he look well, Mr Black?'

Black said nothing but continued to stare intently at Nash. His hand hovered at his waist, ready.

'Is it just the two of you?' asked Nash.

'Our associates are just behind us. Terrible journey down it was, thank you for asking,' said Gray. 'I don't know what this country's coming to. Roadworks, diversions, endless queues. Endless queues, hundreds of thousands of cars, all pumping their poisons into the air, driving us on to the end of days.' He grinned evilly, and sat down again. 'Please, Mr Nash, take a seat.' He gestured to the other chair and Nash sat down. Gray turned to Black and White.

'Mr Black, Mr White, would you mind watching the front, just in case we have unexpected visitors? Mr Nash and I need to talk.'

Black nodded and left the kitchen; White followed. Nash heard the crunch of gravel at the front of the house.

'Is this it, then?' he asked.

'All in good time, Mr Nash, all in good time.' Gray lit a cigarette. 'So how have you been? We heard you settled in very nicely.'

'I suppose so. It's alright once you get used to it.'

'And you've observed all the terms and conditions?'

'Of course.'

'Really? No fraternisation? No expeditions beyond the bounds?' Gray watched him slyly.

Nash shook his head.

'Owen says you've been reading a lot.'

Nash nodded.

'Any recommendations?'

Nash shrugged. 'It was just to pass the time, really.'

Gray put his hand inside his jacket and drew an object from the chest pocket. It was something small, wrapped in tissue, and he put it on the table next to the saucer. He looked about with an expression of distaste. 'Dingy little hovel, isn't it?' He watched Nash for his response and Nash had the feeling that the house was focussed, gathered about him, waiting for something to happen. 'What is it, do you think? Eighteenth century? Older? I'd say older.'

Nash shrugged. 'It feels like it's been here forever.'

'Back then, houses were just shelters really, weren't they? There was no sense of style then, no vision, just exigency. Get the thing done. *Vernacular*, they call it.' He paused and smoked. 'Tell me, Mr Nash, have you ever paid attention to architecture, what it says about its time, its age, what it says about human life, hopes, aspirations?'

'I can't say I have.'

Gray began to unwrap the small thing on the table. He held it delicately between two fingers and unwound the tissue paper. He paused.

'I've been studying it, thinking about it. You might even call it a hobby of mine. I believe it's the most important artform, more than painting, more than literature, even TV or cinema. The houses and buildings we occupy dictate the ways in which we live, breathe, think. They influence our emotions. This house says a lot about the hopes and aspirations of the people who built it, don't you think?' He grinned, sarcastically. 'Have you ever seen a Gothic cathedral? Wonderful, exquisite. The building – the architecture – draws the eye (and the mind) upwards, to heaven. Praise the Lord, and all that. But you couldn't live in it, could you? Good architecture makes life better, easier to live. It's true, I assure you. But most modern architecture is awful. Machines for misery.' He looked around and grimaced again. 'But this place? Oof. It's *abject*, isn't it?'

Nash shook his head. 'I don't know about any of that. But I've grown to almost like it here, actually.'

There were pink flecks on the white tissue paper.

'Who would have thought it? Well, you have been here quite some time. They say familiarity breeds contempt, but perhaps with you it goes the other way.'

Nash's mind was racing, wondering where all this was going, what it signified, what he could infer from it. 'Would you like tea?' he asked.

Gray nodded and Nash filled the kettle, got mugs and teabags. He took a teaspoon from the drawer, his back to

Gray, and as he did so he took the paring knife and slipped it carefully into the pocket of his jeans.

They were silent as the kettle boiled. Nash made the tea and set a mug before Gray, resisting the temptation to snatch at the gun.

'As you said, I've been here a long time, much longer than expected. So, I was wondering…'

'The verdict? Yes, well. The powers-that-be have cogitated and ruminated and have reached a decision. And I am here to deliver it.'

'And?'

Nash watched carefully. Gray began again to unwind the tissue paper.

'The problem, Mr Nash, is that there are *vested interests*.'

'What does that mean? Who are they?'

'People that our people work with. People who take an interest in our organisation's activities.'

'I'm not following. The ones at the hotel? *With* or against?'

'Both, really. It's complicated, and I don't have the time or the will to explain it to you now. Even if I did, I'm not sure you would understand.' He smiled, without emotion. 'What it means is that whatever happened in that hotel room, whoever was at fault, whatever the facts of the case, the rights and wrongs, doesn't really matter.'

He paused to let his words sink in.

'Yes, it's true. It doesn't really matter. Strange, isn't it? It's because things are now out of balance, and equilibrium must be restored. It's the way of things, you see?'

The last pieces of tissue paper were stained pink and dark red. Gray pulled them free and held something up, pinching it delicately between his thumb and forefinger. He looked at it curiously and then set it on the table, next to the saucer. It was a finger. The flesh was pale, white almost. The nail was dirty, decorated with chipped lilac nail varnish.

Nash rose. 'I forgot the sugar.'

He crossed to the counter. From behind he placed a bag of sugar on the table, and as Gray dipped his teaspoon in, Nash plunged the paring knife into the side of his neck and kicked the table leg. The mugs scooted, spilling tea, and the gun span across the table. Gray jerked back and up, his feet slipping on the stone floor, but Nash had him in a lock with one arm and, with his free hand, stabbed the short blade into his neck again and again, releasing an astonishing spray of blood across the room. Gray gasped and tried to get hold of him, twisting. The mugs smashed on the floor and Nash heard running steps on gravel outside. Gray grunted, heaved himself up, and Nash released him so that The Grey Man careered backwards, falling, and smashed the back of his head into the kitchen counter and then slumped to the floor. Black was fumbling with the front door as Gray made a horrible noise – like an underwater scream – and Nash was already at the back door and out, stumbling but moving fast, around the corner of the house, keeping low as Black came into the kitchen from the hallway and fired out at him through the window, showering him with shards of glass. At the front door Nash seized the shotgun, released the safety and turned as Black exited the back door, came careening around the corner in pursuit, gun in hand, feet slipping on gravel and glass. Nash levelled the shotgun, chest high, and fired.

The impact stopped Black in his tracks. He stood still for what seemed a very long time, and then brought his gun up, unsteady, and fired a shot away over Nash's head into the trees. Nash raised the shotgun to his shoulder and took aim, taking his time, as Black seemed to waver, unsure of himself. Nash squeezed the trigger, and the recoil made him step back. Much of Black's head was gone and he took a step backwards and dropped heavily to the ground.

With a harsh chorus of alarm and protest, the crows took to the air, filling the sky above the trees with curses and vexations.

Nash's ears were filled with a metallic ringing, the echoing sound of an anvil being struck by a metal hammer over and over. He lowered the shotgun and broke it, ejecting the spent cartridges. As he took the last one from his pocket and loaded, careful not to scorch his fingers on the metal, he was aware of movement in the trees beyond the log pile: White, running for it.

Everything was happening very slowly, and he felt very calm.

The crows were screaming angrily, and it seemed a strong wind had suddenly blown through the woods, so that the trees swayed and rocked.

Nash went in through the front door aiming the shotgun, expecting Gray to fire at him from the kitchen. But Gray was not in the kitchen. There was a lot of blood on the floor and the back door was wide open. Gray's gun was gone. Nash slowly made his way to the back door, shotgun levelled, and saw a trail of blood leading from where Gray had hit the floor, out onto the unkempt lawn. He followed it, warily, and saw that it went up the steps through the ruined garden. He was about to follow when he heard a car revving on the track below the house. He turned and ran back to where Black lay in a widening slick of blood, and with difficulty extracted the pistol from his clenched hand.

He hesitated. Should he follow Gray? Or White? His impulse was to conceal Black's body but there was no time. And they would see the blood, anyway. He ran quickly to the shed beside the log pile, crouched down behind it and watched as a second black car came out of the trees and came to a halt behind Gray's vehicle. There were two men inside. The driver kept the engine running. He could see them talking and pointing. Black's body would have been clearly visible to them, and the open front door.

With the engine still going, the passenger, a big man wearing the regulation dark suit, opened his door and got out, keeping low. His gun was drawn. He watched and waited for a moment and then ran across to the house, to where Black lay. He crouched beside the body, and Nash saw him recoil when he saw the state of the head. He looked back to the car, to his partner, and drew a finger across his neck. Now, he went to the front door and peered inside. Again, he waited – he seemed to be listening – and then went in.

Now, the man in the car cut the engine and climbed out. He also had his gun drawn but he made no move to join his companion. He waited, watching the house.

Nash leaned against the wood of the shed. It was furred with green moss. At his feet a penny-sized beetle with an obsidian carapace was gamely attempting to climb over a twig. Brown leaves were disintegrating into mulch. Above, the sky was becoming dull and ashy.

Something again stirred the crows to a harsh chorus of complaints. About six feet away, Nash noticed, some bluebells were about to flower.

The first man appeared at the back door and, as Nash and Black had done before, made his way back around the corner of the building to the front door, where the second man waited. They conferred briefly and then both went inside. He saw them through the broken kitchen window and then they disappeared from view. They would be searching the house.

Moving quickly and lightly, the pistol on his right hand and the shotgun balanced in his left, Nash crossed to the house and considered his next move. He heard voices from within – from upstairs, he thought – and crept around the house to where he could crouch below the living room window. He leaned the shotgun against the brickwork. Again, voices from above.

Peering over the windowsill, he had a good view of the staircase in the centre of the room. When he saw feet coming down, he stood and braced himself, steadying the pistol with both hands. As the first figure came into the view on the staircase he fired through the glass. The man went down on his arse on the stairs, a look of incomprehension on his face. As his eyes locked with Nash's, he brought his gun up – in agonising slow motion – and Nash fired again. And again. And again.

The man lay still on the stairs and then slid, very slowly, down onto the floor at the bottom. No one followed him.

There were buds of pink, tightly wrapped in pale green, coming on a climbing rose that clung to the brickwork of the house. A ladybird on a leaf. There were spiderwebs on the underside of the windowsill, the paint of which was cracking and peeling.

He heard a woodpecker off in the distance, somewhere in the woods.

In the kitchen, Nash slipped in the pool of blood and almost went down, but steadied himself against the table. He tucked the pistol into his jeans and went into the sitting room, the shotgun levelled before him. He could hear the second man moving about above him.

'Gray and Black are dead,' shouted Nash. 'You're on your own.'

'Fuck you, Nash,' the second man screamed back. 'There are more coming.'

'No, there aren't,' Nash replied. The man was in the corridor above him. He could hear his movements, hear his breathing even, and see his shadow projected through the tiny gaps between the ages-old floorboards. He considered the man's position and fired the shotgun up through the ceiling, blowing open a hole the size of a plate and showering himself with splinters.

Last cartridge. Nash dropped the shotgun and pulled the pistol from his waistband.

'Fuck you, Nash,' the second man screamed again, and Nash heard him moving along the corridor towards his bedroom, which was over the kitchen.

Nash began to move silently up the stairs. He knew which steps creaked and avoided them.

At the top of the stairs was the small landing (the hatch in the ceiling above), leading onto the corridor which ran along the side of the house and led to his bedroom. Nash crouched there, beside the hole he had blown in the floor from below, and dared a look around the corner. The corridor was empty and the door to the bedroom was open. He could hear the second man's laboured breathing. And something else, muffled, up above him, movement, slow and massive, as if some great creature were stirring, uncoiling itself in the void space of the attic.

'You're on your own, brother,' called Nash. This time the man did not respond. There was a noise that sounded like a window being opened and Nash thought, incredulously, that the man was going to climb out and risk a jump.

He crept along the corridor. As the room came into view, he saw that the second man was indeed climbing up onto the sill of the open window. A floorboard creaked and the man turned, and as Nash fired – over the man's shoulder and out of the window into the trees somewhere far beyond the house – he dropped to the floor and rolled behind the bed. Nash went to fire again but there was only a metallic click. He dropped the pistol and turned on his heel, and as he ran back down the corridor shots came from behind, slamming into the wall to his right, throwing out clouds of dust and plaster. A sudden pain in his arm, like a knife inserted into the muscle and twisted. He threw himself down the stairs, stumbling and slipping at the turn, losing his grip and falling, hitting the bottom step with force, rolling onto his back next to the body of the first man. He could hear the second man coming. He was at the top of the stairs. As he came down, he fired, seemingly as a warning, and Nash wondered how many shots that was.

Now Nash was in the hallway, where he gathered the axe. He pressed himself against the wall behind the door and held his breath. As the second man came through from the sitting room holding his gun before him, he forced all his weight against the door, slamming the man's arm against the doorframe, so that his gun clattered to the floor. Nash stepped past and, using the axe like a poker, jabbed the flat metal head hard into the centre of the second man's face. He staggered backwards which gave Nash room to swing the axe, catching him where his neck met his shoulder. The blade went in, but not far, and, as the man staggered back and sat down heavily on the bottom step of the staircase, Nash pulled the axe out, raised it and brought it down with all his strength on the man's head. It was like cleaving a log.

He got a glass of water from the kitchen, went out of the back door and sat on a chair. The sky was dark, and it looked like rain was coming. It hurt. It really fucking hurt. *I've been shot*, he thought, incredulously. It looked like the bullet had gone right through his upper arm. There was a small dark hole, brimming with blood, where it had gone in, and a ragged wound where it had exited. It really fucking hurt. But in an odd way it only hurt in a superficial sense. It was pain, a sharp and unpleasant physical sensation – overwhelming almost, just for a moment there – but nothing more, simply a physiological reaction to broken skin, punctured muscle, torn flesh (but not shattered bone, thank God). The crows were still complaining, and Nash agreed with them. He was fucking furious.

He contemplated the oily trail of blood leading across the grass. Gray was out there somewhere, wounded and bleeding. White, too. He thought about the black cars coming through the village, perhaps even nudging their way through the spring procession, breaking it up, and then making their way up the track into the woods. It was still only mid-afternoon, and he imagined the fair would be in full swing now. Toffee apples. Cider. Hot dogs. Masks. Was Brigid there? Was she safe? Whose finger had Gray laid on the kitchen table?

He took a t-shirt from his bag and tore it into strips. He bound his arm tightly and the white cotton was soon dark with blood. He returned to the chair by the back door and sat there for a long time. Or at least, it seemed like a long time. Perhaps it was not. Perhaps it was only minutes, or even seconds. He was trying to figure things out. His situation was clear now, but his next move was not.

More would come, obviously. Someone would be expected to call back by a certain time to let them know that the assignment had been completed. If they didn't hear by the appointed hour, they would send someone to investigate. But they would have to drive all the way from the city. So, he had time. Unless there was backup waiting in the village.

There was a lot of blood. On the stairs, at the foot of the stairs, in the kitchen, and on the gravel at the front of the house, where Black lay. He wondered if he should attempt to clean it up.

*The house shivers, ever so slightly.
It waits.*

(31)

He took the gun off the dead man lying at the bottom of the stairs and went out into the woods, following White. He had blundered through the undergrowth, trampling plants and grass, disturbing the soggy carpet of dead leaves that lay upon the ground, twisting and snapping branches, and in several places he had obviously fallen. His trail was clear. Nash kept low – he did not think that White had a gun, but could not be sure – and he went quickly, moving smoothly, not once tripping or stumbling.

He did not have to go far. He soon came to a clearing and saw White on the other side, wavering, as if undecided whether to go on. His smart black clothes were smeared with mud and leaves clung to him. He was limping badly. It looked like he had fallen and twisted or broken his ankle. His beautiful white sneakers were filthy.

Nash approached and White turned to face him, grimacing in pain. For the first time, he looked scared. In fact, he looked terrified.

'What did you do?' said White.

'This is the end,' said Nash. 'It ends here.'

'More will come.'

'I'll be gone.'

'You won't get away with it.'

'Yes, I will.'

Nash raised the gun and aimed. White looked as if he couldn't decide whether to say something more or turn and run.

Nash fired.

After roughly concealing White beneath dead leaves and branches, Nash trudged back to the house. The keys were still in the cars. With great effort he dragged Black's inert bulk across the gravel and forced him up onto the back seat of the second car. Then he dragged the second man, the one he had killed with the axe, by his feet, down the steps into the hallway (his head bumped soggily on the stone steps) and across the gravel to the car. It was heavy work. He took a breather and then pushed the body up onto the back seat beside Black. The two dead men leaned against each other like they were old friends. Perhaps they were. Next, he dragged the first man, the one he had shot on the stairs, over to the car, and with difficulty folded him into the boot. He took the shotgun, the spent cartridges, the paring knife, the axe and the gun he had taken from Black and put them into the car too. The man he had killed with the axe had dropped his gun in the hallway. Nash checked and saw there was still a single round in the clip.

None of them had wallets. No bank cards, no ID. The one he had killed with the axe had a roll of fifty-pound notes in his jacket pocket. Nash took it.

Finally, he went back into the kitchen. The finger lay on the floor in a smear of Gray's congealing blood. There was something horrific about this finger, this disembodied object, something far worse and more affecting than the bodies he had just piled into the car. He picked it up, gingerly, and examined it. A little finger, a pinkie, though it was now a horrible greyish colour. It had been taken off with a neat clean cut. Lilac varnish on the tiny nail. He tried to remember if Brigid had had nail varnish on the last time he had seen her. He could not say for sure that she had or hadn't. He wondered if he should perhaps keep this strange object, save it, just in case. But instead, he carried it to the car and tossed it in with the dead men.

He took a shower – his hands and face were spattered with blood – and changed his clothes and the makeshift dressing on his arm. The clothes he had been wearing, the ones that were covered in blood, he put in the car.

He started the car up and backed it round, and then drove slowly down the track. About a mile from the house a smaller track led off into very thick woodland. Nash had investigated it on foot several times over the past weeks. It looped away from the main cart track and ran a hundred yards or so down a steep section, to a sort of hollow in the side of the hill. It looked like at one time there had been a small quarry here. Perhaps it was where the stone for the house had been dug. Now, it was completely overgrown, and the bottom of it was filled with black water.

Nash stopped the car on the incline above the water and put the handbrake on. He went around the car lowering the windows. With the driver's door open, he leaned in, checked the angle, and released the brake. As the car began to roll forward, he stepped away and watched. It gathered speed and seemed for a moment to be turning away from the water, but then it went over the rim of the quarry and plunged into the water at an angle. At first it seemed to buoy up and Nash thought, for a horrible moment, that it might simply float out into the centre of the pool, like a grotesque funerary vessel; but then the front end dipped under, and water began to pour in through the windows. Slowly it sank, accompanied by loud plopping and bubbling sounds. Nash squatted on his haunches and watched.

Eventually, all of the car was submerged but for a bit of the roof and the lip of the boot. Nash began to gather branches and throw them on, gradually concealing it. If someone was looking for it, and found the pond, they would see it. But if they weren't, they would not. And the chances of anyone coming this way were very slim.

At last, the oily surface of the water was once again still, and Nash wearily made his way back up the track to the house.

Now it was late afternoon. He made himself toast and a mug of tea. Given the circumstances, it seemed surreal to butter toast, put the teabag in the bin, add milk. There was too much blood in the kitchen – sticky and black, now – and so he carried his food through into the sitting room and ate it hunched on the sofa.

He tried to think how, when the next ones came, they would read what they would find. Two cars had come but only one remained. Lots of blood but no bodies. Would they think he had taken the car and escaped? It was important that they not be able to perceive a clear narrative. He retrieved the hammer, found a long nail in the shed, and used it to puncture the tyres of the first car. He took the keys from the ignition and threw them into the undergrowth beyond the log pile.

He considered torching it, burning the house to the ground. He had no doubt that despite the damp that lurked in the walls, it would go up like a firework. It wouldn't take long. Destroy the evidence. Erase Paradise. He wondered if he had been mistaken to hide the car and the bodies in the quarry. Maybe he should have just burnt the lot?

But no, there were hundreds of people gathered in the valley below. Someone would see it, a burning house up on the mountain, how could they not, and then the police and others would come. As it stood, no one visited Paradise. Probably not many knew it even existed.

In the sitting room, he lay on the sofa and listened to the album of Bach's piano pieces for the last time.

Then it was dusk and he must leave. He gathered his things and took one last look through the house. At the bookshelf in the bedroom, he hesitated and then took a fat old paperback with a butterfly on the cover. Into it he slid the family photograph and then stuffed it into his rucksack. The mask seemed to beckon to him. He put it on. He made a point of leaving both the front and back doors open.

He remembered Brigid's words. *I'd go up. Over the mountain.* And he set out, heading up in the gathering gloom. The crows screeched at him, and he didn't look back.

When he came to the spring, he stopped and splashed the bright clear water on his face and drank deeply. Then, as he climbed higher, it began to rain heavily and the fox appeared on the path ahead of him.

'I wondered when you were going to turn up.'

'Bloody hell, Nash. That was a good show. They didn't have a chance.'

Nash shrugged. 'I was lucky.'

'I don't think so. No, they didn't have a chance. So, what's the plan?'

'I'm getting out.'

'Obviously. Where to?'

'Not sure yet.'

'You're going over the mountain?'

Nash nodded. 'There'll be others coming. They might not get here until tomorrow. But they might be in the village already. I can't risk going that way.'

'Fair enough. But crossing the mountain in *this*, at night...'

'What choice do I have?'

'Let me tell you what I think. I think trying to cross the mountain in pitch dark in the middle of a storm is pure folly. You'll break a leg or, worse still, go over a cliff edge. Also, you're exhausted. You're feeling good right now, but that's only the adrenaline. Pretty soon it's going to catch up with you. My advice? Find shelter, rest. Sleep if you can. Go over the mountain in the morning.'

'There's no shelter up there.'

'What about the barrow?'

Nash thought about it. The fox had a point. Even as he mulled it over, he was filled with an intense weariness and knew the fox was right.

'Okay.'

'Follow me. I'll show you.'

The fox led the way. Night came, a black night with dense cloud cover and no moonlight, and with the rain the darkness was awful. Nash stumbled and fell, and knew that without the fox he would be hopelessly lost. The rain was whipped about by the wind and the mountainside became a slick of mud and grime. Eventually, they came to the familiar clearing.

'We're here. This is it,' said the fox. Nash could barely hear the words above the howling of the wind. 'This is where you and I part ways. Get in there and rest till morning.'

Nash watched the fox disappear into the woods and then he crawled into the stone tunnel. The central chamber was dry. He took off the mask and carefully laid it on the ground. He lay down and fell asleep immediately.

And dreamt that he lay on a bed of tiny bones, and that severed fingers crawled over him like worms. That he was in the house called Paradise, trying to light a fire, but it wouldn't catch no matter how many times he tried. That a crow stood on the table and berated him loudly and hoarsely for not getting the fire going, calling him a fucking idiot, a fraud, an imposter. *That he was walking through the woods, and someone was following him, and it was The Grey Man. Then Brigid smiling, holding up a flower for him to examine. Mary Owen, saying* there, there, love. It'll be alright, just you see. *His own mother, turning away and him pleading with her,* please, Mum, please...

He woke in the night, in a complete void. Total blackness. No light. It was as if he had died. And for a moment he wondered if that was indeed what had happened. The rain had stopped but the wind was still blowing, whistling across the entrance to the barrow. He turned over and slept again.

When he woke, faint light was filtering into the chamber where he lay. Damp air. First light, washed out. He sat up and immediately know that someone – some*thing* – was near. He could feel it. He waited. No sound, not even the birds. Something in him was quivering like a bowstring. He was fully awake.

He got to his knees and groped in the darkness until his fingers found feathers. He put the mask on and, taking the gun with its single round, he crawled to the entrance. The Grey Man was waiting there in the pale light. Nash could not believe he was still alive. He looked even more like a corpse than usual. His grey suit was muddy and torn and on one side of his body a great black bloodstain extended from his collar to his waist. His tie was gone, and he had evidently torn a sleeve from his shirt and used it to bandage the wounds in his neck. His hair was dishevelled and stood up from his scalp at awkward angles. His skin, where it was not crusted in blood or dirt, was grey, a pale ghostly silvery grey that was almost white. One hand was crudely bandaged. The other held the gun. Grey metal. From beneath their reptilian eyelids the black eyes watched, unblinking, as Nash crawled out of the barrow entrance and stood before him. The Grey Man was a demon.

They stood quite still, watching each other in silence, for what seemed to Nash like a very long time. Eventually, The Grey Man gestured, to the trees, the sky, the mountain. 'Isn't it beautiful?' he said hoarsely.

Again there was silence and stillness.

'Nash,' croaked Gray, in a voice that was not quite human. 'You—'

Nash shot him.

A tiny black sun flared into existence in the centre of The

Grey Man's forehead. He took a step backwards and fell to the ground.

Nash crawled back into the chamber and retrieved his rucksack. He sat on a cold rock and contemplated Gray's body as he ate biscuits. Very slowly, the light changed to an infinitely pale pink and then gradually a warm yellow, as the sun began to rise above the mountains. Finally, the birds began to sing.

It was cold, despite the golden light, and Nash shivered.

He took Gray's gun and stowed it in his rucksack. Then, pulling it by the ankles, he dragged the body into the trees, away from the clearing. Using a branch, he scraped away the dead leaves and scoured away a few inches of dirt, and then pulled the corpse over. Gray watched him implacably as he worked. The hole in his forehead was a like a third eye, dark and infinite. In Gray's jacket pocket was a phone. He stamped on it and threw the pieces into the trees. He covered the body with dead leaves and then piled ferns and branches on it until it was no longer visible.

Then he began to climb the mountain.

AFTER

( )

On the first day of the Easter holidays, Brigid makes her way up the valley track. She has not been much in the woods in recent weeks but on her last foray – a solitary, melancholy walk that she had hoped would clear her head – she had seen what she was sure was a goshawk returning to its nest, a raft of sticks high up in a tall pine tree. It was amazingly lucky. Goshawks – distinctive, and one of the biggest birds of prey – are notoriously difficult to spot. She formed a plan to monitor the nest. If there were young, it would make a nice project for the holidays, to watch their progress over the following weeks. She walks slowly, taking her time, and before she comes to Paradise she takes a smaller path that climbs up across the hillside, to where there are stands of pine interspersed with ancient oaks.

As she walks, she looks about her. The woods are now changing from day to day, as the vegetation comes fully into leaf and blossom. The first bluebells have flowered in drifts of blue beneath the trees. The fresh shoots and heads of Alexanders, and the unfurling growth of ferns, are almost luminous.

Brigid is glad to be out of the house. The last few weeks of school have been tortuous, and she has found it hard to concentrate on her work. They had all seen the black cars drive slowly through the village on the day of the Lent fair, but no one had seen them return. What did that mean? The procession had been about to start, and Brigid felt happy and proud. She knew she looked beautiful (an unfamiliar sensation), and even she had to admit that the dress her mother had made was gorgeous, pale fabric embroidered with flowers and leaves. Her unruly hair was tied back, and she wore a floral headdress. Everyone complimented her and congratulated her on her 'coronation'. She didn't even mind holding hands with Finch, the boy from the year above who was to be her king. But when the cars went by, and everyone turned to watch them, it seemed to draw the breath from the air, to make all the pomp and ceremony seem silly and unimportant. She knew what they were there for and despite herself she offered a prayer for Nash, for his safety, even if that meant him being taken away, back to the city.

In the days that followed, her mother was grim-faced, taciturn. Brigid was dying to ask her what had happened but knew she should not. Mary Owen spent two full days up at the house, 'putting things in order'. On the second day, when she returned from school, Brigid looked up the valley and saw a thin column of black smoke in the distance, and knew that it was not a good sign. That was his things being burnt. However, when her mother came back and sat wearily at the kitchen table, she had offered Brigid something.

'I think he made it,' she said.

Brigid nodded, had said nothing, and began to set the table for supper.

She comes to the place in the woods and, with her binoculars, looks for the nest. It is a dark round mass high in the crook of a tall pine tree, close to the trunk. She settles to wait. The sunlight around her is dappled and the air is warm. It is a good place to be.

Why had the cars not come back down the valley? It was possible, she supposed, that they had come down much later, in the middle of the night after the festivities had ended. They would not have wanted to be seen, she thought. But then why had they driven through the village so brazenly, at the moment when the largest number of people would be there to witness them?

There is movement in the nest. Yes, it is occupied. How wonderful! For a brief moment the head of the female hawk is in view and Brigid can even see the bright orange of her eye. The female stands and makes adjustments to the nest, and as she does the male arrives, carrying something. They are grey and black, mottled and barred across their muscular chests, their eyes like yellow fire, their fierce beaks deadly. When the male leaves the nest, Brigid sees his agility as he weaves gracefully though the trees and vanishes. They are magnificent to behold, these birds, and Brigid feels that she has been gifted something very special. She resolves to return every day, to check on the hawks and, hopefully, monitor their young as they grow. Should she tell anyone? No, she decides, she will keep it to herself for now.

She had been almost giddy with excitement the first time she met him. For days she had watched him from amongst the trees, chopping wood, wandering through the ruined garden, muttering to himself, stumbling along the muddy paths and ways of the wood, and she had wondered what it would be like to talk to him; what his voice would sound like, if he would be rough or kind, if he would be *interested*. She had been surprised that he was so young. Usually they were old; broken, sour-looking old men in suits who mostly stayed in the house and didn't have any curiosity about what lay beyond the fence, no interest in the woods. And when he had finally stepped out into the open that day, taking her by surprise (for she had been lost in a daydream), she had been almost overwhelmed and had struggled to stay calm. It had been, she thought later, like a scene from a movie.

She liked it when they talked, but she liked it best when they walked or sat together in companionable silence. She liked to think that the fact they didn't need to fill the spaces meant something; that they were in tune, so at ease in each other's presence. Sometimes, after nothing had been said for some time, they would both begin to speak at exactly the same moment, and then both would shut up, smiling and grinning at each other, and fall back into the intimacy of quietness.

For the next week she makes the long trek up the valley to visit the hawks every day. She feels the need to be away from people, to think things through. When her mother offers to take her to Aber to visit the shops and the library, she declines. When some of her friends from school suggest a get-together to have pizzas and watch a movie, she makes an excuse.

She has a lot to think about. As well as recent events, she has a big decision approaching. In the summer she will do her GCSEs. Then she must make a decision about her A levels. It is the next stage, a step closer. University, art school, it is the beginning of the way out. It feels almost within touching distance.

In the woods, watching the nest, she reflects on her desire to get away. The irony of her vigil, watching the hawks as she thinks about flying the nest, is not lost on her. She feels the need stronger than ever now, the need to escape. It is a desire given an edge by Nash and their conversations. He had seemed like an exotic creature to her, an emissary from an alien land. She pictures him in the capital, the neon and steel and glass. Life there must be extraordinary, she thinks. The possibilities. Yet. And yet.

She loves the valley, but she knows she must leave it if she is to become... what? Something. She will become something.

She avoids Paradise, unwilling to visit the scene of whatever happened there. Nonetheless, she wonders, as she has done so many times before, at those people who come in their black cars from time to time. Who they are and what it is they do? How is it that her family is involved with them? It was something to do with her father, but she knows nothing more than that.

She has fixed Nash's face in her mind. She has made drawings of him. One time, he sat for her while she sketched him. He fidgeted, uncomfortable under her scrutiny. He managed five minutes before the embarrassment became too much. But since then, she has drawn him many times. He had an interesting face, she thought. *Has*, she corrects herself. His blue eyes. His shy smile. He seemed humble and she liked that. He also seemed vulnerable, which surprised her. It made her want to look after him, even though he was so much older.

Then, one day, approaching the nesting tree, she finds a feather on the track. It is a wing feather from the male hawk, a miraculous thing, it seems. She takes it as an omen – hadn't she been holding a feather when they first met? – and, after checking on the nest, makes her way across the hillside into the denser part of the woods, to the place where Paradise lies hidden.

The house is the same, but seems smaller, somehow. There is new growth on the creeping plants that grip its brickwork, and the ruined garden is bursting into wild and wilful abundance. She notes the blackened patch in the gravel area, where something has been burnt.

At the front door she pauses and then goes in. It is unlocked, as always. The house is shabby and dark but now it is clean. It has been dusted and even the cobwebs have gone. They will return. They always do. In the kitchen she sees that one of the windows has been broken and a piece of ply nailed across it. She takes a glass and fills it from the tap, drinks deeply. She moves silently through the house. She is looking for signs of him. But there are none. He has vanished into thin air. She wonders sometimes if he was ever really there.

Would he have left a sign? If he was getting out, would he have left a sign for her? If – and it is such a big if – he was getting out, she knows he would not have gone down the valley. They had discussed that. He would have gone up, over the mountain. And so she leaves the house, making sure the front door is shut securely, and makes her way up through the woods, climbing through the trees.

At the barrow, everything is as it always is. Stillness. She sits on a stone and takes in the clearing, the landscape beyond. She crawls down the entrance passage and rests in the darkness of the main chamber with her back against the cold stone. Ancient time. Timeless time. As she makes her way back out towards the sunlight, her fingers touch something on the ground and she picks it up. Back out in the brightness, she sees it is the wrapper from a packet of biscuits. And then there at her feet is another feather.

ACKNOWLEDGEMENTS

Thanks to everyone who helped make this book. To Gary Budden for belief and commitment, Dan Coxon for impeccable editing and Luke Bird for the beautiful cover. To Charlotte Seymour for making the connection, and Ed Wilson, Anna Dawson and Helene Butler at Johnson & Alcock, for support. To Julian Marshall, Sandy Foster, James Miller and Seán Padraic Birnie for valuable feedback. To Emile Cassen, Billy Green, Catherine Johnston, Conor McAnally, Niamh McAnally, Lisa Orban and Nina Smith, for sharing the journey. And as always, to Cecilia, Pablo and Tomas, for everything.

ABOUT THE AUTHOR

Ben Tufnell is a writer based in London. He has worked as a curator in both museums and galleries and has published widely on modern and contemporary art, focussing particularly on artists and art forms that engage with ideas of landscape and place. His debut novel, *The North Shore*, was published by Fleet (Little, Brown) in 2023.

Influx Press is an independent publisher based in London, committed to publishing innovative and challenging literature from across the UK and beyond.

www.influxpress.com
@Influxpress